CASHED
OUT
COLD

CASHED OUT COLD

A JOSIE POSEY MYSTERY

ANNA ST. JOHN

Contents

Praise for Cashed Out Cold

Warmth & Wit. "Anna St. John threads warmth and wit through a genuinely smart puzzle. When a beloved bank teller turns up in a claw-foot tub filled with counterfeit hundreds, Josie Posey does what good neighbors do: shows up, asks the right questions, and won't be pushed off the truth. Between garden-tour rivalries and Peruvian breadcrumbs, this is a brisk, satisfying read with real heart. *Cashed Out Cold* is cozy crime done right."—**Desmond P. Ryan**, author of *A Pint of Trouble* series.

Fresh and Engaging. "With sharp wit, small-town charm, and a heroine you cannot help but root for, *Cashed Out Cold* delivers a delightful mystery that proves life's second acts can be the most intriguing of all. Josie, a seasoned crime reporter who has been reassigned to cover her town's annual garden tour, expects pruning tips and polite society chatter. Instead, she uncovers a local scandal that turns deadly. At sixty-eight, savvy and far more observant than the residents of English Village realize, Josie finds herself digging into more than flowerbeds. What begins as a light community feature soon blossoms into a tangled web of secrets, rivalries, and motives lurking beneath manicured hedges and polished real estate smiles.

Brimming with humor, heart, and a cast of unforgettable townsfolk, this cozy mystery balances clever plotting with genuine warmth. Fans of character-driven whodunits will savor every twist as Josie follows the clues with determination, insight, and just the right touch of sass. *Cashed Out Cold* is a fresh, engaging mystery that reminds us that in a small town, nothing stays buried for long."—**Sarah E. Burr**, award-winning author of the Trending Topic Mysteries and more

me, you will absolutely want to read the other books in this series!"—**Ivanka Fear**, author of the Blue Water Mystery Series and the Jake and Mallory Thriller Series

This Time, It's Personal. "It's almost time for the annual garden tour, and everyone in English Village is buzzing. Each year, the entrants will go to any length to have the best, but someone may have gone too far. When a suspicious death threatens to bring everything crashing down, Josie Posey and the Mahjong Mavens are caught in the middle, and this time, it's personal."—**Heather Weidner**, author of the Jules Keene Glamping Mysteries and the Mermaid Bay Christmas Shoppe Mysteries

A Mystery Brewing. "Something is brewing in the quaint town of English Village, Kansas, and the Peruvian coffee is just the beginning. I love the way author Anna St. John weaves information about priceless artifacts into this story of competitive gardeners and an inexplicable murder. Secrets abound in this tiny town. When Josie and her Mahjong Mavens devise a "rumor mill scheme" to flush out the killer, there's nowhere to hide. This story kept me turning pages to reach the surprising conclusion."—**Daphne Silver**, Agatha Award-winning author of the Rare Books Cozy Mystery Series

A Mystery of International Intrigue. "Josie and the Mahjong Mavens have their work cut out for them again when the small town of English Village is tossed into a mystery of international intrigue. Author Anna St. John continues to delight her readers in this fourth book of her cozy mystery series.

When a new mystery develops in the small Kansas town, its resident sleuth, Josie Posey, is up to the challenge. She and her mahjong-playing friends come to the aid of Chief Marshall even when he tells them to stop meddling in his case. A young woman's curious death is too much to walk away from.

It literally takes a village to solve this puzzling crime, but Josie and her crew leave no stone unturned as they dig into the potential motives of every suspect.

Being a Software Engineer I never thought I would fall in love with cozy mysteries, but these books keep me coming back for more. Maybe because they take place in my childhood home of Kansas, or maybe because I always learn something new within the pages of a well-written Anna St. John mystery.

Although there is no need to read these delightful tales in order, you owe it to yourself to enjoy every book. Just like in any small town, there is more going on than you might think. Josie does more than solve mysteries and you will get to know her better in each one. I can't wait for number five."—**Dan Edwards**, retired software engineer and cozy mystery fan

Chapter One

Wednesday Morning

I f there's one thing I've learned in my sixty-eight years, it's that everyone in English Village thinks they have a secret—but, truth be told, usually the whole town already knows it. So, naturally, when I sat across the desk from Leslie Anderson, the editor of *The Village Gazette,* I could guess what was on her mind. The proprietor at Crystal Pines Nursery had spilled the beans when he sold me a copy of *The Old Farmer's Almanac* earlier in the week.

"You're gonna need this for reference when you dig into the story about our local Garden Tour," the third-generation nursery owner had said with boyish glee. "Those gardeners have zero tolerance for city folks who don't know the difference between seedlings and saplings."

"There is *no way* I would accept an assignment to interview a gaggle of gardeners," I had declared.

He had grinned wider, if that was possible. "Don't be too sure about that," he said. "And when you write their story, don't refer to them as a gaggle. The official collective noun for a group of gardeners is a *sprinkle.*"

Really? It was the sprinkle tidbit that convinced me to purchase the almanac.

A smile must have lingered around my lips at the memory, because Leslie Anderson was quick to ask me about it. She peered at me through her wire-rimmed glasses.

"What's up, Josie? You look like the cat who ate the canary."

"I'm celebrating spring," I said innocently.

"You and me both." Leslie took a stubby pencil from its resting place over her ear and jotted a phone number on the pad in front of her. She shoved it toward me. "Here's the perfect story to get you into the springtime spirit."

"Savannah Sweet?" I recognized the name from the single billboard placed strategically near the entrance to English Village. It featured an attractive woman with a mane of red hair and wide white smile beneath the words: *I'll Help You Find Your Home SWEET Home.*

"You want me to write a feature on a real estate agent?"

This was not what I anticipated.

Leslie shook her head. "Not exactly. Savannah is the promotions chair of the Cleeve Hill Garden Society this year. I want you to write about the Annual Garden Tour. She can give you the details and introduce you to the homeowners included on the tour. We'll send a photographer, but I'm counting on *you* to interview three of the gardeners and tell their stories."

Aha. That's the request I was expecting, I thought.

"No, thank you," I said, pushing the pad back across the desk. "This isn't my kind of story. The gardens are beautiful, but gardeners can be cantankerous. Can't the new guy cover it?"

Leslie slid the notepad to me again. "Look, I know you're a crime reporter, and this Garden Tour doesn't sound exciting, but I can't send a college kid to talk to these people."

"Why not?" I stared at her without blinking and shoved the notepad firmly in her direction. Leslie fidgeted in her seat.

"If you must know, they are the royalty of English Village," she said. "They live in the mansions up on the hill and serve on every important board in town. Some are getting old and crotchety, but they will still talk to *you*."

"Because I'm *old*?" I hoped my editor caught the nuance of a challenge in my question.

The corner of Leslie's lip barely twitched when she answered. "No. Because you're crotchety."

I snorted.

She giggled.

Then we both fell into a fit of laughter. The new kid stuck his head around the corner. "Everything okay here?"

I waved him away and wiped the tears from my eyes.

Leslie inched the notepad my way again. "Seriously, Josie, it's an important story. They raise a lot of money for our parks through this event. And…" she paused dramatically.

"*What?*" I wasn't in the mood for dramatics.

Leslie leaned forward and lowered her voice. "They have hired an artistic director for the gardens this year. I want to know who it is and why they selected him. You're good at mysteries. *Please* write the story."

I sighed and tucked the phone number into my purse. "Okay, but don't blame me if someone gets upset when they think we've given preferential coverage to their neighbor's garden. These stories are far more political than crime cases."

"Which is why you're the best reporter for the job." Leslie stood to signal the end of our meeting.

"Ri-i-i-ight." I stretched the word to be sure she caught my sarcasm, but Leslie smiled and handed me an envelope.

"I almost forgot. Here's the check for last month. You're an excellent reporter, Josie. I can't wait to see what you do with the Garden Tour."

After Leslie shooed me out the door, I climbed into my little red VW convertible, who heard me grumble about all kinds of injustices daily as I circled the winding roads of our village. Piper—as I'd playfully named the car—got an earful once again.

"I can't believe Leslie convinced me to interview the gardeners," I complained, half to myself, and half to the car. "She tricked me, Piper. After all her smooth talk about mysteries and my ability to solve them, I couldn't refuse the assignment."

Maybe the Garden Tour will prove to be a welcome change of pace, I rationalized. I'd been cooped up since December, as the entire state of Kansas stubbornly refused to let go of the wind and snow, during our longest cold streak in decades. The days had been dreary ever since an awkward breakup with my friend Harvey around Christmas. (Although, since we weren't *truly* a couple, a breakup might be the wrong way to describe our decision to go separate ways.)

Anyway, I'd been sulking about the weather for the last few months. During those snowy days, only a weekly game of mahjong raised my spirits. With spring in the air, it was time to end my lingering doldrums and get back into the swing of things.

I patted Piper's dashboard. "Let's go, girl," I said. "We have errands to run."

I took the long way to the bank so I could drive past a meadow dotted with colorful spring wildflowers, then up the curvy incline to the charming neighborhood of Cleeve Hill. All I wanted was a glimpse of the stately homes perched atop the hill—each with a stunning view overlooking the countryside and the lake below. I never intended to stir up trouble.

At first glance, all was tranquil and picturesque; tall oaks formed a canopy over the worn cobblestone streets and cast dappled shade onto the manicured lawns. Every house was unique, but they all had long, red brick pathways stretching from their front steps to the decorative black mailboxes near the curb.

As I approached the end of the block, I noticed a silver-haired woman in a stylish denim dress and knee-high leather boots, staring at me. She stood motionless outside a gate with the number 22 engraved on its face. When I waved, the woman pointedly turned away.

The hair on the back of my neck rose, sending a shiver down my spine. I wondered what I might discover amidst the carefully tended flowers hidden behind each manor.

I'll bet every one of these gardens holds a secret, I thought.

Chapter Two

Wednesday Mid-Day

My cell phone rang just as I stopped at the bottom of Cleeve Hill. I pulled to the curb to answer it.

"Is this Ms. Posey?" A woman shrieked at me.

"Speaking."

"What are you doing snooping around the gardens without talking to me first?" The woman's shrill voice shouted into my ear.

"Excuse me? Who is this?"

"Savannah Sweet. I believe your editor directed you to contact me, and I specifically told her you were not to pry into the Garden Tour event without my guidance."

When I interviewed mobsters in my crime reporting days, I learned never to show my anger or fear in a phone conversation. This woman would not intimidate me. I counted slowly to ten and pasted a smile on my face to keep my voice *friendly* before I spoke.

"Ms. Sweet, you are mistaken. I spoke to my editor less than fifteen minutes ago and haven't arrived home yet. If someone is prying into the story, it isn't me."

"I have my sources, Ms. Posey. You attempted to view the gardens not five minutes ago, and I won't allow it. Do you understand?"

"Your information is incorrect, Ms. Sweet. Why don't we meet for coffee and get this straightened out? I can't wait to hear about your new artistic director for the Garden Tour. Cozy Cups in fifteen minutes?" *I'm ready to duel.*

She sputtered into the phone. "That's impossible. I'm a busy woman with far too many appointments to toss everything to the wind for a spur-of-the-moment coffee."

"Hmm. And yet you called immediately when someone told you I drove down Cleeve Hill Lane? Would you prefer to meet tomorrow morning?"

"Hold while I check my calendar," her clipped words ended with a full minute of silence. I drummed my fingers on Piper's steering wheel as I waited.

Finally, she returned. "I've rearranged my entire morning tomorrow to meet with you. Ten o'clock at Cozy Cups?"

"Perfect." I allowed a tiny smile to creep into my response. Neither of us said goodbye. Checkmate. *I might enjoy the challenge of the Garden Tour story after all.*

I glanced at the clock on the city hall tower and confirmed there was still enough time to make my deposit and have lunch before I joined the mavens for our afternoon game. One trip around the block, and I slipped into the bank drive-through with a single car ahead of me. While I waited, I turned up the radio. DJ Phlash Phelps chattered about hits from the 60s, and I sang along with the Beatles. The lyrics to "Here Comes the Sun" suited my celebration of spring. I was still humming when I pulled up to the window.

My favorite teller was on duty, and I greeted her with a cheery smile. "Good morning, Maryann, what's the latest on your professor from Peru?"

She shot me an anguished look, making me sorry I had raised the subject. Earlier in the week, Maryann had gushed about the lecture she had attended, where the visiting professor had spoken passionately about Peruvian coffee. Perhaps the handsome instructor was no longer in favor.

"Give me a minute, Nellie," she said. I did a double-take when she called me by my best friend's name, but Maryann continued shuffling papers on the workspace in front of her.

Normally calm and organized, Maryann Penny was the opposite of that today. I watched as she removed her thin white gloves, gulped her coffee, and peered at the deposit slip again. Her silky chestnut hair framed her face as it always did, but a deep frown creased her brow.

"Everything okay, Maryann?"

Her chin jerked upward when I spoke, as though she had forgotten I was there. Then she forced a smile, slid her hands into the gloves, and shoved the papers aside. "Yes, Josie. I'm fine. How can I help you?"

I placed my check on the tray. "A simple deposit, but I also need two hundred dollars in cash."

Maryann hesitated as she pulled the check from the exchange box. "The rest goes into your checking account?"

"Yes. The deposit slip is right there with the check. See?"

She placed my check down on a stack of papers beside her, reached again for her coffee, knocked the cup onto its side, and splashed the brown liquid across the counter, dousing all the paperwork—including my deposit—with pale brown splotches. "I'm so-so-sorry," she stammered. "Let me mop this up and…I'll be back with you …"

Maryann grabbed a wad of paper towels from beneath her desk and dabbed the spilled coffee in a frantic series of patting motions. Finally, she tossed the wet towels in the trash, pinched the bridge of her nose, and turned back to me.

"Thank you for your patience, Josie. Are hundred-dollar bills okay?"

Did she just call me patient? No one had ever described me as patient. I nodded my approval, although I would have preferred smaller bills. *No need to cause her extra trouble.*

"Here's your cash and your receipt," she said.

"Maryann?" I waited for her to make eye contact. When she raised her dark brown eyes to mine, I smiled. "You seem a little flustered. Is there anything I can do for you?"

She leaned into the microphone, and her words came in a rush. "Oh, Josie, I'm in a terrible pickle. I need to take care of some urgent business—a legal matter—in the city for the next few days. My mother is recovering from surgery at a spa in Florida, and I have no one to watch Johnny Depp or water the plants while I'm away."

"Johnny Depp?"

"My cat. Also known as JD. Do you know any cat sitters?"

"That's easy. *I'll* do it. How long will you be away?"

"Less than a week, I hope. Are you serious?"

The driver behind me beeped his horn, and I shifted into gear. "Give me your home address, and I'll meet you there at the end of your shift. You can introduce me to Johnny Depp."

Maryann breathed a sigh of relief and passed me her address through the teller window. "You're a lifesaver," she said. "See you at four o'clock?"

"I'll be there." *One cat and a few houseplants. How difficult could it be?*

With an apologetic wave to the car behind me, I pulled onto Main Street and made the quick drive home. Moe met me at the door, wagging his entire body as though I'd been away for days, instead of a couple of hours. I set my handbag on the kitchen counter and knelt to give him a belly scratch.

"How was your morning, boy?" Moe cocked his head, listening to my chatter like he understood every word. I described the emerging wildflowers and told him about my conversation with Maryann.

"I'm going to make dinner for Johnny Depp! What do you think of that?" The story did not impress Moe. He nudged me for a bite of my leftover chicken, nibbled the tiny morsel I provided, and resumed his favorite position, stretched out on the kitchen floor.

He was still there, napping, when I slipped out the door to meet the Mahjong Mavens—that's what we called ourselves—at Nellie's house. She lived a ten-minute drive away, in a quaint, gated neighborhood with native limestone homes and cobblestone streets. Most everywhere in English Village was a quick commute from my cottage on Primrose Lane—a vast difference from Kansas City, where I lived before.

I was the first to arrive for mahjong, so I knocked before I opened the door and stepped inside. "I'm here!"

The house smelled of chocolate chip cookies, and I breathed in the mouth-watering aroma. Nellie called out to me from her kitchen. "How many times have I told you not to knock? Come on in, Josie."

"Sorry. It's a city thing." I set my purse on the kitchen island and turned to hug Nellie. "Anything I can do to help?"

"Could you set up the game? We're playing in the dining room today." Nellie tucked her perfect bob behind her right ear and waved me toward the table. She was striking, even dressed casually—with dark jeans, a crisp striped shirt, and a single strand of pearls at her throat. I hope I will look as polished when I reach her age.

I poured the game tiles onto the table and mixed them thoroughly, enjoying the noisy process and the familiar feel of the cool blocks between my fingers. Then I spread them face down and stacked them two-deep, building four long walls—one against the backside of each rack, where the players would arrange the thirteen tiles they drew for each hand of the game.

The Chinese tile game had a rich history, dating back to at least the mid-1800s. Some said it was much older, originating when all the creatures aboard the Ark played the game during the Great Flood. Still others claimed Confucius created the game in 500 BC, naming it "Sparrow," after the Emperor's favorite bird. I still remember sitting at my Grandma Molly's feet as a child, leaning my head against her knee while she stroked my hair and told me the stories of mahjong.

"Josie! Wake up!" Nellie nudged me out of my daydream. "I swear, you drift off more than anyone I know. What are you thinking?"

"Sorry. Reminiscing about some old mahjong myths my grandmother used to share. She was a masterful storyteller."

"Doesn't surprise me," Nellie said. "That's probably where you inherited your talent for spinning a yarn." She set an icy glass of peach tea in front of me.

I raised the glass to my lips, savoring the sweet goodness.

"Kate and Sharon are coming up the walk," Nellie said. "Let's get this party started."

It was just supposed to be an ordinary Mahjong Wednesday. No one suspected another murder would rock our little town to its core before the weekend, or that I would be the one to discover the victim.

Chapter Three

Wednesday Afternoon

The dining room erupted with laughter as we took our seats. The Wednesday afternoon mahjong game was a standing appointment—part entertainment, part support group—with my closest friends. Officially, we were there to play a few hands of the Chinese tile game. But, like most women's groups, we enjoyed visiting with each other—four gray-haired ladies chatting around the table.

To be accurate, three of us were succumbing to our graying locks, while the fourth resisted the ravages of time. Nellie had a perfect salt-and-pepper bob. Kate's short hair was pure white. My own unruly dark curls now had silver highlights, and I wore it long enough to pull into a messy ponytail when necessary. Sharon still relied on her favorite stylist to maintain her "natural" shade of blonde. We called ourselves the Mahjong Mavens, and we most certainly would not describe ourselves as "old."

Although the game was mostly for fun, we kept score of every hand for bragging rights. While we played, the ladies shared news from around the village long before it reached the pages of *The Gazette.* They knew everyone in town and had played matchmaker to at least a half-dozen couples—including introducing Harvey and me, which turned out to be a mistake, as far as "dating" goes.

Sharon set her drink on the corner of the table and opened her playing card. "It's my turn to win," she declared. With her short blond curls, a fair complexion, and a light dusting of freckles over the bridge of her nose, she looked more like an impish teenager than a grandmother of four.

"Don't be too quick to claim victory," Kate said, setting her game card in front of her tiles. "We haven't even rolled the dice yet." Our self-proclaimed rule keeper, Kate was a stately woman who wore her pure silver hair cropped in a short, sensible cut that drew attention to her lovely blue eyes. She always reminded me of Bea Arthur in *The Golden Girls,* with her wry sense of humor and straightforward comments. At 75, she still had the energy of a woman in her thirties.

On the opposite end of the spectrum, Nellie was the peacemaker of the bunch. "Now, now, ladies. Let's save the trash talk for later," she said. "Does anyone have news to share before we begin?"

"I do!" Sharon jumped into the conversation. "I'm creating a new dessert for The Philbrook Inn restaurant, and I can't wait for you to try it." The youngest of my friends, at 74, Sharon was a prize-winning baker and our designated fashionista. Today she wore a silky turquoise blouse that emphasized her vivid blue eyes. When she insisted the mavens be her official "tasters" for a new concoction, we happily complied.

"You know I can't resist your desserts," Kate said. "What are you making?" A retired U.S. Marine, Kate was all about fitness—until it came to sweets. She spent hours in yoga class and on the pickleball courts, so she could devour Sharon's sugary concoctions without a care.

"Trifles!" Sharon's silver earrings dangled as she spoke. "With luscious lemon cake and strawberries, served in stemmed crystal glasses."

"Sounds extravagant," Kate said. "When can we taste them?"

"That's the fun part," Sharon said. "They are easy to make and fancy to serve. I'll have samples for you next Wednesday at my house, but they won't be on the menu at the Philbrook until spring."

"Spring officially arrives today," I corrected her by quoting my newly purchased copy of *The Old Farmer's Almanac.* "We can plant flowers after the New Moon."

"Hmmm. Well, The Philbrook introduces their spring menu in a couple of weeks," Sharon leveled her big blue eyes at me, and I knew it was pointless to argue with her.

Nellie sighed. "Could we play now, please? I'd like to finish a game before Sharon's lemon cake comes out of the oven."

The next two hours were a flurry of clacking tiles and intense competition as the mavens collected combinations of flowers, winds, and dragons to complete their hands. The first to assemble fourteen tiles into a winning formation shouted out "Mahjong!" ending each round with a chorus of groans from the losers.

After the last game, I tossed my handbag over my shoulder and headed toward the door. "Sorry, ladies, I'm on my way to meet Johnny Depp, so I need to rush."

"Wait. What?" Sharon held up one hand in the universal sign for "stop," and the room silenced.

I responded with an innocent shrug. "I figure if we're spending the next week together, I should get to know him."

Nellie raised a knowing eyebrow. "It's that cat, isn't it? Maryann calls him JD."

"I prefer to call him by his full name," I said. "But yes. She's leaving town for a few days, and I'm watching her plants and Johnny-boy."

"Don't take Moe," Kate advised. "I doubt Johnny Depp is a dog-lover."

* * *

Maryann met me at the door in jeans and a white t-shirt, her glossy brown hair pulled back into a bouncy ponytail. Standing there with a huge multicolored cat draped in her arms, she looked like a college girl, home for spring break. "Come in, Josie. This is Johnny Depp."

I followed her into the living room, noting the cat's broad-chested body, his long, silky fur, and his delightfully bushy tail before Maryann settled into a chair with the pet across her lap. She hoisted the limp feline into a sitting position, and he deigned to open his dark brown eyes for a glimpse in my direction.

"Aha," I said. "His name suits him." The fluffy feline was predominantly white, with random markings of black and gold, but it was his eyes that claimed my attention. They were the color of dark chocolate, and they glistened as he stared at me.

Maryann shifted the heavy cat into the cradle of her arms. "He's a handsome guy," she said. "Ragamuffins are pure white when they're born, so his markings are relatively new. But his eyes have been that same piercing color since the day he was born. When I saw those eyes, I had to name him Johnny Depp."

"Some names are serendipitous," I said. "Is he friendly to newcomers?"

She stroked the lazy cat's chin. "JD never met a stranger. He's three months old and thinks the world revolves around him. He's happiest when he's the center of attention. Watch his claws, though. They can be vicious when he reaches for a toy. The vet will trim his nails next week. He is too squirmy when I try to do it myself."

"How is he around other pets?"

"He's curious, but cautious. I bet he and Moe will be fine together once they get acquainted."

Bored by our conversation, Johnny Depp jumped lazily from her lap and walked toward me. He swished his tail, rubbed against my legs, and curled into a ball at my feet.

"Nap time," Maryann explained. "He plays for about an hour each morning and evening. The rest of the day, he sleeps."

"Sounds like my kind of cat. What else do I need to know?"

Maryann led me into the kitchen and took a handwritten list from the counter. "This should cover everything. Feeding times, treats, favorite toys. The veterinarian's name and number are at the bottom, in case you have an emergency."

"Let's hope *that* doesn't happen," I said.

She walked me through the house, pointing out JD's litter box before showing me her favorite fern, and a variety of lush plants. "You have quite the green thumb," I noted.

Her face turned pink, and she brushed aside the compliment. "Each one is like a friend to me," she explained with a shy smile. "I know it sounds silly, but I talk to them every morning."

"No wonder they are thriving. All living things respond to love," I said.

As we stepped into her bedroom, I saw a photo on the nightstand. Maryann stood next to a tall, muscular guy, his arm wrapped around her shoulders, pulling her close to his side. The wind swept their hair as they stood at the fork of a hiking trail. Both smiled widely into the camera.

"And who is *this*?" I picked up the frame for a closer look.

"Nobody," Maryann snapped. Then she stammered a longer answer. "I mean, er, that's my brother, but *not*."

"Hmm. He doesn't resemble you at all, with his blond hair and blue eyes."

"He's just a friend, *like* a brother. We went hiking together." Maryann tried to brush off my observations.

I raised one eyebrow and shot back at her. "Doesn't *look* like a brother."

Maryann grabbed the photo from my hands and set it back on the table. "Well, he *is*. Anyway, I only framed this picture so my mom could see it." She rushed me into the hall and back toward the kitchen.

A deep frown etched her forehead again, and her hands shook when she handed me a thick envelope and the key to her house. "If anything goes wrong—or you can't reach me on my cell—try the number inside the envelope. I've also included a couple of instructions in case of an emergency."

"Don't worry, Maryann. We'll be fine." I took the envelope and tucked it into my purse. When I looked up again, she was already standing at the door, holding it open to let me out. Her eyes darted toward the two bulging suitcases set next to the couch.

Finally, she turned her clear hazel eyes to mine. "Josie, I…"

"Yes?"

"This means a lot to me. Thank you for coming to my rescue." She brushed a tear from her cheek.

The intensity of her gaze startled me. "It's no problem at all. I'm sure you'd do the same for me."

Even as I reassured her, I heard a little warning bell in my head. *Maryann has more on her mind than an ailing mother and a few business appointments.*

Chapter Four

Wednesday Night

I couldn't shake the image of Maryann's worried eyes as I drove toward home. She planned an early start in the morning, presumably to arrive at her appointment in Kansas City by midday. She had not shared her business or the name of her attorney—if, in fact, it was an attorney she intended to see. Reflecting on our conversation, I realized Maryann had told me nothing about the "urgent business" that had popped up so suddenly.

Is it related to her mother's illness, or something else? I wondered.

When I had pushed to know where she intended to stay on her trip, she claimed she had not yet secured a hotel reservation. Thankfully, she had agreed to text me upon her arrival. At least I would know she made it safely to her destination.

My cell phone rang as I turned into my driveway. I turned off the car and swiped to answer Kate's call. As always, she was brief. "Want to grab an early dinner at The Philbrook?"

"Sure. I could meet you there at six," I said. "That allows plenty of time to feed Moe and change clothes."

Every week since my "Holiday Breakup" with Harvey, Kate had quietly attempted to fill the void. Happily single herself, she found a variety of activities for the two of us to experience. I could always count on her to suggest something fun.

Moe waited for me at the door, his leash dangling from his mouth, looking so comically forlorn that I set my handbag on the floor and stooped down to wrap my arms around his fluffy body. He raised his paw, as I had taught him.

I took his paw in my hand and looked into his dark brown eyes. "OK, boy, you win. Let me switch to my walking shoes, and we'll go to the park."

When I first arrived in the village, before I'd met the Mahjong Mavens and made friends, Moe was my only constant companion. With his goofy personality and unwavering puppy love, he filled my days with laughter. Gradually, we both allowed others into our lives, until we found ourselves encircled by the close friendships that became our family here. I hadn't forgotten the loneliness I'd felt after my husband died, but I would be forever grateful to the women who had so readily opened their hearts to us.

Moe led the way along the familiar path toward our historic park. Tugging gently on the leash, he hurried me along. We turned right at the end of our driveway, followed the sidewalk along Primrose Lane until it curved to intersect with Main Street, then continued two more blocks to the quiet green park. Without prompting, Moe stopped abruptly at my favorite bench and waited for me to sit.

"Aww, aren't you a thoughtful boy?" As I took my place on the bench, he nudged closer, so his body pressed against my legs. It was part of his herding instinct, I knew, but I preferred to believe he enjoyed my company.

From this vantage point, we could gaze upon the bronze statue of our town's namesake, Henry Joseph Nolan 'Hank' English, and marvel at how he inspired a village he never visited. Or we could admire the quaint gazebo where so many events brought people together—for outdoor weddings, concerts, and even children's ballet performances.

Scratching Moe in his favorite spot behind his ears, I relaxed into the quiet of the empty park. Here, on warm summer days, lovers strolled the flower gardens, children played tag, and tourists visited the historic blacksmith shop where my friend, Harvey, spent most of his free time. Today we were alone.

A twig snapped behind me, and I whipped around to see who was there. The flash of a squirrel's tail disappeared up the tree, but the motion directed my attention to another bench near the gardens. A woman sat alone with a book in her hands and a tote bag clutched to her side. As I squinted to see her, sunlight filtered through the trees to shine on her wavy russet-colored hair. *Is that Savannah Sweet?*

Since I'd never seen the woman in person, it was difficult to tell. She seemed shorter than the Savannah pictured on the billboard, but her hair was distinctive—glowing like copper in the sunshine. Before I could rise to call out to the woman, a man in a dark blue running suit jogged across the path in front of her. Neither acknowledged the other's presence, but he dropped something as he passed. It glinted on the sidewalk for several moments before the woman rose from the bench and sauntered over to retrieve it. Then, she casually tucked it into her book and walked toward the parking lot near the library on the opposite side of the park.

"Well, *that* was interesting," I said to Moe. "What do you think just happened?"

He cocked his head as though he waited to hear my theories, but gave no reply of his own.

My imagination raced with explanations for the clandestine exchange. Now I had two puzzling women on my mind—Maryann and Savannah. They remained there, battling for attention, as Moe and I retraced our steps home to the cottage.

By the time I met Kate for dinner at The Philbrook. I was ready to enjoy our meal and shove all thoughts of Maryann and Savannah aside. As soon as our server seated us, I spread my napkin on my lap and turned to Kate.

"Tell me all your latest news," I said.

"You mean, since we talked at mahjong this afternoon?" Kate's eyes twinkled. "There's not much to tell. How was your visit with Maryann Penny?"

At her question, all my good intentions about *not discussing* Maryann vanished. "Something is bothering her, and I can't figure it out," I said.

Kate laughed. "You're not her mother, Josie. Let the girl solve her own problems."

"You're right," I said. "I should do that. But..."

"But?" Kate prompted.

"When I stopped by her house to meet Johnny Depp, she seemed frazzled."

"That's not surprising," Kate said. "She was probably distracted as she packed for her trip."

The logic of Kate's words hit me square in the face, but I wasn't ready to succumb to such a simple explanation. "I don't know, Kate," I said. "It seemed like she had something big on her mind, besides her mother being ill, but couldn't share it."

"Like what?" Kate tilted her head and waited for me to explain.

"Maybe she won the lottery and is meeting with her financial advisers before she claims the money," I suggested. "Or maybe she's running away from a stalker. She looked uptight."

Kate gazed at me over the top of her menu. "What did your Grandma Molly always tell you about your imagination?"

I sighed and recited my grandma's words: "You can't depend on your eyes when your imagination is out of focus."

Kate nodded. "That's the one. From Mark Twain, isn't it?"

"Are you suggesting that I'm mistaken?" I arched one eyebrow.

She laughed so hard her eyes crinkled into tiny slits, and I joined her until my cheeks hurt from smiling. "Let's say there may be a few holes in your theories," she said. "But I *do* delight in hearing them."

Like me, Kate enjoyed fabricating stories about total strangers. She didn't have a malicious bone in her body, but she was happy to observe people and concoct spontaneous imaginary tales about them. Together, we had created fictional adventures for a cook at our favorite barbecue restaurant, two old men playing chess at the park, and a young mother piling three little girls into a minivan at the grocery store.

Still, she couldn't resist reining me in occasionally. "You realize this imagination of yours will get you into trouble one day," she said.

"It already has," I admitted. "Remember when I saw the police chief at the Farmer's Market and assumed he was giving Lorene a parking ticket?"

"And you found out he was simply handing *his wife* a receipt for their purchase."

"That was embarrassing. Lorene should have told me she was married to Chief Marshall."

"Or, you could have minded your own business," Kate smiled to soften the words.

"Agreed. I tried to help a friend without knowing the facts."

Kate raised her wineglass in a toast. "Here's to the facts."

"And to helping our friends." I clinked my glass against hers.

Kate sipped the wine, then looked at me over the table. "Your curiosity and imagination are assets in your role as a reporter and a crime solver. But they may have cost you a long-term relationship with Harvey."

I shook my head. "No worries, Kate. Harvey and I quarreled too much to become a couple. I was accustomed to being treated as an equal partner in a relationship. Harvey wanted a shrinking violet he could shelter and protect. We would have driven each other crazy."

"You can't blame him for worrying when you received death threats," Kate noted.

"Oh, that." I shrugged my shoulders. "Things have calmed down in English Village. I don't think we'll be solving any murders again, soon."

"Let's hope not," Kate said. "Are you *sure* it's over with Harvey?"

"Yes, Kate. Although I would argue that it never really began. Hopefully, Harvey will accept me *as a friend* again someday."

To change the subject, I told Kate about meeting Johnny Depp, and my plans to feed the cat twice a day. "Maryann leaves town early tomorrow, so I will stop around lunchtime and again in the evening. After that, I'll go twice a day, morning and evening."

"That's a serious commitment," Kate said.

"It's only a few minutes to check his food and litter box. Watering the houseplants on Saturday could take an hour with all the pots Maryann has in every room. Easy."

"If you say so," Kate shrugged. "Let me know if you need any help. I'd love to email my kids to tell them I've spent an evening with Johnny Depp."

* * *

I drove past Maryann's house on my way home. A yellow Fiat was parked in her driveway; I wondered who owned the little car. Light spilled from every window. *Maryann must be scurrying from room to room packing for her trip.*

Before I had time to consider the possibilities, my cell phone rang with the tone I had designated for Harvey when we were *almost dating.* We hadn't spoken in several weeks. *Interesting that he would call minutes after Kate brought up his name at dinner,* I thought. I turned onto Primrose Lane and pulled to a stop at the curb.

"Hello?"

"Hi, Josie, it's Harvey."

"Yes," I said dryly, "I recognize your voice."

"I'm doing the art exhibit," he said.

"What?"

"The one in Kansas City. Since you encouraged me to contact them, I wanted you to know."

Instantly, I recalled the short, scholarly man who had approached Harvey at the Summer's End Festival in August. No wonder Harvey wanted to share his news. This exhibit represented an opportunity to gain greater recognition as an artist. Although he and his dad owned the local hardware store, Harvey devoted many hours each week to his hobby—creating decorative wall art and intricate light fixtures from wrought iron.

"That's wonderful," I said. "When do you go? How many pieces will you take? Is it a one-man show?"

He chuckled at my enthusiasm. "Hold on. One question at a time, please."

I listened while my friend provided details. For the first time in months, our conversation felt comfortable and familiar.

"The exhibit is next month," Harvey said. "I'm taking twenty pieces. And, before you ask again, *yes*, it's a one-artist show. They're creating a special display with additional lighting, since my work is all wrought iron. They say it will *illuminate every detail* of the dark metal."

Tears pricked my eyes, and I swallowed a lump in my throat as I realized how important this event was to Harvey's career. "I'm proud of you," I said.

"I wouldn't have had this opportunity without your help," Harvey said.

"You and the mavens made me look good at the festival."

"No, Harvey," I said. "Your beautiful *work* made you look good. We simply provided a place to display it. You deserve this. Congratulations."

Harvey hesitated, and I sensed he had more to say.

"Josie, there's one more thing I wanted to ask—"

"What is it?" I held my breath and hoped Harvey wouldn't venture into anything personal.

"The gallery is hosting a formal opening for the exhibit. I wonder if you and the mavens would attend as my guests? It's on a Saturday afternoon, so you could drive up for the event and return home the same day."

Upon hearing his request, I released the breath from my lungs into an enormous sigh of relief that I hoped Harvey didn't hear over the phone. "That's very generous of you, Harvey," I replied. "I'll tell them about it."

As I swiped to end the call, I felt a weight lifted from my shoulders. I was grateful that Harvey had not asked me for a one-on-one date. *Perhaps we can still be friends, after all,* I thought.

* * *

Harvey's success lingered in my mind through a quiet evening with Moe and the conclusion of the nightly newscast. But it wasn't until I crawled into bed and picked up my book that I understood the significance of his phone call: It was the first time in months that we hadn't bickered with each other.

I set aside the book and switched off my lamp, then pulled my fluffy down comforter up to my chin, careful not to disturb Moe—who already slept soundly at the foot of my bed. Just as I relaxed into that wonderful weightless feeling prior to sleep, my phone pinged with a text. I jerked awake again and retrieved it from my nightstand. I had to squint to read the brief message from Maryann.

"Thanks again for watching JD. If anything stressful happens, make yourself a fresh cup of Peruvian coffee. I've left instructions in the canister on my kitchen counter. You will know what to do."

I rolled my eyes, sent Maryann a "thumbs up" emoji, and pulled the covers back over my head. Then, just before I drifted off to dreamland, my mind triggered two questions:

Why does Maryann think I will stress out? And is Peruvian coffee so difficult to prepare that I need special instructions?

Chapter Five

Thursday Morning

I stood at the serve-yourself coffee bar near the Cozy Cups entrance, scanning the room for the red-headed real estate agent who had berated me for daring to peek at the Cleeve Hill gardens without her. Savannah Sweet sat at a corner table near the window, head bent toward her phone as she thumbed through the screens.

Probably reading important emails. The uncharitable thought flitted through my brain before I could stop it.

While she scanned her messages, I filled my favorite cup and studied her perfect profile. Savannah was attractive in that carefree way of confident women who have *always* been beautiful, with flawless ivory skin and long eyelashes. She wore an emerald-green blazer that complemented her scarlet hair. I could easily visualize her as a former high school cheerleader with dazzling white teeth and a bounce in her step. I knew *this woman* had rendezvoused with the blond secret agent in the park yesterday.

As I approached her table, she glanced up at me. "Ms. Posey?"

"Please call me Josie." I extended my hand. "It's nice to meet you, Savannah."

She avoided my handshake, motioning for me to take the seat across from her. "Sorry, I caught my hand in a broken screen door while I was showing a house to a buyer yesterday."

"Must have been a nasty cut to merit a gauze bandage instead of a Band-Aid," I said.

She shrugged. "One hazard of the job." Her voice was light, but she hid her hand under the table and looked away from my gaze.

When I set my pad and pen on the table, Savannah again waved me off. "Oh, you won't need those," she said. "Something has come up to change my day. I have only a few minutes to talk." She seemed as cool as a cucumber on the outside, but the woman was fidgeting, and we hadn't begun the interview.

"Maybe we should reschedule when you aren't so busy," I suggested.

"That won't be necessary." She reached into her tote and pulled out a folded blue paper. "All the details are here. The dates, times, and locations for the tours, and a brief description of the Garden Club's history and purpose. I've included the names of several people you can contact for supplementary quotes. They are expecting your calls."

"What about your mystery artistic director?" I asked. "My editor specifically asked about him."

"His number is on the list, but please don't mention him to anyone before the article appears." She shot daggers at me with her eyes. "Not even those maven friends of yours."

"What's the big deal?"

"It's all about publicity. We're building suspense for the major announcement. A strategy *you* couldn't possibly understand."

If Savannah had hoped to insult me, I refused to take the bait.

As I reached for the paper, my hand brushed against her bandage, and she winced. "May I ask you one question?"

Savannah shoved her chair away from the table. "You have my number," she said. "Call me anytime."

"About your hand…"

"Yes?" Her eye darted to the bandage, then back to me.

"This happened after we talked yesterday?" I asked.

"Yes. Late afternoon. While I toured an older home with a potential buyer."

I raised my coffee cup to my lips and stared at her. "Really?"

Her face flushed, and she glared at me. "What difference does it make? I really must go now."

It was my turn to shrug. "I was certain I saw you in the park late yesterday afternoon."

"That's ridiculous!" Savannah clenched her teeth and hissed the words at me. "I was nowhere near the park."

"Whatever you say, Savannah," I replied. "But the woman I spotted could have been your twin…and I'd recognize that Gucci leather handbag from a mile away." Her caramel-colored tote featured the bold double-G logo and distinctive red and green webbing reserved for Gucci designs.

She stood, picked up the bag, and hung it over her shoulder. Her voice dripped with honey. "Well, *bless your heart*, Josie. I hardly think I'm the only woman who owns a Gucci."

I looked up at her. "So, the woman in the park *wasn't you?*"

She shook her head, the dark red waves bouncing against her green jacket. "Sorry, no. Call me when the article is ready. I want to check the accuracy before you print anything."

I rolled my eyes. "You'll need to talk to my editor about that."

"Oh, I will, Josie. I *definitely* will."

I watched her exit the cafe and climb into a yellow Fiat. Then, I jotted several quick notes onto my pad. Park Bench? Injured Hand? Yellow Fiat? When I returned to the coffee bar for a refill, Lorene left her position behind the counter and came to greet me. My friend stood only four-foot-ten, but she ran the Cozy Cups Cafe like a drill sergeant. Today, she had pulled her straight black hair into a bun held in place by chopsticks.

"Your guest didn't stay long."

"She's too busy for an interview."

"Or too intimidated by your questions?"

"That's the interesting thing," I said. "She appeared fidgety and agitated before I sat down. We barely talked."

"I wouldn't worry about it. She was here once before and left quickly that time, too."

"Hmmm. Maybe she's always on the go. But the woman seemed anxious. And she wasn't very nice about it. She even pulled that *'bless your heart'* stunt."

Lorene laughed at my imitation of Savannah's words. "We all know what that means," she said.

"The Southern ladies' not-so-subtle way of expressing contempt, disguised within a polite conversation."

"Is Savannah from the South?"

"I didn't notice any accent, but she played the part well."

"It's best to let it go," Lorene said. "Women like that aren't looking for female friends. How about a chocolate croissant to ease the sting?"

I resisted Lorene's offer to taste the pastry, opting to visit Johnny Depp, instead. It was nearly 11 o'clock, and I wanted to catch him during his noon playtime.

First, I walked down the block to The Pet Stop. Barbara Chamberlin's bakery smelled of bacon and biscuits when I entered.

I watched as she slid a tray into the glass case, much like the pastry display in our local donut shop. Barbara's sales strategy was similar, too. "I like to showcase these treats where my puppy customers can see them," she said. "Where's Moe?"

"He's at home this morning, but I'll bring him by later. What do you have for cats?"

"Cats?" The look on her face was comical. She knew every pet owner, and every pet, by name. I was clearly a dog owner.

Laughing at her expression, I quickly explained. "I'm watching Johnny Depp, and I'd like to get him a treat."

She nodded. "Ah. Now I understand. Johnny's heart belongs to Maryann, but you might buy a little of his affection."

Barbara led me to the toy section and recommended a tiny jingle ball with a feather attached, "This should appeal to him," she said. "He loves shiny objects. And he favors the fish puffs, if you'd like to tempt his palate."

I purchased both items, plus a bag of bacon biscuits for Moe. When I turned down Maryann's street, a white commercial van barreling my direction nearly sideswiped me. I pulled Piper to the curb to avoid the driver's careless weaving. I tried to catch the license plate, but the best I could do was glimpse part of an advertisement on the back. *Somebody's in a hurry*, I thought.

* * *

I slipped Maryann's key into the lock and opened her side door—the one she had suggested because it was closest to her driveway—and stepped directly into her kitchen. Johnny Depp failed to greet me. The big white cat with his patches of black and caramel fur was nowhere to be seen. For a moment, I felt a twinge of panic. *What if he had darted out the open door, and I had already lost him?*

Then I remembered Maryann's list. She had provided several suggestions on ways to attract JD to the kitchen. Preparing to take pictures of the cat so I could text them to Maryann, I slid my phone into my pocket, set my purse on the counter, and attacked a container of gourmet cat food with the electric can opener, making all the noise I could. Still no Johnny.

A dishtowel had fallen off its rod, and I wondered, briefly, whether the cat had pulled it to the floor. As I moved around the kitchen, filling his bowls with food and water, I noticed several other things out of place: an open silverware drawer, a toppled coffee cup, and a crumpled floor rug caught my eye.

Either Maryann left in a rush, or Johnny Depp had been performing acrobatics in her absence.

"Here, kitty, kitty," I called out to the cat. "I have treats for you."

The small house was eerily silent as I stepped into the laundry room to check the litter box. I used the plastic strainer to remove a few fresh droppings, relieved to see evidence the cat was still in the house, where he belonged. The plants wouldn't need watering for another couple of days, so my tasks didn't take long.

Eager to befriend JD, I wandered into the living room, the jingle bell ball in one hand and a fish puff in the other. "Johnny? Where are you, boy?"

Here, I noticed more disarray. The pillows were off the couch, haphazardly strewn across the room. Two plants had toppled from the end tables, dirt spread in clumps over the floor. The front door was ajar. There was no way one cat could have destroyed this much in a few hours.

Something is wrong.

The hair on the back of my neck prickled. All at once, I realized I was alone, in a ransacked house. At least, I *hoped* I was alone. I stood motionless in the center of the living room, listening.

My cell phone rang, and I nearly jumped out of my skin, getting the device out of my pocket. The caller ID announced Nellie's number, so I swiped to answer, "Nellie?" I kept my voice low.

"What's wrong?" Nellie's voice was normal, and my moment of panic subsided. "Why are you whispering?"

"I'm at Maryann's, searching for Johnny Depp. He hasn't come to the kitchen for his food, and the house is trashed."

"Describe, *trashed*." Nellie's direct approach was exactly what I needed to make me realize I was overreacting to a quiet house.

"Nothing too serious." I tried to sound casual and confident. "Plants and pillows overturned, and a few rugs out of place."

Nellie's voice became firm in my ear. "Listen carefully, Josie. Maryann is meticulous. She would never leave her home in that condition. And Johnny Depp is a cat, not a burglar. Get out of the house, *now*."

"But I need to find the cat."

"Forget the cat," Nellie said. "Go outside and wait in your car. I'll call Chief Marshall. He can send someone to check the house before you go further."

"Okay." I lowered my voice to a whisper, again. "Tell him the front door was open, too."

"Go, now," Nellie insisted.

I answered her in my best impersonation of my natural voice, in case a robber was hiding in the bedroom. "Sure, Nellie. See you soon."

With my phone still in my hand, I hurried into the kitchen to get my purse. Suddenly, I heard a crash in the bedroom. I grabbed my handbag, raced for the door, slipped on the throw rug, and fell flat on my back. Someone wearing a black ski mask jumped over me, tossed Johnny Depp onto my chest, and dashed toward the door. Johnny tumbled over my neck and landed in a heap, covering my face.

I dragged his limp body off my head, spat cat hair from my mouth, and captured Johnny in my arms. It took me another five minutes to calm him down. And that is why I was still on the kitchen floor, dazed, when the chief arrived.

Chapter Six

Thursday Afternoon

Chief Marshall appeared only minutes after I landed on the kitchen floor with a huge cat on my head. When he barged through the door, I still sat, dazed and cross-legged, with Johnny Depp on my lap. Without a word, the chief gently lifted the cat in one arm and helped me to my feet with the other.

"You okay?" He asked.

"Give me a minute," I said. "I feel a little shaky."

He motioned toward the hall. "Go splash some water on your face."

"Good idea," I said.

I gave JD one final soothing snuggle before I stumbled down the hallway. And then, I screamed.

The chief raced into the bathroom where I stood, frozen, staring at Maryann's bathtub. He took one look into the tub, whipped his jacket off, wrapped it around my shoulders, and spoke firmly into my ear.

"She's gone, Josie. Step away from the tub."

I wanted to follow his instructions, but my feet were stuck to the floor.

Maryann lay, fully clothed, on a bed of cash in the antique clawfoot tub that served as the focal point of the room. *She looks peaceful,* I thought. *As though she napped on the soft piles of currency that filled the tub.* I tried to reach out to awaken her. My arm remained frozen at my side.

The chief spoke again, but his voice sounded faint, and I heard only a few words. "Out of here…" He stepped forward to block my view of the tub and pulled at my arms, turning me toward the door.

I nodded my head and shuffled a few steps, leaning on the chief for support. From the corner of my eye, I saw a flash of something silver, but when I tilted my head to focus on the object, my knees buckled. It was natural to feel wobbly, I supposed. Still, I hated that I fell to the floor again, this time in a dead faint of my own. I had hoped to *assist* Chief Marshall, not create additional work for him.

When I woke for the second time, with a walloping headache and a heavy weight on my heart, I figured I'd suffered from cardiac arrest. Voices called my name.

"Josie? Are you okay?"

I opened my eyes a tiny slit. I was flat on my back on Maryann's living room floor. Johnny Depp curled on my chest, and Nellie leaned over him, peering into my face. Chief Marshall towered behind her, obstructing my view of the hallway.

As I tried to lift my head, the chief silently raised his index finger, pointed it at me, and then raised it to his lips in the signal for "shush." He clearly intended the gesture for my eyes only.

I stared into his dark eyes without speaking and gave what I hoped was an imperceptible nod.

Almost immediately, my cell phone rang on the floor beside me. Nellie picked up the phone while I struggled into a sitting position.

"Hello, Sharon," she said, in a voice so natural that I almost believed everything was okay. "Josie's fine. She walked into Maryann's house and bumped into an intruder…"

The chief stood firm, hands on hips, between Nellie and the bathroom, where he effectively blocked further encroachment on his crime scene.

Unaware that Maryann's dead body was less than fifty feet away from where we sat, Nellie chattered on. "Yes. Knocked her down. She experienced a bit of shock. The chief says she fainted. Now that she's awake, we will be leaving. Chief Marshall wants us out of here."

The one-sided conversation was making me crazy. I grabbed the phone from Nellie's hand. "Let me talk to her."

"Hi," I said. "I'm okay, but feeling a little dazed. Could you come over for lunch? I'll fix soup." Then Sharon insisted *she* would prepare the meal, and Nellie argued *she* would cook.

Finally, Chief Marshall ordered Nellie to take me home to rest. "Our officers will secure the crime scene. Josie can come to the station to make an official statement after lunch," he said. "Meanwhile, keep her as quiet as possible. No questions. No conversations. Just lunch and a nap."

"Yes, Chief," Nellie agreed.

For good measure, the chief turned to face me. "Promise me you won't discuss *anything* you've seen today."

An image of Maryann's body popped into my head, and my eyes filled with tears. I swallowed hard, nodding back at him.

"I need to hear you say it, Josie," Chief Marshall said.

My voice came out in a whisper so low I didn't recognize it. "I promise, Chief. I won't say anything until we talk this afternoon."

After that, Nellie loaded Johnny Depp into his crate and drove me directly home. Moe greeted the cat with caution when Nellie carried him into the cottage and established his litter box and kitty condo in my laundry room. This would be his home for the next couple of days. While Moe and Johnny might become friends in a day or two, I was reluctant to have them share a common space too soon. Plus, Johnny had sharp claws, so he could easily scratch Moe's face or shred my drapes, if provoked.

If he stays here long, I'll need to have the vet trim those claws, I thought.

With the pets settled, Sharon grilled a cheese sandwich, and Nellie heated creamy tomato soup. I devoured both and went directly to my bedroom for a nap.

Three hours later, I woke to discover that Nellie and Sharon had cleared the lunch dishes and left a note on the kitchen island. Nellie's handwriting scrawled across the page:

"We've fed Moe and taken him for a walk. Johnny is sulking in the laundry room. Chief Marshall had a couple of officers return your car. It's in your garage, but you *may not* drive it. I will give you a ride to the station. Call when you're ready."

My head still throbbed, but I wanted to help find Maryann's murderer. I dialed the chief's number.

* * *

Johnny Depp went with me to my official interview at the police station. I sat beside him in the back seat of Nellie's car for the short drive and carried his crate into the conference room as though the cat belonged there. The chief didn't raise an eyebrow. He simply closed the door, placed a bowl of water on the floor, and motioned for me to open the crate so Johnny could roam freely about the room.

I'd been inside the station many times, but never as a suspect—or even a witness—to a crime. Usually, I helped ask the questions. Now I felt a little silly that I couldn't describe my attacker.

"No, I can't identify the intruder," I repeated for the umpteenth time, as Johnny Depp clung to my lap in the interrogation room of our village police department.

"It happened too fast," I said. "I was getting my purse to hurry out the door, and the next thing I knew, I was flat on the floor with a ball of fur on my face. Johnny Depp hindered my view."

Chief Marshall stared at me, his black eyes hopeful. "Please, Josie. You were in the house several minutes before the guy ran out the door. You must have seen *something*."

"All I remember now is finding Maryann in the bathtub," I said, struggling to get Maryann's sweet face out of my head.

"That was after I arrived," the chief noted. "*After* you opened the cat food. *After* Nellie called. *After* the intruder knocked you down."

"I know," I answered miserably. "But that's all I can see. Maryann, dead, in a bathtub filled with cash. Who would do that? And why?"

"Don't you worry. We'll get to that. For now, I need you to focus on what you recall."

The chief was the most patient and persistent interrogator I had ever known—and I'd come across several in my previous career as a crime reporter turned crime solver. He always interviewed a witness three times. My situation was no exception. The first time, he listened while I told him what happened, from the moment I entered Maryann's house until we discovered her body in the bathroom. The second time, I repeated my story, while he asked probing questions along the way. How tall was the intruder? Did I notice anything different about the way he walked? Did he have any distinguishing marks?

The third time he interviewed me, the chief asked about my surroundings. Did I notice anyone on the street as I entered the house? What about disparities inside the home? Had anything changed since I toured the house with Maryann a day earlier?

"Her tub was empty before," I offered, helpfully. "Where did all that money come from?"

Chief Marshall rolled his eyes. "If you don't mind, *I* will ask the questions."

I closed my eyes to concentrate. Then I opened them in a flash. "What about the picture? The one of Maryann and the blond man. Did you find a framed photo on her nightstand?"

The chief skimmed the crime scene photos on his cell phone. "There are a lamp and a book. No photograph."

"When I was there yesterday, Maryann grabbed the photo out of my hands. She seemed embarrassed that I noticed it."

"Would you recognize the man in the picture?"

"Maybe." I thought about the tall man with his arm around Maryann. "At first, she said he was her brother, then she said he *wasn't*. I couldn't see any facial similarities. They were total opposites. Do you think it's important?"

"It's worth exploring. Possibly, her brother has something to hide, and she didn't want to talk about him. Or the man in the photo isn't her brother at all. Either way, the photo is missing. If we don't find it somewhere in her house, one of two things happened—the intruder stole it, or Maryann moved it."

"Which means it *could be* important," I said.

I watched as Chief Marshall jotted a note on the pad in front of him. Over the past couple of years, we had become good friends, putting our heads together to solve some unusual murder cases. I hoped he would allow me to assist on this one.

"What shall we do now?" I asked.

"*We* will do nothing." The chief's ebony brow formed deep creases as he scowled at me.

"But…"

"But nothing. You're already too close to this case. As far as I can tell, you were the last person to see Maryann alive."

"Next to her killer," I corrected him. "Which is why you need my help. I saw how upset she was at work yesterday morning. I was in her home to meet Johnny Depp in the afternoon. And I discovered her body today. No one is more familiar with this tragedy than I am."

The chief pushed away from the conference table and walked to the coffee machine across the room. It was one of those new-fangled pod contraptions, and I was relieved to see it. In the past, the only coffee available at the station came from a glass pot that inevitably sat too long on the burner, giving the brew a char-broiled flavor unpalatable to anyone but the chief himself.

"New pot?" I asked.

Chief Marshall shrugged. "It's on loan from Lorene. I promised her I'd try it for a week."

"That seems fair." I kept my tone neutral but made a mental note to thank the chief's wife for her efforts to update the station's coffeemaker. In my opinion, the new pot was long overdue.

I waited, stroking the cat's silky head and ears, while the chief pressed the button and let the machine work its magic. The rich aroma filled the room.

"Coffee?"

I nodded. "Yes, please."

Neither of us felt a need to fill the silence as the chief went through the motions of coffee-making. We both knew he was thinking about my pitch to help with the investigation. He filled a second cup, dropped two sugar cubes in his, poured a spoonful of powdered cream into mine, and added a plastic stir stick. Then he hiked his pants a little higher onto his waist and returned to the table with both cups.

"You're going to need this if we're working on another case together," he said.

I grinned up at him. "Partners?"

"I figure the best way to protect you is to put you somewhere I can monitor you." The chief still looked worried, but I caught the hint of a smile at the corner of his mouth.

"What does that mean, exactly?" A seasoned strategist, the chief often suggested innovative ways to tackle a case, so I was curious whether he intended to put me in protective custody or some other form of lockdown.

Chief Marshall took a drink of the scalding hot coffee without flinching. "How would you feel about a consulting position with the police department?"

I sat up straight and clasped my hands tightly together, trying to contain my excitement. "Really? You want to hire me to work with you? Would I have an office? Do I get a uniform? How much would I make? Can I have a badge and a gun?"

The chief leaned back in his chair and laughed so hard I thought he would bust the buttons right off his khaki shirt. "Whoa. Hold on, there. I'm considering a part-time advisory position, not a spot on the SWAT team."

"Oh."

"Josie, you know I can't put a regular citizen out on the streets to chase after a murderer—especially a mature, retired woman like yourself."

I placed my palms firmly on the table to steady myself before I spoke. "Did you say I can't be a real deputy because I'm an *old woman*?"

Startled by my outburst, he blinked and then raised his arms in surrender. "Now, now. You know I didn't mean it that way."

"Now, now?" I felt my blood pressure rising. "Don't you *'now, now'* me, Earl Marshall. You should know better than to patronize me."

Normally, the chief considered me an equal—someone with a sharp mind and more than a little common sense. But occasionally, he forgot I had a brain at all, and treated me and my friends like little old ladies who had nothing better to do than volunteer at the local bake sales. It was true we were all mature—in our sixties or better. Every one of us was retired, with time to commit to community projects. But that didn't mean we had forgotten everything we'd learned in those years, checking our brains at the door when we left our respective jobs to begin our golden years. In fact, I was in awe of my maven friends and their abilities to apply their cumulative wisdom to solve complicated problems every single day.

I understood why any ordinary man would get confused, but I expected more from the chief. *He*, of all people, had benefited most from the combined deductive powers of our small but mighty group. These thoughts raced through my head as I sat, glaring at him, until finally, he spoke.

"My apologies." The chief tilted his head and appeared baffled that he had offended me.

I waited for a beat, staring back at him.

"That's better," I finally said. "Now, tell me more about the job you are proposing."

Chief Marshall leaned back in his chair and launched into a list of duties for my new position. I listened and tried hard not to groan. He wanted me to assist with research, help with a few interviews, and keep my eyes and ears open for rumors around town. I was to report daily, contact no one without permission, and avoid all dangerous confrontations. When he had finished his job description, he said, "How does that sound, Josie?"

I sipped my coffee, reluctant to shatter the hopeful look on his face. Then, I set my cup on the table and answered honestly. "The last time I received instructions like these, they were from my mother," I said. "I was sixteen and grounded for a week."

"You think I'm being too restrictive?" The chief raised one bushy black eyebrow quizzically.

"To put it mildly."

"What did you have in mind?"

"You give me a business card with an official title of some sort. Make it impressive: *Senior Crime Consultant*, or something like that. I'll only use it if I need to get access to talk to someone and my journalism credentials don't work. I'll use my personal laptop and phone. No office at the police station, though. Nobody will talk to me if I'm too close to you."

The chief gave me a nod so tiny anyone else might have called it a tic. I figured it was a "yes", so I continued.

"I get to attend your briefing sessions and see all your evidence. I won't say a word in the meetings. I'll filter questions or ideas through you. And I won't use any of the information to report on the crime story until we solve the murder."

Chief Marshall scratched his head. "How is this different from you going rogue and doing your own detective work, as you have in the past? If you join our briefing meetings, you will have even more information at your disposal." The chief made a legitimate point. I was asking for more freedom, not less.

"Well-ll-ll," I stretched the word into at least three syllables. "The business card may open doors I couldn't get into before. I'll be a real member of your team, showing up every day to get assignments. You'll know who I'm going to see, and most of what I plan to ask, before I leave the building. You can keep tabs on me, like my mom used to do."

"Somehow, I doubt your mother had a firm grasp on all your activities as a teenager," he said.

"This is really the best way to solve the murder *and* keep me safe." I gave him my most persuasive, wide-eyed innocent look.

"I could lock you in a cell until all of this is over," he suggested.

"But then I couldn't help you fill in the gaps. You're already short-staffed, and I'm affordable. What's the worst that could happen if I made a few phone calls or researched Maryann's background?"

"I don't want to imagine the worst thing," he said. "About your affordability…"

"Yes?" I smiled up at him.

"This is an unpaid consultancy. If you're able to dig up evidence that leads us to the murderer, we'll publicly acknowledge your valuable help at our news conference."

"Deal." I extended my hand across the table.

"Deal." The chief took my hand and shook it firmly.

As he stood to signify the end of our meeting, Chief Marshal slid a single sheet of paper across the table. "Here's a list of additional officers I have invited to join us," he said. "Now, get out of my station and show up for work tomorrow. We start our briefings early. Be here at eight o'clock."

"I will," I said, heading toward the exit.

"And Josie?" Chief Marshall spoke just as I reached the door.

I paused on the threshold. "Yes?"

"Say nothing about Maryann until after the briefing. As far as the public knows, you interrupted an intruder—not a murderer. We don't know what caused Maryann's death. We're trying to reach her mother before we announce anything to the media."

The image of Maryann's body flashed into my head. I squeezed my eyes shut to erase it, but my mind refused to let it go. "I understand," I said. My voice sounded calm, although my legs were still unsteady.

When Chief Marshall dismissed me with a tilt of his head, I slipped out the door and stood in the hallway, where I inhaled deep breaths of air until I finally stopped trembling. Then I pasted a smile on my face and walked toward the exit.

The chief wants me as his partner.

Chapter Seven

Thursday Evening

Nellie insisted on driving me home again after my session with Chief Marshall. This time, Kate tagged along, and I was grateful that I didn't have to face either of them alone. It would be nearly impossible to hide the truth—that Maryann was dead—if either of them asked me to give them a full account of the morning's events.

I climbed into Nellie's back seat for the five-minute ride and listened as they instructed me to put my feet up, eat a hot meal (prepped and in the fridge from Nellie and Sharon's earlier visit), and get a good night's sleep. They walked me inside and made a fuss of checking the house for intruders.

After the two declared my house "safe" for the evening, I shooed them into the living room where I had released Johnny Depp from his crate. He and Moe were now curled together on the rug in front of the fireplace.

"See?" I waved my hand toward the pair. "There's no need to worry. I have two ferocious animals to protect me."

"Yes," Nellie agreed. "But we still want you to lock your doors and keep your cell phone nearby."

Kate shot me a worried look from the sofa. "How was your interview with the chief?"

"Fine," I answered. "I remembered nothing helpful, but I'll try again tomorrow."

"Tomorrow?" Nellie prompted.

"Yes. I'm going to the station first thing tomorrow morning," I said. "It turns out, the chief made me an offer I couldn't refuse."

Kate leaned forward in her seat. "Spill it," she said. "What have you gotten yourself into now?"

Reporting to my friends about the chief's "job offer" brought a smile to my face, but Kate and Nellie had the opposite reaction. Both women protested when they heard the news. "No! No! No!"

"I thought you'd be happy for me," I looked from one shocked face to the other, as we sat in my cozy living room.

Kate spoke first. "It sounds dangerous. You've already been attacked, and the police haven't identified the intruder. What will happen when you ask questions around town?"

"I agree," Nellie said. "How did your conversation with the chief turn into a job interview? Haven't you learned anything from your previous encounters with criminals?"

"Chief Marshall believes this arrangement will allow him to keep tabs on me. I'll practically be sitting under his nose when I'm at the station. He won't send me out to see anyone he considers armed and dangerous. I'm doing research. It will be as safe as sitting at the library."

I folded my hands on my lap.

Nellie rolled her eyes, and Kate tapped her fingernails on the table. Neither of them said a word. Finally, I gave them one last argument. "Look, I'm not some hot-headed schoolgirl. I'm a grown woman, and this is what I want to do. It's a short-term assignment I know I will enjoy. Can't you accept it and support my decision?"

Kate sighed. "Promise me you'll call if you get into a situation where some thug is threatening you."

"Thug?" I giggled. "Did you really say 'thug' to describe a bad guy? I've *never* heard you say that word."

She smiled at me. "I'm a United States Marine, Josie. I have an *entire vocabulary* you've not heard."

Nellie threw her hands in the air. "I give up. You've been solving crimes for a long time. You might as well make it official. Maybe the burglar will think twice about harming someone who works for the police department."

"That's what I told the chief," I said. "No worries. We'll have this case closed in a few days."

Kate nodded. "Sooner, if the chief can reach Maryann by phone and find out whether someone had threatened her."

I ducked my head and studied my hands to avoid looking at Kate. "Right," I said. "Sooner would be better."

* * *

When they had gone, I tried to follow their instructions. I heated the meal Nellie had prepared, changed to pajamas, and leaned back in my recliner to watch the six o'clock news. So far, no one mentioned a suspected break-in on a quiet street in English Village.

I switched through the channels, pausing on the NBC affiliate station where Chief Meteorologist Lisa Teachman stood in front of a huge weather map. Lisa was my favorite of the broadcasting professionals based in Wichita, close to English Village. I appreciated her no-nonsense reporting style and her willingness to share her knowledge with school children.

Tonight, she affirmed my belief that spring had arrived. "Temperatures will continue to rise," Teachman noted. "If you're a gardener, it's time to prepare for planting season."

She smiled directly at me before she turned to the news anchor, who grinned back at her. "That's wonderful news, Lisa," he said. Then he turned to face the camera. "Next up, I'll be sharing good news for coffee lovers, right after the break. Stay tuned to learn about a professor in nearby English Village who claims the best coffee comes from Peru."

"What?" I blurted the word aloud, even though I knew the anchor couldn't hear me. Moe raised his head at my outburst.

"No worries, Moe," I assured him. "The nice man on television is going to talk about coffee."

My thoughts wandered back to Maryann's suggestion that I try a cup of her favorite coffee. *This is the second time in two days that someone has mentioned*

Peruvian coffee.

Moe dropped his head to the floor and sighed as though to show that humans paid far too much attention to news programs.

Meanwhile, my mind was spinning. This was a perfect opportunity to gather intelligence about the oft-mentioned coffee. I waited impatiently through the commercial break before the news anchor returned to the screen. His eyes focused on the teleprompter as he gave a flawless introduction:

"For those who will travel the world in search of the perfect cup of coffee, your quest may be over. According to tonight's guest, the best brew comes from Peru—and it is now available in nearby English Village."

The anchor gave a slight nod toward the camera, slapped a smile on his face, and waited for the news clip to roll. And waited. After an awkward pause, he apologized. "Sorry, folks, we are having technical difficulties." He paused for another moment before continuing. "We'll try again tomorrow night. Tune in, won't you? And now, for local sports…"

Disappointed, I switched off the television set. "They didn't even say the guy's name," I complained to Moe. "I'll have to research it myself."

I carried my empty coffee cup to the kitchen sink, gathered my notebook and laptop, and returned to the living room, determined to organize my thoughts before the morning briefing.

It didn't take long to create a list of questions to consider. At the top, I noted my primary questions in the order every trained journalist followed: Five "W's" and an "H."

Who? The victim: Maryann Penny. The intruder: Unknown.

What? An innocent young woman was found dead.

When? I had last spoken to Maryann around 4:30 p.m. on Wednesday. She texted me around 10 p.m. *Less than 24 hours ago!* Sometime between last night and noon today, the young woman had died.

Where? The crime occurred in Maryann's home, a cozy cottage on a quiet street, in the safe little town of English Village.

Why????? I jotted an extra series of question marks beside the word. *If we can determine why Maryann died, all the other questions will answer themselves,* I thought.

How? With any luck, the forensics team would answer this question. I hoped for solid evidence from fingerprints, blood samples, footprints, and more.

I closed my laptop and stood to pace the floor between my kitchen and dining rooms, mumbling to myself as I walked. Moe, accustomed to my unorthodox way of sorting through the facts, barely noticed the rambling, one-sided conversation. Johnny Depp slept with his eyes shut tight, blissfully unaware of my pacing. After several minutes of the senseless repetition, I resorted to my tried-and-true "note card system."

Pulling a stack of 4x6 cards from my kitchen drawer, I settled onto a barstool with my pen in hand and scribbled random thoughts onto the cards. One card focused on the unanswered questions regarding Savannah Sweet: Injured hand, park bench, yellow Fiat. Another included stray observations about Maryann: Distraction at work, Peruvian coffee, urgent business. When I came to a stopping point, I grouped the cards into stacks. One collection described the crime scene: Disarray, intruder details, missing photo. More cards related to the cash in Maryann's bathtub: How much cash? Can we trace it to a source? Why leave so much money at the scene? Did it come from the bank where she worked?

Clearly, I had far more questions than answers. I decided my strategy for the morning briefing would be a simple one: *Listen and Learn.*

Based on the list of names Chief Marshall had shared with me, his investigative task force had ballooned from his small staff of four to a whopping nine, including me. The chief had recruited three experienced police officers "on loan" from nearby small towns, plus a rookie from the Sunflower County Sheriff's Patrol. Although I had no reason to doubt their capabilities, I wasn't eager to share my thoughts with anyone but the chief. I vowed to keep my mouth shut until I developed a plausible explanation for Maryann's death.

Meanwhile, I had told my friends I thought we would solve the case quickly, and I still believed it could happen…right until my first meeting with the investigative team.

Chapter Eight

Friday Morning

The mismatched assembly of law enforcement officers greeted each other with awkward handshakes and clipped conversations as they reported for duty at The English Village Police Station. Unaccustomed to working together, they grumbled about being summoned to assist with a small-town break-in.

When Chief Marshall introduced me as a *Senior Crime Consultant*, the shock was palpable. No one shook my hand or welcomed me aboard. Instead, they put their heads together, whispered comments to each other, and ignored my presence.

"Who needs a reporter's help, anyway?" I heard one patrolman complain.

I helped myself to a cup of coffee and sat in the back row, waiting for the briefing to begin.

The chief thanked everyone for coming and directed them to be seated. Then, he shared preliminary information: No cameras. No cell phones. No discussion without permission to speak. The room drew eerily silent.

Officer Devon—not my favorite, because of an awkward encounter when I first arrived in the village—projected slides onto a large screen at the front of the room. Chief Marshall dimmed the lights and began his overview of the crime scene photos.

"I have requested your presence today because this intrusion was not a routine break-in." Chief Marshall paused until he had undivided attention.

"We need all-hands-on-deck to solve this crime," he said. "That means morning briefings six days a week until further notice."

The chief cleared his throat and clenched his hands on the sides of the podium. When he spoke, his voice shook with emotion. "Unfortunately, we're dealing with something far more serious than an attempted burglary."

I bit my lip to hold back my tears. Except for Devon and another policeman who had taken evidence at the crime scene, the chief and I were the only ones who knew what was coming next.

"After the assailant attacked Ms. Posey and fled the scene, we discovered a woman, deceased, in the bathroom." Chief Marshall tipped his head toward Devon, who forwarded to the next slide. It was a photo of Maryann resting peacefully in the bathtub filled with cash.

The room erupted; everyone shouted questions and clambered for attention. The chief raised his hands to command silence.

"The woman is Maryann Penny," Chief Marshall continued. "We found no signs of forced entry," the chief explained as pictures of the intact door locks filled the screen. "We have not yet established the cause of her death."

Again, the officers shouted out their questions until Chief Marshall lifted his hands to quiet them.

Bonnie Jackson, the young officer from the Sunflower County Sheriff's Department, raised her hand, and the chief motioned for her to speak.

She squinted at the photograph on the screen. "I have a question," she said. "Is that bathtub filled with *money?*"

Chief Marshall's firm voice filled the room. "Yes, the tub contains piles of paper currency. Why? We don't know."

The chief squared his shoulders and surveyed the officers gathered in front of him. "Frankly," he said, "this case is baffling—that's why you're all here." He motioned for Officer Devon to forward the slideshow.

Pointing to the screen, he read the three bullet points aloud. "We have no suspect, no murder weapon, and—as I just mentioned—no cause of death. At this time, we believe the intruder killed Maryann Penny. The house was in disarray, Maryann's body was staged on top of the cash, and the guy ran from her home—knocking down Ms. Posey as he escaped.

Three officers on loan from other nearby towns fired another series of questions at the chief.

"How can there be no cause of death?"

"What do we know about the victim?"

"Did Josie describe her attacker?"

The chief pointed to each of the officers as he replied to their questions. "Obviously, *something* caused Maryann's death. We're working with the coroner to determine what it was. So far, we've found nothing."

He motioned to Devon, who forwarded to a slide of the bathroom floor, where a pipe wrench lay partway concealed beneath an overhang of the lower cabinet. The glint of silver sent my mind reeling back to the moments before I fell to the bathroom floor in Maryann's home.

This is what I saw from the corner of my eye, I thought.

"We discovered his wrench at the scene," the chief said. "Our forensics team is searching for fingerprints or identifying marks to determine whether the tool was used to subdue the victim."

He walked to the doorway and switched on the lights. "Ms. Penny was thirty-three years old. Single. A teller at the English Village State Bank. She had an ailing mother and a cat. No confirmed boyfriend."

Motioning toward where I sat in the back of the room, the chief continued. "Josie provided a contact number for the deceased's mother. We've called, but no one answers."

Bonnie raised her hand. "And the attacker?"

"Josie could not identify the individual. We're dusting for fingerprints today. Meanwhile, let's get started with the investigation."

Scanning the mixed group of law enforcement officers gathered in the room, Chief Marshall issued three additional instructions: "Keep the details of this investigation confidential. If anyone asks, you are free to confirm that we are investigating a potential burglary and the death of a local woman. Do not label it as a suspicious death. And do not speak of the cash found at the scene. We're withholding this information from the public."

Suddenly, the overwhelming lack of evidence hit me smack in the face. *No motive. No weapon. No cause of death. No suspect. We are starting from ground zero.*

Chief Marshall doled out assignments, with reminders to report any progress on Saturday morning. He tossed me the easiest of the tasks. "Josie, contact Maryann's employer. See what you can learn about her work relationships, any recent changes in her behavior, and additional emergency contact information they may have."

We walked out of the conference room, single file; I trailed at the rear. The officers headed toward their cubicles in the center of the building, and I made a beeline to my corner of the conference room. A few people gathered near the coffeepot for refills. I waited for them to disperse before I pulled my cell phone from my bag.

The moment I turned it on, the phone lit up with unread text messages and missed calls. I did a quick inventory, noting three from Leslie Anderson, my editor at *The Village Gazette*, and multiple contacts from my maven friends— all insisting that I return their calls ASAP. Apparently, the news of Maryann's death had already reached them.

I scurried to the chief's office to alert him that someone had already leaked information to the public. He folded his hands on his desk. "Some things are out of our control, Josie. It's possible one of Maryann's neighbors witnessed a team loading the stretcher into the coroner's van. Or, the leak could have come from the coroner, himself. Either way, it makes our job more difficult."

"Yes," I said. "I'll do what I can to limit the information in the news story for *The Village Gazette*."

"Keep the public statement simple," Chief Marshall said. "Police are investigating a break-in at a local home, where the resident was found dead at the scene. The deceased has not been identified, pending notification of next-of-kin."

"What do I tell Maryann's boss, Mr. Wentworth?"

"The truth. Maryann has died. We don't know the cause of her death."

"And if he asks if her death was suspicious?"

The chief squared his shoulders. "Tell him we are exploring all possibilities."

* * *

Ten minutes later, I phoned Leslie with the chief's statement and sent a group text to Nellie, Kate, and Sharon. The message was brief: "Thanks for checking on me. I'm okay. Police are investigating the break-in. We cannot announce the identity of the woman discovered dead at the scene. I'll get back to you when I can."

My response wouldn't satisfy any of them, but it was the best I could do for the moment. Instead of dwelling on all the things we didn't know, I made my call to Maryann's boss, Wayne Wentworth. I'd met Mr. Wentworth when I opened my bank account, and I appreciated his friendly welcome—such a departure from the formalities of big city banks where the top officers hid in glass towers.

Here in English Village, bankers often served on nonprofit boards, coached kids' soccer teams, and attended every major event. Wayne and I had seen each other many times, and he took my call immediately. "Good morning, Josie. What can I do for you?" His cheerful greeting confirmed what I already assumed—he didn't know Maryann was dead.

"I need to visit with you, if you have a few minutes," I said.

Without hesitation, he agreed. "I was about to walk next door to the cafe for my coffee break. Would you care to join me?"

"Could we meet at your office?" I countered. "It's a private matter."

"No problem at all. Come on over. I'll wait for you."

If the banker was curious about the reason for my call, he didn't ask. He understood the importance of maintaining confidentialities, and may have assumed I wanted to discuss a financial transaction. I walked the short distance from the police station to meet him. Mr. Wentworth's graying hair glowed like a halo as he crossed the lobby to shake my hand. Although he appeared to be in his fifties, he walked with a bounce in his step and a broad smile on his face.

We threaded our way between customers to reach his corner office, where he motioned me to take a seat as he closed the door. I swallowed the lump in my throat and stared at him without speaking. His normally jovial face became serious, and he pushed away from his desk, coming instead to sit in the guest chair beside me.

"What is it, Josie?" Wayne leaned forward, his gray eyes peering into mine. Oddly, I noted his eyes matched not only his hair but also his suit and the silver striped tie around his neck.

I took a deep breath and exhaled. "I have bad news to share, and I don't know where to begin."

Wayne Wentworth clenched his jaw and reached over to grab a box of tissues from his desk, setting them on the table between us. "It's best to begin at the beginning," he said.

Taking another deep breath, I clasped my hands in my lap and raised my eyes to face the banker.

Chapter Nine

Friday, Mid-Day

The color drained from Mr. Wentworth's face, and he fell forward, burying his head in trembling hands. The banker was visibly shaken by my announcement of Maryann's death. Concerned that he might faint, I rushed to request a glass of water from his assistant.

"Mr. Wentworth isn't feeling well," I told her.

Then I returned to his side.

"Maryann is gone?" He stared at me with blank eyes, forcing me to repeat what I had told him.

"Yes. I'm terribly sorry. I know it's a shock. I am the one who discovered her, dead, in her home." I was careful not to mention the bathtub or the cash.

"But, how? Why?"

"We don't know yet, Wayne. That's why I wanted to speak with you. Can you tell me anything more about Maryann's life? Her friends or family?"

"I…I can't," he stammered, clearly struggling to comprehend my words. His reaction seemed extreme, in his position as the teller's boss. *Was Maryann more than an employee to him?*

The secretary knocked softly on the banker's door before she opened it to hand me the glass of water.

"We need to reach out to her family," I said, giving him the water glass. "Do you have an emergency contact number in her HR file?"

The banker gulped the water down and set his empty glass on the table.

He inhaled a deep breath. "Give me a moment," he said in a shaky voice.

I folded my hands on my lap while he composed himself, finally returning to my question.

"I am—er, *was*—quite fond of Maryann. She was one of our brightest employees. I can't believe she died so unexpectedly. Could it have been a heart attack?"

"The cause of her death is still under investigation," I replied. "There was an intruder in her home. With no sign of a forced entry, we can only assume it was someone she knew or trusted."

"Maryann was *killed*?" Mr. Wentworth's gray eyes opened wide as he stared back at me.

I repeated the words Chief Marshall had suggested. "The police have not determined how, or why, Maryann died. Naturally, they will investigate every possibility—including murder."

The banker leapt to his feet and began pacing the floor in front of his desk. "That's impossible! Everyone loved Maryann."

"It seems difficult to believe," I agreed. "Did she have a particular friend? Someone she ate lunch with each day who might know about her personal life?"

Mr. Wentworth shook his head. "I'm sorry, I don't…Let me introduce you to Corky Markham, Maryann's supervisor. She will answer your questions."

* * *

"Maryann was a lovely young woman—a bright girl, beginning her first proper job," Corky said as we sat at the tiny conference table in her cluttered office. She gave me a sidelong glance before she added a surprising punch: "Although she certainly wasted a lot of time on the phone during her coffee breaks."

I wondered why Corky cared how Maryann used her personal time, but let the comment slide. Without taking a breath, the woman painted a picture of a vastly different Maryann than the one I knew.

Corky sifted through the bank's HR files, jotting down details from

Maryann's life while she shared her own opinions about the junior employee. "I tried to take Maryann under my wing," Corky lowered her voice and leaned toward me as though sharing a deep secret. "However, like most young people, she loved to shop. She had trouble living within her means and was always asking for a raise. Did you ever meet that ex-boyfriend of hers?"

Corky didn't wait for me to answer.

"If you asked me, it was a stroke of good fortune when he dumped her for the redhead. That two-faced real estate girl from the billboard and Maryann's ex deserved each other, if you know what I mean."

I bobbed my head until my neck hurt, listening to Corky's stories. "Hmmm," I said.

"Lately, she's been much happier. My guess is she's sweet on that new curator, Tony Something, at the Art Gallery. He invited her to the new exhibit the same day he opened his account here."

"Tony?"

Corky tapped her finger on my notepad. "Write it down. He's a foreigner. We all know they could be trouble."

I cleared my throat and stood to signal the end of our conversation. "Anyone else?"

She shot me a sidelong glance. "Mr. Wentworth had a thing for Maryann, too. Everyone knew it."

"A thing?"

"He *mentored* her, personally. Gave her his full attention. Recommended a couple of college courses to help her career. *You* know. They were close."

"*Romantically?*" I couldn't imagine the jovial Wayne Wentworth cheating on his wife. The man was a pillar of the community.

"Oh no. No. *No.* I wasn't suggesting *that*," Corky said. "He favored her, that's all."

During our forty-five-minute conversation, Corky provided a rambling description of Maryann's personal life that contradicted my own impressions of the young woman. She gave me a list of phone numbers for Maryann's hairstylist, her dentist (the ex-boyfriend), and her mother. I left the bank with the list in hand and my head reeling from the astonishing new background information on my favorite, shy bank teller.

Maryann was a spendthrift with a broken heart and a bank president who doted on her. Who would have guessed?

The chief expected a report, but I went directly home. I needed a walk with Moe to clear my head. Then, I would make additional calls to discern whether Corky's stories were true—or a total fabrication.

Nellie called as I walked in my front door. "How's the knot on your head?"

"Better. My headache is gone. But I started my new job this morning, and I'm more confused than ever."

"I hoped you would come to your senses and turn down the chief's offer." Nellie's tone signaled her disapproval. I could almost see the frown on her face.

"Are you kidding? This is my dream job, but I could use your help."

"Thought you'd never ask," Nellie said. "How about tonight? The mavens are dying to know what's happening."

"My house for potluck?"

"See you at seven o'clock. I'll contact everyone and get the food handled. You take care of beverages."

* * *

I made two calls in rapid succession. The first went directly to Chief Marshall's voicemail. I kept the message short. "Hi, Chief. I've spoken to Maryann's employer and will send you a list of her emergency contact numbers. See you tomorrow."

Next, I dialed Kate. She and I often walked our dogs together. The chief had requested that I consider an old-fashioned buddy system when I wasn't in his office. Although I felt a little silly about it, he had a point. Walking alone, I was an easy target—especially if Maryann's intruder feared I could identify him. With Kate by my side, and two dogs to protect us, we should both be safe.

She picked up on the first ring. "Josie! I hoped you'd call. How *are* you?"

"Better today than yesterday. Do you and Bacon have time for a walk?"

"Meet you at the park bench in five minutes."

I filled Johnny Depp's water bowl and stroked his tummy. "We'll be back soon," I promised the cat.

Then I slipped my phone and house key into my jacket pocket, fastened Moe's leash, and headed toward our meeting spot.

Kate waited by our favorite park bench with her Goldendoodle, Bacon, by her side. I still remembered the day Kate announced she had chosen "Bacon" as her new puppy's name. "He doesn't answer to anything else," she had explained. "I made it official." We had a good laugh over that, but the name stuck, and now it fit him perfectly.

Bacon was Moe's best friend. The pair often enjoyed play dates together at Kate's house or mine. They always greeted each other warmly, spent a few minutes wrestling in the grass, and then snoozed in the sun. Now the two dogs fell into a familiar rhythm, prancing side by side down the sidewalk ahead of us.

"Tell me everything," Kate said. "Rumors are running wild in the village. Is it true that you discovered Maryann's body when you went to feed Johnny Depp? That must have been terrifying."

"It was."

"I guess your instincts were right when you sensed Maryann was distraught, Josie," Kate said. "She must have had a good reason to be worried."

The sight of Maryann, sleeping peacefully on top of that vast pile of cash, flashed briefly in my mind. I couldn't tell Kate the details, so I changed the subject.

"See that bench across the park? The one over by the flower beds?" I pointed toward the shady area beyond the gazebo and the Hank English statue."

"Yes, I see it," Kate said.

"Wednesday afternoon, Moe and I were resting near the gazebo when I noticed a woman sitting on the bench. She was pretending to read a book—keeping her head down, but never turning the pages."

"Who was it?"

"Savannah Sweet."

"The woman on the billboard?" Kate's voice rose an octave. "I've never seen her in person. Does she look as beautiful in real life as she does on that sign?"

"I guess," I said. "She was shorter than I expected, but with the same gorgeous hair and smile."

"Haven't seen her around here before," Kate commented. "I heard she spends most of her time with the country club set. She's always busy. It's odd that she would choose to sit on a secluded park bench in the middle of the afternoon."

"It gets odder," I said. "While I watched, a tall blond man jogged directly in front of her and dropped a key—or something shiny—on the sidewalk. As soon as he passed by, she closed her book, picked up the object, and walked away."

"Hmmm. Sounds like a scene from a spy thriller."

"That's what I thought. But when I met her for coffee yesterday before I went to Maryann's, she swore I was mistaken. Said she wasn't in the park at all."

"You met her for coffee? Why?"

"Good question." I tugged on Moe's leash as we approached our normal resting spot, and he came to a halt beside me. Kate and I sat together while Bacon and Moe lay panting at our feet. "Savannah oversees publicity for the Garden Tour, and I'm writing an article about it for *The Gazette*. She wanted to tell me how to do my job. We didn't exactly get off on the right foot."

"Because you questioned her about being a spy?" Kate raised an eyebrow.

"Oh, no. When she denied being in the park, I didn't mention the spy thing. I'd already made a poor impression by driving past the gardens on Cleeve Hill without her permission."

"I thought Cleeve Hill Lane was a public street."

"Apparently, the mansions are off limits during preparations for the Garden Tour. People there are quite secretive about their plants."

Kate clapped her hands and laughed. "I *love it* when you get yourself into English Village politics," she said.

I rolled my eyes at her. "I warned my editor not to give me this story. I really don't have the patience for it."

"Savannah will get over it when you write a beautiful description of the gardens on display."

"Which reminds me, I'd better get back home and make some calls. I scheduled a couple of interviews for this afternoon."

"What about Maryann?" Kate's forehead creased with concern. "Everyone says you're the only one who can identify the intruder and help figure out how she died. Are you making any progress?"

I frowned. "Not yet. As usual, I have more questions than answers. I'm hosting dinner for the mavens tonight to help me sort through it. I hope you can be there?"

"I wouldn't miss it," Kate said. "Maryann was a good person. We need to find out if someone killed her…and why."

The words were barely out of her mouth when I glimpsed a tall blond man jogging directly toward us. I grabbed my friend around the waist and pulled her off the sidewalk onto the grass. "That's him! The jogger!"

Chapter Ten

Friday Evening

We gathered around my Grandma Molly's beautiful antique table. Nellie had organized a feast, as always. She provided a chicken casserole from the ever-ready stash in her freezer. Kate brought salad and bread. I had chilled wine ready to pour.

At the last minute, Sharon waltzed through the door with fresh flowers and one of her famous prize-winning pies, plus a package of napkins proclaiming: GARDENERS SPEND ALL DAY IN THEIR BEDS. She tossed them on the kitchen counter to be certain I saw them.

I laughed at her choice. "I doubt the ladies on Cleeve Hill would appreciate these, but I certainly do," I told her.

For the first time since I had discovered Maryann's body, I felt the tension in my neck relax as my friends took their places in the dining room. Moe stretched out on his favorite rug near the fireplace, and Johnny Depp curled next to him. The two had quickly become friends.

I put Sharon's flowers into a vase and set them in the center of the table. The mavens were already fidgeting, so I suggested we share a moment of silence for Maryann before we started our discussion.

When I closed my eyes, the image of Maryann in the bathtub appeared again, and I rubbed my temples to clear it. I must have been the last to raise my head because Kate cleared her throat and nudged me with her elbow to get my attention.

"Why don't you begin by telling Sharon and Nellie what happened this afternoon?" she suggested.

Kate kept her face serene, but her eyes held a hint of mischief. I smiled at her and launched into the story.

"As you already know from our previous crime-solving adventures, this woman is *fearless*," I tilted my head toward Kate.

"Nonsense," she said. "You pegged the guy as a potential spy. I simply attempted to help identify him."

"A spy!" Sharon clasped her hands and bounced in her seat. "Is he the intruder? Tell us more."

"He may be an ordinary jogger," I said. "But something suspicious is going on, and we need your help to figure it out."

For the next few minutes, I described my awkward introduction to Savannah Sweet, the interaction between Savannah and the jogger in the park, and Savannah's reaction to my question about her appearance there.

"She's hiding something," Nellie said.

"Yes, and there's the question of her injured hand," I added. "I don't believe her story about snagging it on a broken screen door."

"Two lies in one conversation," Sharon noted.

"She could be a liar and still not be involved with Maryann's break-in," Nellie said.

"Agreed," Sharon said. "But why fib about *both* her injury *and* a visit to the park?"

"Unless she's afraid the truth will implicate her in something nefarious," Nellie said.

Kate took a sip of her wine and set her glass on the table in front of her. "When Josie saw the same jogger in the park again this afternoon, she pointed him out to me."

"Wait? You saw him again today?" Nellie asked.

"The man ran directly toward us," I explained. "I wanted Kate to get a close look at his face. But she shoved Bacon's leash into my hand, whipped out her phone, and snapped a photo of the jogger as he ran past."

"Kate!" Nellie exclaimed. "What were you thinking? This man could be a murderer."

Sharon leaned across the table to fire out additional questions. "What happened next? Did he try to take the phone away?"

I chuckled. "No. We were lucky. The guy wore headphones and trotted by us, focused on the path ahead. He didn't notice two nondescript old ladies and their dogs standing on the grass—just *four feet* from the sidewalk—as he ran."

Nellie shrugged. "Of course not," she said. "Everyone underestimates us. Even Chief Marshall sees us as harmless elderly women."

"But I took the picture!" Kate waved her phone in the air, and two sets of hands reached up to take it from her. Sharon was the first to grab it.

"Let me see," Sharon said, holding the screen up to her face. "It's a great shot, Kate." She continued to study the photo. "He's a handsome young man, isn't he? I don't know him, but I'd guess him to be about thirty-five. He lifts weights, too. Look at the way his t-shirt stretches across his chest..."

"Give it to me," Nellie said, taking the phone from Sharon. She stared at the picture for only a few seconds before she yelled out, "I know him. That's David Lang."

"Your *dentist*?" Sharon stared at Nellie. "You never told us Dr. Lang was a hunk."

"You never asked," Nellie said. She looked at the photo again. "He *is* good-looking, isn't he?"

All eyes were on Nellie as we waited for details.

"What do you know about him?" I asked. "Is he single? He resembles the man pictured with Maryann in a framed photo she had on her nightstand."

Nellie shrugged her shoulders. "Obviously, he's not my type—he's way too young—but most people would say he's *charming*," she said. "As far as I know, he's never been married. He's probably in his late thirties. The dental assistants flirt with him while they clean my teeth."

I took the phone from her for another look at Dr. David Lang's handsome face. "Maryann's boss gave me a phone number for Maryann's dentist, but I didn't connect him to the nightstand photo until now," I said. "Can you find out more about him?"

"Absolutely," Nellie agreed. "His office is open on Saturday mornings. I'll call them tomorrow."

Sharon brought the conversation back to Maryann and her mysterious death. "Tell us what you remember about the intruder, Josie."

"Unfortunately, it's all a blur. I've repeated my story to the chief three times and haven't given him anything helpful."

"Start at the beginning," she prompted. "What happened that first day? How was Maryann when you spoke to her at the bank? Did you notice anything unusual when you arrived to meet Johnny Depp?"

Nellie poured a glass of cold water and handed it to me. All three of my closest friends leaned forward, waiting for me to speak. I saw the concern in their eyes and knew I had to try harder to remember every detail.

I sipped the water, inhaled a deep breath, and cleared my throat.

Kate kept her gaze leveled on mine. "Go ahead, Josie. We're listening."

My voice came out stronger than I expected. "I started the day with a meeting at *The Village Gazette*. My editor, Leslie Anderson, asked me to write a story about the Garden Tour. I didn't want to do it, but she talked me into it."

"Did anyone else attend the meeting?" Nellie pushed for me to recall more details.

I paused a moment to visualize the room where Leslie and I had met. "No. The intern heard us laughing, but I don't think he listened to our conversation."

"What happened next?" Sharon asked.

"I was supposed to call Savannah Sweet for information on the Garden Tour," I admitted. "But I drove up to Cleeve Hill instead, to get a sense of the preparations that might be in progress."

"And…?" Kate prompted.

I shrugged. "And *nothing*," I said. "If people were working on their gardens, I couldn't see them from the street. One older woman stood beside her mailbox as I drove past. When I waved at her, she gave me the cold shoulder."

"Maybe she didn't see you waving," Sharon offered.

"Oh, she *noticed* me," I said. "A few minutes later, Savannah called to chew me out about sneaking around the gardens without her permission. Apparently, she enjoys bossing people around."

Sharon shook her head. "You've missed the mark on this one, Josie. Savannah is one of those people who behaves like a bully to cover up her insecurity."

"Hmmm," I said. "She didn't sound insecure to me."

"Believe me," Sharon said, "I serve on the Garden Tour committee with Savannah. She gets snippy when you question her authority, but she's basically a nice person. Want *me* to ask her a few questions? She likes me."

"Yes, please!" I hadn't considered that the attractive, successful real estate agent might have an inferiority complex.

Nellie tapped me on the arm to get me back on track. "What happened after the call from Savannah?"

I closed my eyes to concentrate. "I drove to the bank. Maryann worked in the drive-through. She wore gloves, like she always does, but she appeared distracted. She spilled coffee on the counter. I tried to calm her down. She said her mom was ill, and she needed to leave town but couldn't find anyone to take care of her cat and water the plants. When I offered, she was ecstatic." I opened my eyes. "Does anyone know her mother? The police haven't been able to reach her."

The mavens responded with a chorus of "Nos", so I returned to retracing my day.

"After the bank, I went home to let Moe out. Then we played mahjong. At four o'clock, I drove to Maryann's house to meet Johnny Depp. I noticed the photograph on her nightstand with a handsome blond man in it. At first, she claimed it was her brother, and then she changed her story to say he was *like a brother* to her. Either way, I'm pretty sure the picture was of Maryann with Dr. Lang. Is he her brother? A boyfriend? Or just her dentist?"

Again, none of my friends had answers, so I wrapped up the summary of Wednesday's activities. "I returned home and took Moe for a walk. That's when I saw Savannah Sweet and Dr. Lang in the park—which was surprising because she said her calendar was jam-packed with appointments. Then

Moe and I walked home. Harvey called. And that was it for the day."

"Wait! Harvey called?" Sharon pounced on the new information. "I thought you two were *kaput*."

I took a sip of my wine and waited for the mavens to calm themselves. "Don't get your knickers in a twist, Sharon. It wasn't a *personal* call. Harvey wanted to share some news with *all of us*."

"Let's hear it," Nellie said.

"A Kansas City gallery has invited Harvey to show his work in a special exhibit. Remember the owner who admired Harvey's booth at the *Summer's End Festival?*"

"That's big news," Kate said.

"Yes. Harvey says we will all receive invitations to attend the opening reception, since *we* made his work look gallery-ready."

"How kind of him to say so," Nellie said. She motioned to the floating chandelier above our heads. "Remember when you questioned this creation because you thought it was too beautiful to be functional, Josie?"

"I never said it wasn't functional."

"Humph," Nellie replied. "You most certainly did."

"But that was before you and Harvey became *a couple*," Kate pointed out, emphasizing her last words.

I threw my hands in the air and leveled a stare at Kate. "How many times do I have to tell you, Harvey and I were *never* an actual couple?" I asked. "There's *no way* I could be with a man who gave me the ultimatum that Harvey did."

"Which was?" Nellie pushed for details.

"Which was to make promises I couldn't keep," I said quietly. Although I understood my friends wanted more details, I had no desire to relive the arguments that had ended my budding relationship with Harvey.

Sharon raised her hands to signal a time-out. "Let's not dwell on the past," she said. "I'm happy for Harvey, and I vote that we all attend the reception to show our support."

"I second," Kate said. "We can talk more when we receive the invitations."

We cleared the table and gathered around my kitchen island while Sharon sliced her pie, and I packaged the leftovers from our meal. I'd hoped the diversion of dessert would signal an end to the evening, but Nellie wasn't ready to let me off the hook so easily.

Before I tasted my first bite of the pie, Nellie faced me, again. "Continue your tale about Maryann, Josie. What happened the next morning? Include every detail."

"I've already told you. I had coffee with Savannah, who denied being in the park and lied to me about her bandaged hand. She must have hurt herself between the time she rendezvoused with the dentist at the park and her meeting with me the next morning."

"Let's make a note of that," Kate said. "Then what happened?"

"I went to the Pet Stop to buy a gift for Johnny Depp. Then I drove to Maryann's house, and—"

I stopped talking, focused on remembering that day. "Wait! I remember seeing a van. Or possibly a delivery truck."

"What van?" Nellie leaned toward me. "You never mentioned a van before."

"It was white," I said. "I turned down Maryann's street, and a big commercial vehicle nearly sideswiped me. I pulled over to prevent being hit."

"Think, Josie." Nellie's voice was firm. "Can you identify the van? Was it driving away from Maryann's house?"

"I don't know where he came from, only that he was driving fast. I tried to read the license plate as it raced away, but all I could see was an ad on the back. It was a picture of a faucet and tools. It said something about Stan. A slogan, I think."

"Could the driver have been Maryann's intruder?" Nellie asked.

"Someone was still in the house when I went inside, so I doubt the driver was the one who decked me," I said. "But maybe he *saw* something—or *someone*—that frightened him."

"I don't know, but we're going to find out," Nellie said. She whipped out her phone and began a Google search, but Kate was faster.

"It's that plumber," Kate said, snapping her fingers. "The one who calls himself *Stan, the Man.* Stan Hermann is his name."

"I know the secretary who works in his office," Sharon said. "She used to be a file clerk at Will's law firm."

Kate nudged Sharon. "Let's pay her a visit tomorrow morning. Maybe she will give us a copy of his house calls for that day."

"Anything else?" Nellie looked at me expectantly.

I rubbed my temples, where the throb of a headache formed once again. "A couple of names popped up when I interviewed Maryann's employer and coworker," I said.

"What names?" Kate prompted.

"Her boss," I answered. "Mr. Wentworth broke down when he learned Maryann was dead. I sensed he knew more about her than he shared."

"I've got that one," Nellie said. "Tim and I have known Wayne Wentworth for as long as he's been in English Village. He loaned us the money to open Tim's furniture store. We'll talk to him."

Kate studied me from across the table. "And the second name?"

"What?" My brain wasn't processing her question.

"You said *a couple* of names popped up in your meeting at the bank. Wentworth was the first. Who was the second?"

"*Tony Something*," I tried harder to recall Corky Markham's description. "A new guest curator at the Art Gallery?"

Kate's face lit up in recognition. "Of course. Tony Dell. I read about him in the gallery's newsletter this morning. I'll drop by and pick up a pamphlet about his exhibit tomorrow after Sharon and I visit the plumber's office."

"Thank you, ladies." My eyes pricked with tears as I gazed around the table at my friends. Each of them had volunteered to help me gather information I might not find on my own.

"What would I do without you?" I raised my wineglass for a toast. "Here's to solving the case."

"And keeping you safe," Nellie added.

If only it were that simple.

Chapter Eleven

Saturday Morning

The morning briefing session brought several surprises, beginning with another new team member. The guy entered the room moments before Chief Marshall arrived. He wore khaki slacks and a white shirt with a lanyard around his neck. I tried to make eye contact, but he dodged my efforts and took a seat in the back row without speaking to anyone.

The meeting began routinely, with the chief calling on each person to make their reports. Officer Devon had pulled text messages from Maryann's phone and tracked the identities of her recent callers. He distributed copies of the stapled printouts, and I added mine to the stack of notes in front of me.

If anyone wondered about the new guy, they didn't interrupt the meeting to ask. We had all learned to follow Chief Marshall's lead.

When the chief pointed to me, I noted that a photograph I had observed in Maryann's home Wednesday was missing on the day she died. "I saw the man from that photo jogging in the park this week. My friend says he is Dr. David Lang, a local dentist," I said. "We don't know his relationship to Maryann."

Rookie Officer Bonnie Jackson groaned at my suggestion. "You've got to be kidding," she said. "We don't have a copy of this photograph you *claim* to have seen. Yet you're certain a jogger in the park is the man from the photo?

And he is coincidentally your friend's *dentist?* What an amateur."

"Enough," Chief Marshall silenced the officer. "Ms. Posey is a part of this team until I say otherwise. We will consider the information she provides, just as we accept the findings from other team members. But I would like to get a copy of that picture."

"But her observation is nothing more than a wild guess." Bonnie barely controlled the fury in her voice. "Josie is reckless. She could ruin a man's reputation by naming him as a murder suspect."

The chief ignored the officer's outburst. "Moving on," he said, pointing to a quiet detective in the second row. "Romano, what do you know about the fingerprints?"

Romano stood to give his report. "We've captured six sets of unique prints, but only matched two of them to people who were inside the victim's home," he said. "The majority belonged to Maryann Penny. Several prints from the kitchen and living room matched the prints we collected from Josie Posey. We retrieved three prints from the wrench handle. One was Ms. Posey's. The other two have not yet been determined. The tool is professional grade— more likely from a licensed plumber or tradesperson, than from a household toolbox."

My mind flashed to the swerving white van, and the mavens' theory that it belonged to the local plumber. *Could the owner of the wrench be Stan (The Man) Hermann?* After Bonnie Jackson's reaction to my earlier report, I wasn't ready to mention the van. Besides, it might have been in the neighborhood on a legitimate service call.

I bit my tongue and said nothing.

Officer Devon raised his hand with a question. "Has the coroner determined a cause of death yet? Even with fingerprints, we can't assume the wrench we discovered on the bathroom floor was a murder weapon."

Chief Marshall rewarded Devon with a nod. He walked to the whiteboard at the front of the room and picked up a marker. "Here's what we know," he said.

In big block letters, the chief wrote: CAUSE OF DEATH. "This may surprise you, but the coroner sees no evidence of any injury. We found no blood on the wrench, and no wound on Maryann."

An audible gasp filled the room, and Chief Marshall turned to face the puzzled officers. "This is the strangest crime scene I have ever encountered," he said. "It looks as though someone rendered Maryann unconscious, filled the tub with cash, laid her gently on top of it, and left her there."

"Are you saying she wasn't murdered?" An officer from nearby Lindsborg called out from the back row.

The chief shook his head. "There's no doubt the victim's death is suspicious," he said. "Her home was in disarray, which shows there may have been a physical struggle. And yes, there was an intruder. But a murder? We simply don't have enough evidence to be certain."

Confusion erupted as the puzzled officers shouted more questions at the chief.

He raised his hands to silence them. "Here's the interesting part," he said, turning back toward the whiteboard. This time, he wrote only one word: MONEY.

The officers sat on the edges of their seats, ready to learn about the cash discovered at Maryann's home. "The perpetrator used 5,000 hundred-dollar bills to fill the tub."

"What? Who would kill someone and leave a half-million in currency at the scene?" Bonnie Jackson bounded from her seat and walked to the coffee machine for a refill. "It's crazy."

The chief raised one eyebrow. "Technically, he left nothing valuable behind," he said. "The bills were counterfeit."

Again, the chief's announcement generated a roar of astonished reactions. He raised both hands in the air and the conversations rumbled to a halt.

Chief Marshall waited until it became so quiet that all I could hear was the old round clock ticking on the wall. Then he glared at the faces staring back at him. "I hope I don't need to remind you that this investigation is confidential," he said. "You are *not* to share details of this case, our evidence, or our theories, *with anyone*. This includes your personal speculations about Maryann's cause of death, or the money found in her home. Is that clear?"

After every head nodded, the chief continued. "I want to introduce you to a new member of the team, U.S. Secret Service Agent John Evans."

The quiet man in the khaki pants stood to speak. "Some of you may know that the USA formed the Secret Service Agency in 1865 to investigate and prevent counterfeiting. Our investigative mission has grown over time, but our primary purpose still involves safeguarding the payment and financial systems of the United States." He swept his eyes across the room. "That's why I'm here," he said.

Chief Marshall reclaimed the podium for a couple of additional announcements. "You may see Agent Evans around town as he investigates the currency we found in Maryann's home. Please don't reveal his occupation until we make a formal announcement later this week."

He gestured to the back of the room. "I have posted today's assignments on the bulletin board. Take the card with your name and get to work. We have a crime to solve."

Everyone filed out, collecting their cards from the array thumb-tacked to the board. My heart raced a little as I attempted to guess what job the chief had chosen for me. Refusing to appear too eager, I pulled my card off and slipped it into my notebook. When all the officers had cleared the conference room, I returned to my seat and opened my laptop. Then I removed the card, flipped it over, and stared at the handwritten note.

"Go home," it read.

* * *

Chief Marshall waited for me in his office. "Have a seat, Josie."

"No, thank you," I stood in front of his desk, holding the assignment card in my hand. "Care to explain this?"

The chief sighed. "You're off the case," he said.

I glared at him and asked the logical question: "Why?"

"We found your fingerprint on the wrench in Maryann's bathroom. You are officially a person-of-interest now."

"What?" I was genuinely stunned by the news, and my next words came out in a stammer. "But-but-but you *know* I didn't kill her! I'm the one Maryann's intruder slammed into as he ran out her door."

The chief's dark eyes didn't waver. "Please sit down, Josie."

This time, I did as he asked. My knees felt like rubber, and I clutched the assignment card in both hands, trying to figure out how I had suddenly become the prime suspect in Maryann's murder.

Chief Marshall spoke gently. "Tell me about the wrench, Josie."

My head bobbed up and down as I realized what must have happened. "Yes! I noticed the wrench as I fell to the bathroom floor. It was after I saw Maryann's body. Remember? I fainted. I guess my hand must have touched it then. There's no other explanation."

I saw the resolve in the chief's dark eyes. He counted off the facts on three fingers. "One: the last number Maryann called was yours. Two: you found her body. And three: your print is on the wrench. Do you understand why you're on our list to investigate?"

Jumping to my feet, I paced the floor. "No," I said. "No. No. NO. That's impossible! What about the intruder who knocked me down?"

"You are the only one who reported an intruder, Josie. We have no evidence—other than your word—that anyone else was there."

My voice shook as I asked, "And the unidentified partial print on the wrench?"

"We will investigate it, but we have no further leads on whose it might be."

I turned on my heel and walked to his door. Then I shot out one last suggestion over my shoulder. "Check out Stan Hermann."

"The plumber with that catchy jingle?"

"Yes. I saw his van speeding away from Maryann's house that day. Maybe he's missing a wrench."

Without another word, I stomped out the door and climbed into my little red convertible with as much dignity as I could muster. Still fuming over my unceremonious dismissal from the job I had accepted two days earlier, I grumbled aloud to Piper as I drove home.

"This is the first time they've fired me off a case so quickly," I huffed. "It's not fair."

Piper's motor hummed in agreement—at least, I imagined it did. I used the next five minutes to regale the little car with my sad story. By the time I pulled into my garage, my anger had given way to a mild pity party.

Inside the cottage, I made a fresh cup of coffee and settled into my favorite reading chair with a notepad and pen. Johnny Depp plopped on my lap, and Moe lay across my feet—both providing comfort in response to my sulky mood. During the drive home, I had concluded: The chief was dead wrong about his decision to pull me from the case, and I would *prove* it to him.

* * *

Before I figured out what to do next, I made my calls to the gardeners. All three seemed happy to hear from me—Savannah Sweet had arranged the interviews, and they trusted her. As luck would have it, the ladies were eager to show off their gardens that very afternoon. The chief might not want to see my face, but the ladies of Cleeve Hill couldn't wait for me to arrive. Since their homes were on the same block, I scheduled thirty minutes at each one.

My journey to the gardens was a short ten-minute drive, with a vastly different result than the unauthorized peek I had attempted earlier in the week. This time, spring was in full bloom at the mansions along Cleeve Hill Lane. Colorful pots lined the sidewalks—bright yellow daffodils, orange tulips, purple irises—each home featured a different palette of dazzling flowers.

In contrast to the secrecy I had encountered earlier in the week, today the ladies waited on their front porches to greet me.

I stopped first at the daffodil house, the home of Mrs. Evelyn Greenwood, the self-declared matriarch of Cleeve Hill. The woman held her head high, her back ramrod straight as she led me through her foyer and down the hall to a spacious sunroom that opened to the rear gardens. As she stepped outside, her demeanor softened. My breath caught in my throat at the sight of the botanical wonderland that spread before me, and her face lit up with a gracious smile.

"Surprised?" She laughed with childlike delight at my reaction to the array of flowers so artfully arranged throughout the spacious estate.

"Spellbound," I said, meaning it.

A riot of color hung from arbors and spilled out of fountains, filling every corner with luscious nooks for wandering, reading, or relaxing. "We call it the Secret Garden," Mrs. Greenwood explained. "We want our guests to get lost in the heady fragrance of flowers as they stroll from one point to another."

"How do you coax these blooms so early in the season?" I imagined dozens of gardeners planting fall seeds and sheltering them with heated teepees during the harsh winter.

"Oh, my dear, we don't actually *grow* these plants," she said, her voice dripping with condescension. "We buy them from Florida greenhouses, and our local workers install them."

"Really? Isn't that terribly expensive?"

"Naturally. But look at the beauty it creates. Surely you can see the value?"

I bobbed my head in agreement. *"Naturally,"* I repeated.

But my lesson in the competitive world of gardening had just begun.

Chapter Twelve

Saturday Afternoon

Evelyn Greenwood led me to a corner bench near the bubbling fountain and motioned for me to take a seat. "We have always prided ourselves on the quality of our gardens," she said. "This year, we hired Savannah Sweet to help us set a higher standard."

I pulled my notepad and pen from my handbag and waited for her to continue.

"We added a Peruvian theme to the gardens and brought in Tony Dell, the new curator at the art gallery. Our goal is to attract gardeners, historians, and educators from throughout the Midwest."

Mrs. Greenwood studied my face, as though to gauge my reaction, so I responded with my brightest smile. "My goodness," I said, "you ladies are ambitious."

"Frankly, we need the money to support our charities," she said. "We will still offer a local ticket price to the residents of English Village, but outsiders will pay double that cost for admission."

As she described the pricing structure, I made notes for my article. "You are certain to generate additional funds," I commented.

Mrs. Greenwood lifted her chin. "There's more," she said. "Each gardener will also plan high-dollar events—like private showings and VIP parties. I fully intend to host more guests, *and raise more money*, than my neighbors. I'll start with a Peruvian Coffee Hour at one hundred dollars per person."

"Is it a contest?" I asked.

The matriarch raised one eyebrow and gave me a slight Mona Lisa smile. "Of course not, Josie. We always work together to accomplish our goals."

I'd barely stepped off Mrs. Greenwood's front steps after touring her garden when her neighbor, Leticia Cornwall, waved at me with a pink handkerchief she clutched in her frail hand. "Hurry this way, Ms. Posey," she insisted. "You must view my garden while the afternoon sun is still high in the sky."

To accommodate her, I strode quickly down the Greenwoods' long sidewalk, dashed across 50 feet of decorative stone pavers separating the two houses, and jogged back up Mrs. Cornwall's walk—reaching her stately columned porch only slightly out of breath. She greeted me graciously, with a trace of kindness in her voice. "It's lovely to meet you, Ms. Posey."

"Please call me Josie," I said, smiling at her.

"I shall, if you call me Leticia," she replied.

With the formalities behind us, the diminutive Mrs. Cornwall turned to escort me through a wide hallway dripping with chandeliers and straight to the French doors leading to her garden. The contrast between the two women was striking. Leticia was shorter and slimmer than the regal Evelyn Greenwood. Wisps of silver hair escaped from beneath her sunhat as she hurried through her tour. She reminded me of a woodland sprite, dancing her way along the pathway, and fluttering her hands as she spoke of her vision for a true English-style garden.

"I must show you the terraces," she said. "We have one for dining, another for formal tea parties, and a third for children's events."

We walked along the flagstone paths to the terraces, admiring the features of each. Afterward, Leticia led me beyond a labyrinth of vertical hedges to a quiet reflecting pond brimming with lily pads. Tiny lights dotted the trees, and the scent of hyacinth blossoms filled the air. "This is enchanting," I said.

"Thank you, Josie." Leticia motioned for me to sit beside her on a small garden bench. "If you listen to the stillness, you will feel your spirits lift."

"I understand," I said. "Thoreau wrote, '*We can never have enough of nature.*'"

Neither of us spoke again for several moments, as we enjoyed the quiet spot. Leticia broke the silence when she turned to face me, a sparkle in her eyes. "Can you keep a secret?" she asked.

I smiled back at her. "Is it about the gardens?"

The older woman clasped her hands together and beamed at me. "Yes. And I believe you need to hear it."

"Then, you *must* share it," I said. "I promise not to tell anyone else until you give me permission."

Leticia pointed to a ledge of rock that jutted out from the stone wall that surrounded the pond. "We plan to install art pieces into each of our gardens, just as they do in Peru! Soon, an antique Peruvian artifact—an ornate, hand carved trunk covered in finely tooled leather—will be displayed right here," she said.

"What a wonderful idea," I said. "Visitors will discover authentic artifacts among the flowers."

"Yes!" Leticia agreed. "The new curator at the art gallery has donated priceless artwork for each garden."

"Tony Dell? For someone new in town, this is a generous gift," I said. "He must have an affinity for beautiful gardens."

Leticia lowered her voice to nearly a whisper. "We aren't supposed to talk about it, but Evelyn will have a large stoneware vase from the Inca Period—1200 AD."

"That's impressive," I said as I scribbled the information onto my notepad.

"Wait till you hear what Florence will display," Leticia confided. "It is *magnificent.*"

"Tell me," I urged.

Leticia shook her head. "All I can say is that it is perfect for her rose gardens. Ask Florence for details."

* * *

From the serenity of Leticia's garden, I made my way to the third home on Cleeve Hill. Before I could knock, Florence Crockett opened her door wide and pulled me inside for a private conversation. "I'm afraid we may have gotten off to a poor start, dear," she said, wringing her hands. "I'd like to extend my apologies, and I *do hope* you'll accept."

Astonished at her apparent distress, I stammered a reply. "There's no need to apologize-" I began, but the determined woman interrupted.

"Surely you remember," she said. "It was Wednesday, I believe. I stood at my mailbox. When you drove by the front of the house and waved, I ignored you."

"Ah, yes. I remember."

"I'm truly sorry," she continued. "I regret behaving rudely."

I smiled at the woman. "Let's forget the past and begin again, shall we? I'm sure you have been under a great deal of stress as you prepare for the Garden Tour."

"It's more complicated than that," she confided. "I believed Savannah Sweet sent you to check on us. The woman irritates me, with her heavy-handed methods. We hired her to help with promotions, not to assume full control of our event."

"I see." The words came out of my mouth even though I still didn't grasp her meaning.

"After you drove by, I called to give her a piece of my mind," Florence explained. "We're working hard up here—not to mention investing significant dollars—and I don't need a money-grubbing real estate agent looking over my shoulder."

Florence Crockett has an independent streak. No wonder Savannah was cranky when she phoned me that first day. I smiled at the woman's feisty attitude, but she misunderstood my admiration for condescension.

"I'm serious," Florence said. "Since Savannah took charge of the event, we have paid more fees, but netted less. She tells me not to worry my little head about such things, but I do."

"Perhaps she is trying to lighten your burden by handling the paperwork," I suggested.

"Humph. I suspect Savannah is more concerned about lining her pockets." The woman peered at me with sharp eyes. "I may be eighty-six years old, but I was an accountant in my day. I know when someone is cooking the books."

"Aren't the funds you raise designated for charities?" I asked.

Florence pointed her finger at me. "Yes! That's the goal. We want to net more money each year, not less." She grasped my arm to lead me into her garden. "Come," she said, "I will prove that you have saved the best garden for last."

We stepped out of her home, and the heady fragrance of roses assailed me. The blooms filled every corner, artistically arranged over heart-shaped trellises and garden walls. Vibrant colors greeted me at every turn as we threaded our way through what Florence called her "Garden of Love."

She led me to a raised platform of white marble in the center of the garden. "This is where my special exhibit will be," she announced with pride. "It is a model of Victor Delfin's most famous sculpture, *El Beso*. He's a Peruvian artist, and the full-sized sculpture is in *Parque del Amor,* which translates to *Love Park,* in the floral district of Lima."

"Goodness gracious," I said, echoing the phrase my Grandma Molly had always reserved for truly astonishing news. "*El Beso* means *The Kiss*, right? It will be perfect in your Garden of Love."

"You must come to my *Wine and Chocolates* event," Florence said. "I'm charging one thousand dollars per person, but it's all for a good cause. And the cocoa from Peru is excellent."

I thanked her kindly for the invitation, all the while wondering whether *The Village Gazette* might purchase a ticket for me to attend. I imagined Leslie Anderson would blow a gasket at the suggestion.

As we ended our tour, I promised to return when the sculpture arrived. Florence assured me I would not be disappointed. She accompanied me down the front walk, where I climbed into my car and started the ignition.

Before I drove away, I jotted notes for further contemplation: *How far will the Cleeve Hill cronies go, to outdo each other with extravagant displays? Is Savannah skimming Garden Tour profits for herself? Why is Tony Dell giving away Peruvian artifacts? Why are they so focused on Peru?*

All thoughts of the Garden Tour flew from my head when my phone rang with another call from Harvey. I swiped to answer it. "Hi, Harvey, what's up?"

His words came out in a rush, as though he had practiced them before he dialed my number. "It's none of my business—especially after how I reacted to your murder investigations earlier—but I heard a home invader knocked you down. *As your friend*, I wanted to make sure you're okay."

"I'm fine, Harvey."

"No black eyes or broken bones?"

"No," I said. "I landed flat on my back with a cat on my face. Nothing injured except my pride."

Harvey laughed at my description. "Good," he said. "Sorry to bother you."

"No problem. I appreciate your call."

"Keep my number on speed dial," Harvey said, "in case you need a friend, or *anything*."

"I will," I said, because that was the polite thing to do. It was nice of him to call, but I was pretty sure I wouldn't reach out to Harvey unless I had a genuine emergency. *I'm not ready to be more than friends*, I thought.

Chapter Thirteen

Saturday Evening

Later that evening, Kate arrived for dinner. Since the two of us were "singles," we made it a point to cook together one night a week. It had been Kate's suggestion, after Harvey and I came to an impasse on our relationship—if our occasional dinners out qualified as *a relationship*.

As soon as she walked in the door, Kate tossed a brochure on my kitchen island and pulled an apron from a drawer. "I brought you the flyer about the Peruvian artifacts exhibit," she said. "There's a picture of Tony Dell inside."

"Thanks." I moved the brochure to the pile of paperwork I'd left on my dining room table. *There will be time to read it later,* I thought.

I always looked forward to the meals Kate and I prepared. Left on our own, each of us would most likely have thrown together a sandwich or salad. Together, we tried out new recipes while we caught up on the day's events.

Kate stirred the marinara sauce and handed me the spoon to taste it.

"Yum."

"Need more garlic?"

"No, it's perfect."

I sipped my wine at the kitchen island and chopped lettuce for a salad while she cooked. Her short silver hair gleamed in the light, and she wore the same floral print apron Harvey had borrowed the last time he stirred up a recipe in my kitchen. "You remind me of Harvey," I said.

Kate raised her eyebrow.

"He was always comfortable in an apron," I explained. "He wore a protective leather apron when he worked on his art pieces at the blacksmith shop, a khaki tool apron at the hardware store, and *that* floral apron for cooking." I pointed to the one Kate had selected from the stash in my tea-towel drawer.

She laughed. "I've always admired men who aren't afraid of their feminine side," she said. "Was that what attracted you to Harvey?"

"No," I said. "It was partly his auburn hair—which he had despised as a child. And, the way he walked, with that unconscious grace of a natural athlete. But, most of all, I liked his lopsided smile and those brilliant blue eyes with crinkles at the edges."

Kate glanced at me over the steaming pot of spaghetti sauce. "It sounds like you miss having him around. What *really* happened between you?" She cut a slice of lemon, squeezed a few drops of juice into the sauce, and deftly tossed the rest into the wastebasket without missing a beat.

"I miss him, but not the way you might think," I said. "Harvey is a good man, as *a friend*. Unfortunately, during the few months when we spent more time together, he became increasingly overprotective. He meant well, but he wanted me to stop investigating crimes and become a mild-mannered retired woman."

"Ahh," Kate said. "That would *never* have worked."

I laughed at the droll expression on her face. "What? You don't think I can be mild-mannered?"

"Not every day," she said. "If he's honest with himself, Harvey would probably say your adventurous nature is one trait he admires in you."

"It doesn't matter now," I said. "We have both moved on."

"Give it some time," Kate suggested. "You could still become friends again."

* * *

As we ate the pasta, I told Kate about my interviews with the gardeners on Cleeve Hill.

"Evelyn Greenwood's garden was straight out of a fairytale," I said. "It was the most gorgeous place I had ever seen—but that was before I visited the next two."

"I'm not surprised," Kate said. "I've heard that all of those gardeners on Cleeve Hill buy tons of supplies from Harvey's hardware store to prepare for the show each year." Kate buttered another slice of bread. "If my hairstylist has her facts straight, the ladies spend thousands of dollars on specialized gardening mulch, organic fertilizers, and fancy drainage systems."

I laughed. "Never doubt the tales you hear at the salon."

"You've got that right," Kate said. "They know all the inside scoop. I once told my hairdresser I was planning a surprise party for my sister in Iowa. Two hours later, Sissy called to tell me she knew about the party. Turns out the lady in the chair next to me told her daughter, who knew the caterer in Des Moines, who told another friend, who lived next door to my sister."

"Secrets spread faster than the headlines, around here," I said. "No wonder the gardeners are so touchy about keeping their plans confidential."

"Can't blame them," Kate said. "They work hard to make each year more beautiful than the last. Tell me more about the other gardens you saw this morning."

"Leticia Cornwall designed a traditional English garden for the spring tour. It features a large stone dining terrace, a children's play area, a separate tea terrace, and a wildlife pond. Low-cut box hedges border the slate pathways, and the flower beds overflowing in pink, white, and blue petals. Her hyacinth blossoms are huge."

"Did she invite you for tea?" Kate's eyes twinkled.

"Scoff if you must, but the woman had already staged a silver tea set on a white wrought-iron garden table."

"Impressive," she said. "What did her neighbor, Florence Crockett, create?"

"Oh, Kate," I sighed as I answered, "the Crockett garden is incredible—filled with roses, roses, and more roses."

"It sounds lovely," Kate said.

"You need to experience it for yourself," I said. "Walking along the flagstone path is like strolling on a wedding cake. The fragrance is hypnotic. Florence said she had always loved roses, so she decorated her entire garden with them this year. Vining roses covered an arched trellis, decorated a quaint garden gate, and grew in every nook and cranny. She called it the *Garden of Love.*"

Kate nodded. "I saw the garden she created last year. The woman is a certified Master Gardener, and it shows."

"This year, they have added an extra element to the Garden Tours," I said. "It's a central theme that ties the various gardens together. I'm sworn to secrecy, but it's a showstopper."

My friend rolled her eyes. "It sounds mysterious," she said, "but I won't press you to divulge any details."

I stood to clear the dishes, and Kate joined me in the kitchen, setting the salad bowl and remaining breadsticks onto the island. This was as good a time as any, to tell her the news I had avoided throughout dinner.

"I'm off the murder case," I said.

Kate turned to study my face. "Why?"

I took a deep breath, then let the words flow out in a rush. "The chief says I'm a person-of-interest."

Kate blinked, then waved a hand. "That's ridiculous. Does he think you talked to Nellie on the phone from Maryann's kitchen, then knocked yourself out before she could get there to revive you?"

"My fingerprint is on a tool the killer may have used to hit Maryann on the head. The blow didn't kill her, but somehow, she had heart failure while she was lying on top of all that cash in the bathtub."

"Wait! You never told me you found her in the bathtub. What cash? I thought you discovered her body on the bathroom floor and fainted, falling beside her."

"Oops. I wasn't supposed to say anything about the money. *Promise me* you won't mention it to anyone else. The chief is going to kill me." I paced back and forth the length of my kitchen island, while Kate stood staring at me.

My phone pinged with a text, and I pulled it from my pocket. "Unknown caller."

I took a screenshot of the message, then passed the phone to Kate, who read it aloud:

"KEEP YOUR MOUTH SHUT."

She set the phone on the counter and shoved it back toward me. "Someone thinks you can identify them." Her voice had turned to steel, and I saw the look of determination in her eyes. "You need to share this with Chief Marshall."

"We shouldn't assume the text refers to the investigation," I said. "It could be a reminder from the garden show ladies; they don't want anyone to reveal their big promotional idea before the show begins."

Kate cocked her head and stared at me. "Either way, the text is ominous. Forward it to the chief, *now.*"

I tried to reason with my stubborn friend. "He won't like it," I said. "Besides, he has more than he can handle, already."

Kate placed her hands on her hips. "It's not the chief you need to worry about," she said. "It's the person who sent you this message."

When I glanced down at my phone again, the text had already disappeared. I sighed, sent my copy of the text to Chief Marshall, and waited for his reply. "This won't be pretty," I told Kate.

"Doesn't matter," she said. "He needs to know, so he can deal with it. Consider the message a compliment. The sender sees you as a threat."

I laughed, but Kate did not look amused.

"Seriously," she continued. "You have already touched a nerve for someone close to the murderer. They must believe you have the inside track on identifying them, or there would be no reason to resort to scare tactics."

Kate's words reminded me of my grandmother's advice from long ago. A bully on the playground had threatened to punch me in the face if I tattled he had stolen my friend's doll. I ran directly home to the cottage, crying all the way. Grandma Molly dried my tears and marched to the boy's house for a conversation with his mother. She returned fifteen minutes later—the doll in hand. The boy never misbehaved again.

"You must not allow a bully to keep you from doing the right thing," she told me. "If you had been afraid to tell me, he would have continued to threaten you."

With renewed resolve, I stretched to my full five-foot-three height and smiled at Kate. "You're right," I said. "I have no intention of stepping away from this investiga-"

Before the words were out of my mouth, my cell phone rang again. I swiped to take Chief Marshall's call and pressed the speaker so Kate could hear the conversation.

"Yes, Chief."

"I don't like the tone of the text you forwarded."

"Me, neither."

"Doors locked?"

"Yes."

"You alone?"

"Kate's here. I can ask her to stay for a while." My friend nodded 'yes' at the suggestion.

"Good. I'll get an officer to swing by your house to check the exterior. Kate can head home afterwards. Our team will also patrol the neighborhood overnight."

"Got it."

"Keep your outside light on and your phone charged."

"Yes, Chief."

"Call, text, or flip off the porch light to signal us if you're in danger."

"I will."

"And Josie?"

"Yes."

"You're still off the case."

"I know."

"*Sure* you do." Chief Marshall grunted on the other end of the call and neither of us said goodbye.

Kate raised her eyebrows as I returned my phone to the counter. "We'd better make another pot of coffee. It could be a long night."

A tiny ringing noise whirred in my head, and I could not shake the feeling that it might be important. Frustrated when the thought eluded me, I scooped the last of my coffee grounds into the coffeemaker. Then I wrote

"Coffee" on a Post-it note and tacked it to my refrigerator door.

At least I will remember to restock my pantry, I thought.

Chapter Fourteen

Saturday Night

At the chief's request, Kate stayed after dinner to babysit me. Although I didn't believe I was in danger, I appreciated her company—particularly as the sky grew dark outside.

At first, she sipped her coffee and watched me turn my dining room table into a blizzard of notecards and reports. Then, intrigued by the process, she grabbed a handwritten list I had strategically placed beside her cup. "This looks simple," she said, waving the page in front of my face.

"I *told* you my job was mostly online research," I said. "Would you like to help?"

She sighed heavily and muttered under her breath. "I might as well make myself useful."

I slid the laptop across the table toward her. "Tackle the items on that list," I said.

We worked as a team, Kate scouring the internet for bits and pieces of information on the obscure details I had identified. While she searched, I read the reports I had taken from the chief's morning briefing.

Officer Devon had found nothing suspicious in Maryann's phone records, but I was determined to look more closely. I'd scanned them quickly the first time and was about to do a thorough item-by-item analysis when Nellie phoned. Again, I put the call on speaker mode, so Kate could listen, too.

"I'm off the case," I told her. "The chief says I'm a suspect. He may reprimand you for speaking to me.”

“Fiddlesticks,” she replied. “All the more reason to find the actual killer. Aren’t you curious about what we learned from Wayne Wentworth?”

“Kate is here, too,” I said. “We are holding our breath in anticipation.”

“Tim and I pulled the banker aside after our homeowner’s association meeting tonight. Wayne is the president this year, and he has his hands full with a brouhaha over fencing in the neighborhood. Everybody agrees it’s okay to have a fenced yard, but the newcomers want to use cedar planks instead of wrought iron. The bylaws call for wrought iron. Well, you can imagine!”

Listening to Nellie’s tale, I remembered why I preferred crime stories, not politics, when I was a full-time journalist. I interrupted her rambling. “How did you get Wayne to talk about Maryann?”

“We stayed for coffee until all the neighbors had gone around 8:30 p.m. Then, we told him how sorry we were to hear about the death of his employee.”

“And?”

“You were right, Josie. His affection for Maryann went way beyond an employer’s concern, or a typical friendship between co-workers. He *loved her.*”

“They were *involved?*”

“No, Josie,” Nellie said. “Wayne Wentworth loved Maryann like a daughter. *He was her father!*”

“How can that be? Maryann’s last name was Penny. I’m sure she told me earlier that her mother lived alone. Her dad died a few years ago.”

“Wayne said Maryann never knew,” Nellie explained. “Wayne dated Maryann’s mother, Lois, in college. They broke up, and Lois married John Penny two months later. Maryann was born the next fall. After John died, Lois finally told Wayne the child was his.”

“Yet she didn’t tell her daughter?”

“When Lois learned Maryann had accepted a job at the bank—working for her biological father—she felt karma had intervened. Lois wanted Wayne to reveal his true status to his daughter and to share his health records and other pertinent information with her. He planned to speak to her on Father's Day."

"How sad," I said. "Wayne Wentworth was Maryann's real father, but he never told her."

I thanked Nellie for her efforts and ended the call.

Kate poured fresh cups of coffee, and we scribbled a new notecard: "Wayne Wentworth/Maryann's father."

I sat staring at the card until the words blurred in front of my face. Kate waited for me to speak. Finally, I looked up at her. "I don't see how this changes anything," I said.

"No," Kate agreed. "Wayne wanted Maryann to live so he could reveal his connection to her. I can't think of anyone who would kill her to keep that a secret."

Except his current wife and family? The thought flitted across my mind, but I kept it to myself as we returned to work in a companionable silence.

I focused on the printout of Maryann's phone calls. I had already compiled a list of unique numbers Maryann called during the week before she died. Now, I ranked the numbers by frequency to determine which of them Maryann dialed most—crossing through each line with a yellow highlighter as I counted it.

The system was tedious, but thorough. In the end, my efforts produced several surprises. Maryann called her mother every day, sometimes twice a day, until two days before she died. She called the bank twice that week—both at eight o'clock in the morning. She made four calls to Kitty-Kat Hotel, a boarding facility on the edge of town. Five calls to the Art Gallery.

I studied my list and wondered about the purpose of each call. *Why did the calls to her mother cease two days before the business trip to Kansas City? Who did she call at the bank, and why call at all, if she would arrive there in minutes for work? And five calls to the art gallery in two days?*

Kate and I had just turned on the ten o'clock news when Nellie called again. "I was so intrigued by the Wayne Wentworth connection that I forgot to tell you what I learned about my dentist," she said.

I punched the speaker button. "Kate's still here," I said. "You have our full attention."

"I spoke to Dr. Lang's receptionist earlier today. She's in her fifties, a lovely woman. She says David doesn't talk about his personal life at the office, but he *is* single."

Kate and I listened as Nellie shared the details of her conversation. "Dr. Lang works out at the Corner Gym, across from his office, every morning. Mostly he lifts weights, but he's also training for a marathon race. He often has breakfast at Cozy Cups Cafe and is partial to their maple pecan waffles. His favorite color is green. And he orders flowers from the Garden Cart for special occasions."

"She offered this information out of the blue?"

"Of course not, Josie. It took some coaxing. I told Dorothy—the receptionist—that I wanted to introduce Dr. Lang to my niece if he wasn't seeing anyone. Since Dorothy is a bit of a matchmaker herself, she was happy to help."

"Did you ask about the real estate agent? Savannah Sweet?"

"Sorry, I couldn't figure out how to bring up her name. I'll work on it, though. Monday morning, I'll be at Cozy Cups for an *early coffee.* Who knows," she added, "maybe I can share a table with my dentist."

"Thanks, Nellie," I said. "I'm scrambling to connect the dots, and every little bit helps."

"Yeah, yeah. I know. *You're off the case.*" She chuckled into my ear. "Guess that means you'd better work faster."

Kate laughed. "We're going as fast as we can," she said, leaning into the phone I had laid on the counter.

"We?" Nellie repeated. "I thought you were supposed to *keep an eye on* Josie, *not* become her partner in crime solving."

"Look who's talking," Kate responded. "I'm not the one ambushing my dentist at breakfast."

A text from Chief Marshall interrupted the good-natured ribbing. "Gotta go," I told Nellie. "My *former boss* is sending new instructions."

Kate and I read the message together: "All is clear. Send Kate straight home. An officer will monitor your street tonight."

"Looks like you're off duty," I said to Kate.

"For tonight, at least." She returned the list of research assignments, now completed. "Give me another list if you need additional help. This one was *way* too easy."

"You can be my assistant any day," I said.

As Kate gathered her things to leave, she made a point of checking all the locks in the cottage—windows and doors—then reminded me to turn on the porch light and set the deadbolt on the front door.

As she drove into the darkness, my phone pinged again. This time, the Caller ID announced someone I'd never met: Professor Tony Dell. His message was crisp and clear:

"SORRY TO TEXT SO LATE. THIS IS TONY DELL. FLO SAYS WE SHOULD TALK. MONDAY MORNING WORK FOR YOU?"

It took me a minute to figure out that the "Flo" he referenced was most likely Florence Crockett—although I could not imagine a world in which the society lady from Cleeve Hill responded to the nickname "Flo." Neither of her neighboring gardeners referred to Mrs. Crockett by the shortened name—and they had known her for many years. Apparently, the professor from Peru had a closer relationship to Florence Crocket than I realized.

Regardless, his invitation to meet saved me the trouble of tracking him down. Since the conversation would focus on the Garden Tour, I had no reason to clear the appointment with Chief Marshall in advance.

I am free as a bird, I reminded myself. *If our discussion veers onto the subject of Maryann's work at the art gallery, it is no one's business but my own.*

Without further hesitation, I selected a "thumbs up" emoji and pressed "send."

Done. I thought. *I can't wait to ask the professor if he noticed anything strange in Maryann's behavior the week before she died.*

Chapter Fifteen

Sunday Morning

By the time I crawled out of bed on Sunday morning and opened the back door so Moe could patrol the yard, I already felt better about Chief Marshall's decision to kick me off the investigation. My position as a "senior consultant" wasn't helpful anyway, I decided.

Unburdened by an official role with the police department, I could spend my time doing whatever I chose, without constant supervision from the chief. With no plans for the day except to attend an early worship service, I was footloose and fancy free.

Johnny Depp trailed me to the kitchen, where I turned on the coffeemaker and filled food bowls for Maryann's cat, and my fluffy dog.

Before I could toast my English muffin, Moe returned to the back door with a bright orange tennis ball in his mouth. I saw the hopeful gleam in his eyes, but pointed to his toy basket. "Drop the toy, and eat your breakfast," I said. "We will play this afternoon."

He gave me a sad-eyed look but quickly forgot his disappointment when he spotted the bits of bacon sprinkled on top of his dog food.

While JD and Moe gobbled their meals, I told them I planned to solve Maryann's murder case without the help of Chief Marshall. Like always, Moe listened attentively.

"I will follow my own leads," I said, as I lathered a slab of butter onto the muffin. "I'm a perfectly capable adult."

Moe tilted his head in agreement.

"Besides," I continued. "The chief already gave me a stack of files to read. He can't take them back now."

My fluffy pooch sauntered across the kitchen to rest his head on my knee. "You are the best dog detective ever," I assured him. "We will work on this case together."

The decision made, I dressed for church and drove the short distance to English Village Chapel, spotting the spired limestone building long before I pulled into the parking lot.

Kate sat on the polished pew one row behind Nellie and Tim, and I took my usual place beside her. Then, just like every Sunday, we settled into Pastor Pinkerton's sermon and allowed the ordinary problems of our lives to drift away.

After the service, Sharon hurried from her place with the choir to catch up to me in the parking lot. She had a sparkle in her eyes. "I spotted Savannah Sweet on the other side of the sanctuary," she said. "I'll have a word with her and call you later with any *intel*."

"*Intel*, Sharon? Really?" I raised an eyebrow at my friend's use of yet another "spy" word. The mavens insisted on using police jargon these days.

"Yesss," she hissed. "Intel. It's short for *intelligence*."

"I *know* what it means," I said with a trace of sarcasm. "We could *use* some intelligence in this investigation."

With that, Sharon dashed away to catch Savannah Sweet, and I returned home to dig into Maryann's text messages. Out of sixteen pages, only three caught my attention. I felt certain they were break-up texts to her ex-boyfriend, but the numbers didn't match any on her list of voice calls.

The first read: "YOU DON'T UNDERSTAND WHAT YOU ARE ASKING OF ME." The second, to the same number said: "I CAN'T DO THIS ANYMORE." I made a note to include the texts in my growing pile for Chief Marshall, if he invited me to return to the investigative team.

The third text was all too familiar. It was the one Maryann sent *to me* the night before I discovered her body. This time, as I read the words, a few key phrases jumped out at me: "IF ANYTHING STRESSFUL HAPPENS, MAKE

YOURSELF A FRESH CUP OF PERUVIAN COFFEE. INSTRUCTIONS IN THE CANISTER. YOU WILL KNOW WHAT TO DO."

I buried my head in my hands. *How could I have forgotten to retrieve the note from Maryann's coffee canister?*

I had first assumed the late-night text was a friendly word of encouragement; now it seemed ominous. Had Maryann hidden instructions on how to prepare Peruvian coffee? Or something more? There was only one way to be sure: I had to get my hands on that canister.

From my experience with the chief, I knew he was likely to spend a couple of hours after the morning service in his office, clearing out paperwork. If I hurried, I might catch him there. I called the number I still had on the speed dial.

He answered after the second ring.

"What is it, Josie?" The chief sounded exhausted.

"I, uh, wanted to check in with you," I said. "Would it be possible for me to stop by Maryann's house this afternoon to pick up a few things for her cat? I still have the key, but didn't want to go there without permission."

"Our investigators completed their work yesterday, so the house is no longer off-limits," Chief Marshall said. "Are you okay to return to the house on your own? I could have an officer accompany you…"

"Thank you, Chief, but I'll be fine. It's broad daylight, and I won't be there long."

"Suit yourself, Josie," Chief Marshall said. "Make it quick and let me know if you run across anything unusual."

Since the chief was in such a cordial mood, I kept talking. "By the way," I said in my most casual tone, "Have you reached Maryann's mother yet?"

"You know I can't share that information," Chief Marshall answered without a trace of the friendliness he'd shown earlier.

"But I thought…"

"Don't think, Josie," he said. "When I said you were off the case, I meant it. And that goes for your mavens, too. You're already receiving threatening texts. Don't make things worse."

"You need our help," I said.

"For what? *I'm* a trained professional."

"We hear things." I snapped at the chief for implying that the mavens had nothing to offer.

"Like what?"

Chief Marshall's comment sounded like a dare, and I couldn't resist a taunt of my own. "Wouldn't you like to know?"

"This isn't a game, Josie," the chief scolded me. "I doubt that you have heard anything our investigators don't already know."

"Oh, yeah?" I shot back at him. "Wayne Wentworth is Maryann's biological father." The words were out of my mouth so fast that I didn't have time to regret saying them.

The chief was silent.

"Chief? Are you still there?"

"Why didn't you share this earlier?" The rumble in Chief Marshall's voice sounded almost as dangerous as Moe's deepest growls.

"I'm off the case, remember? Besides, I only learned about it late last night."

"That's no excuse for hiding evidence. I could charge you with hindering an active investigation."

"Good grief," I said. "He's *her father*, not a co-conspirator in a crime."

"Are you certain of that?" The chief's question was like a slap in the face.

I waited several seconds before I answered. "I'm not positive about anything," I said.

"What else haven't you told me?" Suddenly, I felt like a teenager again, arguing with my mother.

"What haven't *you* told *me*?" I countered. "You said we could be partners on this case, then you fired me the moment your evidence placed me at the scene of the crime—which everyone already knew, because *I* discovered her body."

"Your fingerprints were on the wrench in Maryann's bathroom."

"Which was lying on the floor where I fell when I fainted. I could easily have touched it as I tried to catch myself."

Chief Marshall didn't acknowledge the logic of my argument. He skipped to another topic instead. "I suppose you have identified a list of suspects."

"I have." I agreed. "Five possibilities, so far."

"Do you have motives?"

"A few. Nothing substantial." I hoped I sounded surer of myself than I felt.

"Have you figured out *who* committed the murder, and *how* he did it?"

"You mean, like Colonel Mustard in the bathroom with a wrench?"

"Yeah, like that," he said, and I could hear the mockery in his tone.

"No," I admitted.

"Good," the chief said. "Then keep your speculations to yourself."

"Even if I discover important clues to Maryann's death?"

The chief hesitated before he answered. "If you somehow stumble onto something, type your notes and drop them by my office after hours. I don't want anyone to see you here at the station," he said. "And I would prefer that you and your mavens not stir up more trouble."

"You can't stop us from talking to a few people around town, Chief," I said. "I want a chance to clear my name."

"Trust me, Josie. The best thing you can do is stay home and leave this investigation to our officers."

"If you insist," I said. "But I should reach out to Lois Penny soon for a discussion about Johnny Depp. Besides…I want to talk to her."

"Our investigators will handle that."

"No, Chief. Your team will interrogate her about *legal things*. Her whereabouts the day of the murder. Her relationship with her daughter. The money. I won't talk about *any* of that."

"What would *you* ask her?" The chief sounded skeptical, so I tried to reassure him that my intentions were honorable.

"Nothing of consequence," I said. "I'll offer my condolences. Tell her Maryann looked peaceful when she died. Find out what she wants to do about Johnny Depp…"

"We'll see." He spoke with the same dismissive tone my parents used when I made an impossible request as a child.

"But Chief–" I began, but he interrupted my plea by exhaling heavily into the earpiece of my cell phone.

"Don't push me, Josie. I'll let you know when it's okay for you to contact

Mrs. Penny."

He ended the call, and I counted myself lucky that he had approved my return to the scene of the crime for cat food. I made a mental note to approach him tomorrow about calling Lois Penny. *If I ask enough times, surely he will allow it,* I thought.

Fortunately, I didn't have to wait for permission from the chief, after all. Before I could gather my things to head toward Maryann's place, my cell phone rang. I nearly dropped the phone when Lois Penny introduced herself.

"Is this Josephine Posey?"

"Yes."

"I hope you don't mind taking my call, Ms. Posey. My name is Lois Penny. I believe you knew my daughter, Maryann."

"Thank you for reaching out to me, Mrs. Penny. I wanted to phone you, but with the investigation still ongoing, the chief advised me to wait."

"I understand," she said. "But I have so many questions. Chief Marshall barely gave me any information, and I won't see him in person until tomorrow."

"Maryann was a lovely, caring young woman. I'm genuinely sorry for your loss," I said.

Lois paused for so long I wondered if the call was disconnected. Finally, she continued, with a catch in her voice. "I spoke to Maryann's, 'er, *boss*, at the bank," she said. "Mr. Wentworth said you were one of the last people to talk to my daughter before she died. I hoped you could help me make sense of it."

I bit my tongue to keep from admitting that I knew Maryann's boss was also her biological father.

"Yes," I answered in what I hoped sounded like my normal voice. "How can I help?"

"May I ask… How well did you know Maryann?"

"We met when I moved into town a couple of years ago," I said. "She was always friendly in her job at the drive-thru window, but I didn't really know her socially," I said. "Although we saw each other around town, at our local festivals and events."

"Did you notice anything unusual about her behavior in the days before she died?" Mrs. Penny never used the word "*murdered*" when she referred to Maryann's death. I wondered what she had been told about the crime.

"Maryann appeared distraught at work on Wednesday."

"In what way?"

"She fumbled around as she handled my deposit. She called me by the wrong name, spilled her coffee, and became confused at what would normally be a routine transaction."

"I see…" Mrs. Penny's voice cracked when she continued. "If you weren't close to my daughter, can you tell me why you were the one to discover her body? I was told you entered her home and found her dead."

"I'm sure the chief would prefer to give you the details," I said. "All I can say is that Maryann had asked me to care for her plants and her cat for a few days. She planned to be out of town, so she gave me a key to her house. When I arrived, I assumed she had already gone. Instead, I found her body."

"That must have been a terrible shock."

"It was," I said. "If it brings you comfort, you should know she appeared to be sleeping peacefully."

"I always worried about Maryann," Mrs. Penny said. "She had few friends, and a limited social life. She moved to English Village a few years ago to take the job at the bank, but I assumed she did it to be near her best friend, Sissy. The two were always close—although Sissy was as confident as Maryann was shy."

Her reference to the name "Sissy" rang a bell, but I couldn't make a connection in my mind, so I moved to another question. "What about boyfriends?" I asked. "I heard Maryann dated a dentist for a few months. Was she seeing anyone new?"

"Oh, yes, *the dentist*. Sissy had introduced him to Maryann, so I had high hopes for that one. But recently, my daughter met somebody new. A professor, I think. I suggested she should take it slow."

"What did she tell you about him?"

"Only that he had dark hair," Mrs. Penny said. "I tried to get more information, but she was reluctant to provide details."

"Could I ask you a personal question, Mrs. Penny?" Johnny Depp curled onto my lap as if he sensed our conversation was a serious one.

"What is it?"

"Maryann told me you were ill," I said.

Mrs. Penny lowered her voice. "Yes. I found a lump. It was breast cancer. The surgery is behind me, but it was more traumatic than I anticipated. Maryann was concerned about my recovery. That's why she encouraged me to spend a week recuperating and healing at a private spa in Florida before beginning radiation treatments next week."

"Ah, I'm so sorry you're going through this and losing your daughter at the same time," I said. "Were you aware that Maryann had planned a business trip to Kansas City while you rested at the spa?"

"No. I knew she was stressed, but I assumed it was because of my surgery. She *always* confided in me…but not this time. Whatever prompted her trip must have come up unexpectedly."

Stroking Johnny Depp's soft fur, I asked one last question. "I've been caring for Maryann's cat. We are getting along fine, but I wonder whether you would like to take him home with you?"

"My health situation is uncertain, Josie. I need to focus on getting well— without the additional responsibility of a cat. Are you willing to keep him? I know Maryann would approve."

"I'll give him a home for now," I said. "If you change your mind later, reach out to me."

As we ended the call, I asked Lois to consider our conversation *confidential*. "Please don't mention it to Chief Marshall when you visit with him tomorrow," I said. "The chief has asked me to step away from the investigation, and I don't want him to think I contacted you without his permission."

"But *I* called *you*," she said.

"And I'm glad you did."

"Ms. Posey?" Maryann's mother hesitated to continue.

"Yes?"

"Thank you for being Maryann's friend."

I set my phone on the kitchen island and lifted Johnny Depp up to my eye level. "Looks like you're officially a member of the family," I said.

Unimpressed by his new status, Johnny bounded to the floor and sauntered to his water bowl.

Then I jotted a few additional notes on my pad. Lois Penny had named two unfamiliar people during our call. It was time to get back to work.

But first, I need a break, I thought.

And I have a powerful craving for Peruvian coffee.

Chapter Sixteen

Sunday Afternoon

Before I left the house, I took a few minutes to clear my workspace. My dining room table looked like someone had made a tossed salad from index cards and Post-it notes. The haphazard piles made sense to me, but it was time to restore some order to the chaos before Johnny Depp turned the mess into his own personal playground. I added the names Lois Penny had given me to my deck of cards and sorted them into neat stacks I could rubber band into logical sets. No matter how many times I shuffled the note cards, I couldn't make sense of Maryann's murder.

Who wanted Maryann dead? And why?

My list of suspects was brief, but I made a stack of cards, anyway. The top card had no name. It read: "Suspect Unknown. Motive: Prevent Maryann from revealing the source of counterfeit money."

Dr. David Lang was suspect number two. I figured the "ex" is always a person of interest. Maryann could easily have pushed his buttons, angering him to the point of harming her.

The third card named Wayne Wentworth as a suspect. Perhaps his reaction to Maryann's death derived from guilt, rather than love. He had access to bundles of money. How far would he go to protect his reputation if Maryann discovered the banker was involved in money laundering or other illegal activities?

Stan Hermann appealed to me as suspect number four. His vehicle was in the vicinity the day of the murder, but had gone missing afterwards. *Did the wrench belong to him?* Card five had only a first name: Sissy.

I was still staring at the five cards scattered on the table in front of me when Sharon called.

"How are you feeling?" she asked.

"Frustrated."

"Still waiting for a breakthrough?"

"I'm working in the dark," I said. "The chief won't tell me anything, so I'm throwing darts at the wall. What did you learn from Savannah?"

Sharon sighed. "Not enough. She's hiding something, but I don't know what it is. She gave me a different story about her injured hand than the one she told you—said she burned it, picking up a pot of boiling water without a mitt."

"I wonder why she is lying about it?"

"I don't know," Sharon replied, "but you were right about her boyfriend. She's dating the dentist now, although they haven't gone public yet."

"Why the secrecy?"

Sharon laughed. "From what I can tell, Savannah enjoys the drama."

"Drama?"

"Yes. Dr. Lang and Savannah are both active on social media. The word on the street is they want to make a big splash by announcing their relationship to adoring fans during a carefully planned video event tied to the Garden Tour pre-party. I don't know if the rumors are true, though."

"They are setting up a public relations stunt about their personal lives to generate more followers on social media?" The notion that anyone would care more about notoriety than privacy flabbergasted me.

Sharon must have felt the same way. "It's crazy, isn't it?" she asked. "I don't know which one of them is more arrogant—David or Savannah. If they compete for followers, maybe they deserve each other."

"Funny," I commented. "That's what Corky Markham said when she told me the two were dating."

"Both of them are eager to be in the spotlight, but I don't see any connection to Maryann—except that Dr. Lang may have dated her briefly before he met

Savannah," Sharon said.

I doubted Savannah was the type of person to welcome competition for a boyfriend's attention. "Did Savannah mention Maryann when you spoke to her?"

"Only to say that she heard Maryann had died. She appeared genuinely sad about it; she said they were friends. When I pressed her about whether Maryann dated the dentist, Savannah said Maryann was too shy for Dr. Lang; he preferred someone flashy—with star quality."

"What about the budget for the Garden Tour?" I asked. "Did Savannah share it with you?"

"I'll have it tomorrow," Sharon said. "Savannah claimed the event had declined before she assumed control. Now that she is in charge, they have enhanced the gardens and recruited prestigious judges to attract more visitors."

"Go big or go home," I said, picturing the sales pitch Savannah made to the gardeners.

"Savannah has convinced the Cleeve Hill Garden Society their investment will pay huge returns," Sharon said. "She told them it's a sure thing."

"I hope she's right," I said. But as Sharon ended the call, I couldn't help remembering the Robert Burns line my Grandma Molly always quoted: *"There's no such uncertainty as a sure thing."*

Somehow, Sharon's news made me more confused than ever about the popular Savannah Sweet, who claimed to be Maryann's friend. *Did the two women argue over Dr. Lang? Why tell conflicting stories about her injured hand? What is she hiding?*

As I pondered the question, I created another note card for my growing suspect list. This time, I wrote the name in bold letters: Savannah Sweet.

Then I stacked the sets of cards on the table, refilled JD's water bowl, and grabbed Maryann's keys from my dresser drawer. It was time to check out the Peruvian coffee Maryann had recommended as a stress reliever.

I opened the garage door, and Moe raced me to the little red convertible parked inside. After one look at his sweet face, I could not bear to leave him behind. *It will be good to have his company as I return to the scene of Maryann's murder,* I reasoned.

Moe wriggled onto the back seat, and the two of us set out on a Sunday drive. The mid-afternoon sun beamed high in the sky as we rounded the first curve of Primrose Lane. Steering the little red VW through the neighborhood, I felt young and carefree—at least, I did until Piper's radio played Jan and Dean's hit from the 60s, "The Little Old Lady from Pasadena." Listening to the lyrics, I was abruptly reminded that my young and carefree days had receded to a tiny speck in the rearview mirror.

When we approached Maryann's home, I switched off the radio, parked in her driveway, and braced myself for the ordeal of unlocking the side door to enter the same kitchen where the intruder had attacked me only a few days earlier. With Moe by my side, I took a deep breath and pushed through the door.

The scene that greeted me was warm and inviting, with rugs and plants returned to their rightful places, and pillows tucked onto the couch where they belonged. The police had left behind the telltale signs of fingerprint dust, but someone had done their best to restore Maryann's home to order.

Avoiding the hallway that led to Maryann's bathroom, I walked directly to the kitchen counter and instinctively reached for the second canister. The largest one most likely held flour, I reasoned; the next size would be perfect for coffee.

Sliding the ceramic crock away from the wall, I pried the top open. Immediately, the heady scent of fresh coffee escaped from the airtight container. At first glance, I saw nothing unusual. Just the typical coffee scoop poking up from the grounds. Disappointed, I lifted the scoop for a closer look. And there, hidden beneath the surface where the scoop had rested, I saw the corner of a plastic bag jutting above the coffee. I tugged to pull it from the container and was rewarded for my efforts. Inside the baggie was a blue marker and a folded sheet of blue paper with my name on it.

Yes! Anything worth hiding in a coffee canister should be valuable enough to earn my job back, I thought.

As I reached for the bag, I heard a low growl rumble from Moe's throat. A flash of red and blue lights bounced off the clock that hung on Maryann's kitchen wall—it was the reflection of a police car, entering the driveway to block my own little convertible. Without hesitation, I shoved the plastic bag into my pocket, closed the clasp on the canister, and returned it to its original location. Quickly, I opened the kitchen cabinet and tossed several cans of cat food into a paper bag and rushed to the door. Before Officer Devon could turn the knob, Moe and I pushed the door open and stepped outside.

"Hello, Officer," I said calmly.

He tilted his head in a polite response. "Ms. Posey."

"I came to pick up more cat food," I said, motioning to the bag in my arms. "We were just leaving."

"Mind if I look inside the sack?"

I rolled my eyes before I handed him the bag.

The officer lifted each can, studying every label as though he suspected I might have stolen green beans or soup from Maryann's cupboards. I didn't dare to protest, for fear that he might want to search my purse and pockets as well.

"My apologies for the inconvenience," Officer Devon said. "The neighbor reported a stranger on the premises. Chief Marshall made a note of your intended visit on our log, so I figured it was you. Still, I had to respond to the call."

"I understand," I said, even though I didn't. "Am I free to go?"

"Yep. I'll move my vehicle." Devon hitched up his pants. "Want me to escort you home?"

Are you kidding me? I caught myself before the words came out of my mouth and answered him in a more civil tone: "No, thank you. I can handle the ten-minute drive. Moe will protect me."

Moe and I returned home the same way we came, except I didn't play the radio. Officer Devon had sucked the joy out of our afternoon ride. I patted my pocket to reassure myself that the baggie and note were still there. I couldn't wait to read Maryann's special instructions.

This beats a message-in-a-bottle, any day, I thought.

Chapter Seventeen

Sunday Evening

I speed-walked into my cottage and dropped the bag of cat food onto my kitchen island, eager to read what might have been Maryann's last words before her death. Slipping on a pair of thin latex gloves to preserve any potential fingerprints, I unzipped the baggie and placed the folded note onto the counter, leaving the pen inside the bag. My hands shook as I spread the paper flat. The first side contained instructions on how to prepare Perfect Peruvian Coffee, but the back side began with a handwritten letter from Maryann.

"Dear Josie, if you are reading this, you must desperately need coffee. (HA!) I trust you will discover the essence of Peru in every sip. I'm sorry to run away, but I cannot escape the mess I have made without help. Please take good care of Johnny. Your Friend, Maryann," followed by a smiley face.

Reading the letter, I realized Maryann tried to flee from her troubles, but her killer had other plans. How frightened she must have been, to pack only a few bags and leave everything else behind. Below the message was a PostScript. "P.S. Solve these riddles to learn the secrets you seek."

Excited at the prospect of deciphering Maryann's clues, I scanned the three puzzles that followed:

Riddle One seemed easy enough: *If you wish to dig for gold/Do not waste your time/Rare dollars for the bold/In antique vessels you will find.* I was pretty sure the "rare dollars" alluded to counterfeit money, and I figured Maryann's clawfoot bathtub must be the "antique vessel" she referenced. If so, it wasn't much of a clue, since we already found the tub full of money.

Riddle Two tied a profit-making venture to the counterfeit money. *If vast profit is your goal/You cannot trust your eyes/For when the truth be told/The money-tender lies.* It was impossible to determine whether Maryann referenced the counterfeit operation as having "vast profit for a goal" or someone else. I needed to identify the "money-tender" to solve the riddle.

Riddle Three summed up my feelings and was no help at all. *If you are confused/And don't know what to do/Read between the lines/For the answers to the clues.* Maryann must have been confused, herself, if she thought this riddle held any answers. I lifted the paper up to the light but could see no trace of pencil markings or any other hints "between the lines."

Stumped, I refolded the blue paper and returned it to the baggie. The riddles were simply too vague to point me toward a specific conclusion. This exercise had not produced the results I had hoped.

I can't share these with Chief Marshall until I can make sense of them myself. I thought.

Moe sensed my frustration and wandered into the kitchen to lean against my legs. I sighed and reached down to scratch his favorite spot, behind his ears. When my fluffy dog decided it was time for a break, there was no use arguing.

"You're the boss," I said. "Give me a minute, and we can take a short W-A-L-K."

My sweet dog knows how to spell, so he headed straight for the front door. I didn't keep him waiting long. By the time I zipped up my jacket, he had plucked his leash from the toy basket and held it in his mouth. I grabbed my house keys and phone, and we walked out the door.

It was already dusk, but Mrs. Abernathy waved from her porch across the street, just as she always did. *The woman must have a sixth sense about our comings and goings*, I thought. The sidewalk along Primrose Lane was clear and smooth, just like always. There was no reason to expect any trouble— which is why it surprised me when we approached our favorite park bench, and Moe let a deep growl escape from deep in his throat.

He halted in front of me, nearly tripping me. I froze in my tracks, then slowly turned my head from side to side, searching for anything amiss.

"What is it, Moe?" My voice was a whisper, but the dog heard me.

He backed closer to my legs and growled again. Louder. Still, I could see no danger ahead. We hesitated there, with the sky on the brink of twilight, and I suddenly regretted not inviting Kate and Bacon to join us.

The rumble in Moe's chest turned into a roar, making the hair rise on the back of my neck. Still, I could see nothing in the darkening canopy of the trees ahead.

Wait. Was that a rustle from the shrubs near the bench? At the exact moment that I registered the thought, Moe tugged at his leash, spun me in the opposite direction, and dragged me back toward Primrose Lane.

I swiveled to look at the shady pathway behind us in time to see a shadowy stranger emerge from the bushes and run away. He was dressed in black, with a ski mask and a dark hoodie covering his face and head. Without the mask, he could have passed as a jogger. *This was no jogger.* He looked suspiciously like the intruder who decked me at Maryann's home, and he ran like the wind, crossing the park toward the library parking lot.

Moe and I raced back to the cottage without further incident, although I paused every few feet to make sure no one was following us. When we arrived, safe and sound, inside our own front door, I sank onto the floor and wrapped Moe into a big hug. "You are the best dog ever," I said.

We were still sitting on the floor, leaning against the front door and debating whether to report "a stranger in the park," when my phone rang. It was Chief Marshall.

"Hello." My voice shook a little despite my best effort to control it.

"Josie? Is everything okay?" The chief was quick to notice that something was definitely *not* okay.

"We're fine," I assured him. "Moe and I had a brief encounter with a stranger in the park tonight, but nothing happened."

"Tell me, Josie," he said. "What was it that *didn't happen* in the park?"

I knew it would be impossible to evade his questions, so I kept the story brief. "We took a walk. Moe growled at someone lurking in the bushes. The stranger ran away, and we raced back home. End of story."

"Did you recognize this stranger?" Chief Marshall asked.

"It was dark," I said.

"Describe him," the chief insisted.

"Medium height. Dark clothes. Ski mask and a black hoodie."

"Did he say anything to you?"

"No," I answered in a stronger voice. "Honestly, Chief, I think the guy was more afraid of us than we were of him. He hightailed it the other direction, toward the library parking lot."

"Still," the chief said. "I don't like the idea of a masked stranger hanging out in the park after dark. We'll check the cameras and see if we can determine where he went."

"Thank you," I said, meekly. "How did you know to call me?"

Chief Marshall chuckled. "Pure coincidence," he said. "I wanted to let you know we finally reached Lois Penny. She had been at a health spa with limited access to her telephone. She's coming into the station tomorrow, so I will ask her your question about Johnny Depp."

"Oh, 'er, that won't be necessary," I said.

"No?"

"Since you're in a sharing mood, I should probably tell you I already spoke to Lois Penny."

"After I told you not to?" I heard the anger building in the chief's voice.

"Hold on, Chief. I didn't call her. *She* called *me*. We talked for only a few minutes, and I didn't ask her anything important. I promise."

"Uh-Huh. Do me a favor, Josie."

"Whatever you need," I said.

"Get me a written report on your conversation while it's still fresh in your mind."

"Yes, sir." I answered meekly.

My tame reply did not fool the chief. "What else have you done?" he asked.

"What do you mean?" I answered in my best imitation of an innocent voice.

"I assume you've told the mavens about the cash at the crime scene?" Chief

Marshall retorted.

How could he know?

"Only Kate," I said. "It slipped out unintentionally. But I *didn't* mention that the money is fake."

The chief was not impressed. "I asked you to keep it quiet," he said. "Does *anyone else* know?"

"Not from me."

The phone line went silent. "Chief? Are you still there?" I asked.

"Yes, Josie. I'm here," he answered, his voice as cold as steel. "Can you hear me?"

"Yes."

"Back away from this case before you get hurt. Understand?"

"But Chief—"

"And don't go out after dark without my permission."

"Again, with the grounding? I'm not sixteen, Chief."

"Well, you act sixteen."

He ended the call with another caution to lock my doors and keep my cell phone charged, but we came to an impasse on the "grounding" discussion.

Fifteen minutes later, I emailed my "conversation report" to the chief just as Nellie showed up at my door with a tray of sandwiches and a couple of old high school yearbooks in her hands.

I'm sure she caught the look of surprise on my face as I welcomed her inside. "What's up, Nellie?"

"Don't ask me," she said, shrugging her shoulders. "I'm just here for the pajama party."

Chapter Eighteen

Sunday Night

I suspected that Chief Marshall was the mastermind behind the pajama party, but Nellie insisted Kate dreamed it up as a way of keeping my mind off the murder case. Either way, Nellie was the first to arrive, followed by Kate and Sharon.

Before I could greet them, Kate—the artist of our group—unpacked her easel and set a whiteboard in place near the head of my dining room table.

"We think it's time for brainstorming," she explained.

"So, you're *not* here for a pajama party?" My head whipped from Kate, to Nellie, and back again.

Finally, Nellie responded. "I must have misunderstood the purpose of the party," she said, with a twinkle in her eye. "But I dug up a couple of old yearbooks in case you wanted to check out Maryann's teenage years."

"That's a relief," I said. "I haven't hosted a pajama party since my college days when my roommates and I stayed up all night to complete our term papers."

"The chief suggested we stop by to check on you," Kate admitted. "He said you spotted a masked man at the park. I figured you'd be working on the investigation. Anything we can do to help?"

I grinned at their smiling faces. "Always," I said. "Your choice: Loose Ends? Or Fishing Lures?"

"Ohhh, I love loose ends," Sharon said. "Let's start with those."

Grabbing a stack of notecards from the table, I sorted through them until I found Maryann's mystery texts. "Here are two messages I found in Maryann's phone log," I said. "In the first exchange, the unknown caller texts: *ONE MORE TIME.* Then, Maryann replies: *"YOU DON'T UNDERSTAND WHAT YOU ARE ASKING OF ME."*

Nellie took the card from my hand and studied it. "This looks like a boyfriend's plea for another chance," she said. "What does the second text say?"

"The message was shorter," I said. "He texts one word: *PLEASE.* Maryann replies: *"I CAN'T DO THIS ANYMORE."*

"Interesting," Sharon said. "*Someone* wanted to see her again."

"Who was it?" Kate asked.

"Don't know," I said. "The chief pulled me off the investigation, so I didn't call the number to see who sent them."

"Let's do it now," Nellie said.

"We *have* to call the number," Kate said. "You can hang up after we see who answers."

Kate made a good argument. No harm could come from knowing who sent the texts to Maryann. We could always give the lead to Chief Marshall.

While my friends leaned in to listen, I put my phone on "speaker" mode and dialed the number, almost certain Dr. David Lang would answer. Instead, we all held our breath while the phone rang four times before going to a recorded message: "You have reached a number that is no longer in service. Please check your number and dial again."

We groaned in unison.

"Well, *that* wasn't helpful," Sharon stated the obvious.

I circled the texts from Maryann's records and set them aside. "I'll add these to my stack for Chief Marshall," I said. "He can trace the number through the cell phone provider."

"What else is on your list?" Kate asked.

I shuffled through the note cards again, in search of names with question marks beside them, stopping at one that read: *Maryann's Sissy,* which made me think of Kate.

"Here's one that's perfect for you, Kate," I exclaimed. "Maryann's mother mentioned that someone named 'Sissy' introduced her daughter to the dentist. Could it have been your sister?"

Kate shook her head. "I doubt it, Josie. My sister lives a seven-hour drive from here, near Des Moines. Sorry."

"You're sure she said *Sissy*?" Sharon asked.

"Yes. Lois said the two were close."

Sharon grinned from ear to ear. "*You* know her, Josie. Remember the rude real estate agent? She uses her given name, *Savannah*, now. In grade school, she was a perky little thing who went by her nickname, *Sissy*; I was her second-grade teacher."

"Aha! Perhaps Savannah told the truth about being Maryann's friend," I said.

Nellie pointed to the yearbooks on the table. "Flip through those pages, Kate. We're looking for Savannah 'Sissy' Sweet in high school. She was a senior about fifteen years ago."

We pored over the pages, searching for photographs of Savannah Sweet and Maryann Penny during their high school years. A few minutes later, our efforts paid off.

"Found it!" Kate said. "Here's a photo of them together. Look at the caption: DOUBLE TROUBLE—SISSY SWEET AND MARYANN PENNY WIN STATE TENNIS TOURNAMENT."

"This is big," I told the mavens. "It's a connection I've been searching for, and you knew it all along."

"It confirms that the two knew each other, but it doesn't point to murder," Kate said.

"If Savannah introduced Maryann to her new boyfriend, as Lois indicated, the two friends must have also talked about the dentist. Savannah is likely to have valuable information about that relationship," I said.

"They look so young," Kate said.

"And happy," Sharon added.

"See if there are more pictures," I said. "Put Post-it notes on them so we can review the entire batch for details about their friendship. Neither of them had a public Facebook page or other social media back then. This old yearbook may be our best way to learn more about them."

"We still don't know who received Maryann's breakup texts," Nellie said.

"Not yet," I agreed. "But I know another way to identify Maryann's killer. We will lure him out of hiding, like a fish from the river. Are you ready to hear about it?"

Nellie rolled her eyes. "I've never caught a fish worth keeping, but let's hear your plan."

We poured another round of coffee, and the mavens listened as I outlined an idea that had popped into my head after my encounter with the stranger in the park.

"Instead of sifting through nonexistent clues, I want the murder suspect to reveal himself," I said. "And you can help me make that happen."

"What did you have in mind?" Sharon asked.

"It's simple," I said. "We pretend that I have remembered the identity of the intruder who attacked me. We leak the information that I intend to meet Chief Marshall at a specific time and place, to reveal the killer. Naturally, when the murderer tries to prevent me from keeping the appointment, the chief will arrest him."

Three faces stared at me, but no one was smiling.

"I need your help to spread the rumor that I am about to name the murderer," I said. "Understand?"

Nellie was the first to speak. "How's that bump on your head?"

"Almost gone."

"Good, because I'm considering giving you another one. Maybe it will knock some sense into you."

"Now, Nellie…" I began, but she hadn't finished.

"I'm serious, Josie. This plan is dangerous. You could get hurt." She held her hands in the air. "I'm out."

Ever the peacekeeper, Kate spoke out. "Wait one minute; we haven't heard the details yet. Where would you be, while all of this is taking place?"

I took a deep breath. "Here's what I forgot to mention," I said.

"In the interest of safety, I would trade places with Officer Bonnie Jackson, staying at her apartment while she moved into this cottage. "I would not tell anyone that part, because it's important that we act normal."

Sharon took another sip from her coffee mug and set it back on the table. "I'd say nothing about this situation is *normal.*"

"Which is why it requires a unique approach," I said.

"Has the chief okayed this plan?" Kate asked. "If *he* agrees to it, *I* will."

"Not yet," I admitted. "I wanted your support first. Since the plan requires a coordinated effort across the village, it won't succeed without you."

Sharon ran her fingers through her short curls. "I don't know, Josie. We can circulate rumors, but how can we be sure they will reach the murderer?"

Nellie laughed at the question. "English Village is a small town," she said. "If we tell people to keep quiet, the rumors will spread faster than lightning."

Her comment reminded me of the story Kate had shared about her sister's "surprise" party, and I made a mental note to include her hairdresser on our list of rumor-spreaders.

"Let's talk about the rumors we want to circulate," Nellie said.

"You're *in?*" I asked her.

"Yes. After we nail down the details and the chief approves," she said. "We can't let you do this alone."

I passed notecards and pens around the table. "There are three rumors to spread. Somehow, we must make them sound believable."

"The first message is that I know his identity," I said. "This could be because I suddenly woke up and recalled who attacked me. Or I received an anonymous tip, or discovered a new piece of evidence."

"Whatever we decide to use, the rumor needs an element of truth to it, so our suspect will believe it," Kate said.

"Oh, this is going to be fun," Sharon clapped her hands. "I know who I want to tell."

"Let's not get ahead of ourselves," Nellie said. "We have to make sure we're all telling some variation of the same story before we pick who we will call."

Sharon looked at the scribbled list she had already made on her notecard. "Hmmm. Okay. I'll save these names for later."

I slid her notecard closer and peeked at the list, pointing to the top name.

"Cross off Linda Witkoski," I said.

"Why?" Sharon protested. "She knows everyone in town!"

"That's true," Kate shrugged her shoulders, "but the woman is a saint. If you tell her to keep a secret, her lips are sealed. She never, *ever*, gossips."

"Good point," Sharon said, drawing a line through the name. "What's the next rumor, Josie?"

"We should circulate the news that I have figured out a motive for the killing," I said. "It isn't enough to know who the intruder was, if we can't explain why he wanted Maryann dead."

Nellie clasped her hands in front of her. "The motive is the hardest part," she said. "I don't know why anyone would kill that nice young woman. Do you, Josie? Even an ex-boyfriend makes little sense, if *he* broke up with *her*."

How do I answer without referring to the cash found in Maryann's bathroom?

"All we need to do is make the killer *believe* we know why he did it," I said. "We don't have to give details. Let's circulate a rumor that I was excited when I discovered evidence inside Maryann's house about why he killed her."

"Ohhh, I like that," Sharon said. "We could hint that you refused to tell anyone, but the chief—not even your closest friends know the truth."

A wave of guilt washed over me at the accuracy of her words, and I recalled the famous quote from Sir Walter Scott's poem: *"Oh, what a tangled web we weave, when first we practice to deceive!"*

"Great idea," Nellie said. "It should put our killer on edge because it sounds exactly like something Josie would do. That makes it a credible rumor."

"Credible, but false," Kate commented. "Even better."

"Plus, it keeps him focused on me, as the only one with the answers," I said. "No reason to put you in danger, too." *At least I have a good reason to withhold the information about the bathtub of cash,* I thought.

Kate nodded. "I agree," she said. "What is the final rumor to spread?"

"It's the easiest of all," I said. "We want the killer to believe I'm meeting the chief at the scene of the crime, to show him my proof."

The smiles on my friends' faces disappeared.

"Bad idea," Nellie said.

"I don't like it," Sharon added.

"Me neither," Kate said.

I took another gulp of my coffee while the three of them discussed their fears for my safety. Finally, Nellie turned to me again. "Why not say you're meeting the chief at his office? That would be much safer."

"You expect Maryann's murderer to walk into the police station and interrupt my meet-up with Chief Marshall?" I asked. "That's ridiculous—and also higher risk."

"How is it more dangerous?" Sharon put her hands on her hips as she challenged me to explain.

"If he thinks I'm transporting the evidence, he will *attack me* for it. But if he believes we found incriminating evidence at Maryann's house, he will *go there* to retrieve it. The chief can put surveillance on the house to catch him if he shows up before our meeting time."

"Okay, I get it," Kate said. "But what's the evidence that the police missed?"

"Who knows?" I said. "All we must do is *claim it exists*. That should be enough to make him search the house ahead of our arrival."

"You're right," Kate said. "The perp will believe our story."

"Perp?" I raised an eyebrow.

"Hey, if we're going to be detectives, we may as well use the jargon," she said.

We talked for another thirty minutes, figuring out how to spread rumors and catch a killer. Then we agreed to have lunch at Cozy Cups for a final overview, before I proposed our plan to the chief.

The Mahjong Mavens are on board with the plan, I thought. *Now I need to convince Chief Marshall that our scheme will capture the killer. Easy peasy.*

Chapter Nineteen

Early Monday Morning

After the mavens left, I sent a text to Chief Marshall, requesting a time to meet. I couldn't wait any longer to share Maryann's coffee canister riddles and the new information I'd gathered from my friends.

I turned off the lights and climbed into bed early, hoping for a good night's rest. Instead, I dozed in bits and pieces, my eyes popping open every hour. Too keyed up to sleep, I abandoned the battle, rising at 4:00 a.m. and tiptoeing into the kitchen to start a pot of coffee. Moe followed me every step of the way, confused by the early wake-up call, but unwilling to allow me out of his sight.

I paced the floor, trying to shake the uneasy notion that I had overlooked something important. Uncertainty nagged at the corners of my mind, with Savannah "Sissy" Sweet, Professor Tony Dell, and Nellie's dentist all jumbled together without rhyme or reason.

"What am I missing, Moe?" I asked the fluffy pooch, who still marched behind me like a Dr. Watson to my Sherlock Holmes.

Moe tilted his head, strolled to his toy basket, and returned with Lamb Chop—her ludicrous red lips and long eyelashes were the perfect remedy for my anxieties. I took one look at her silly face and laughed. Then I knelt to wrap my arms around the dog and his toy.

"Thank you, boy," I said. "You reminded me it's time to stop worrying and start working."

I grabbed a pen and notepad, flipped open my laptop, and turned on my cell phone to discover three overnight voice messages from Leslie Anderson. *Does the woman never sleep?*

First, my editor wanted an update on the murder investigation. "And make it *pronto*," she said.

Next, she reminded me I had promised her a story about the upcoming Garden Tour. "Those Cleeve Hill ladies are driving me crazy."

In the third message, Leslie inquired about my encounter with the stranger. "I heard someone almost accosted you in the park. Hope all is well," she said.

Life in a small town, I thought. *If the mavens have any doubts about our Operation Rumor Mill plan, this should reassure them.*

Time to get serious about tracking down Maryann's killer, I decided. Without a morning briefing to attend, I would nose around on my own. I scribbled a list of tasks onto the notepad in front of me.

1. Write articles for Leslie
2. Review Maryann's phone records
3. Call Savannah Sweet
4. Visit Art Gallery
5. Lunch with mavens
6. Photo session on Cleeve Hill

One glance at the kitchen clock told me it was too early to make phone calls. I doubted anyone would want to talk to me at 6:00 a.m. To pass the time, I ate breakfast in my pajamas and hammered out the two stories for Leslie, keeping both as brief as possible.

Local Bank Teller Found Dead
Police Chief Earl Marshall today identified the woman found dead in her English Village home as Maryann Penny, 32, who worked as a teller at a local bank. Details of Ms. Penny's death are being withheld, pending a police investigation.

Garden Tour Gives Nod to Peru

The Cleeve Hill Garden Society will present a Peruvian-themed Garden Tour this year, incorporating touches of the South American country into each display. The sprinkle of gardeners is hard at work, installing exhibits for the tour, which opens to the public next week. Professor Tony Dell, a visiting curator at the English Village Art Gallery, has consulted on the project.

I typed a quick email to Leslie, attached the articles, and pressed "send" just as the clock ticked 8 a.m. Despite the early hour, I guessed that Savannah Sweet might already be on her way to her office. Taking a chance that I could catch her, I placed the call. She answered on the first ring.

"What do you want?"

"Sorry to call so early, but I have a few questions *only you* can answer," I said.

"I'm headed to the coffee shop," Savanna said. "You've got five minutes."

"Right," I agreed. "I'll be quick. The paper will run a two-paragraph story about the Garden Tour, promoting it as a 'nod to Peru' and mentioning Tony Dell as a special consultant for the big event. Does that sound okay, or do you want to see the story before it runs?"

"I want to read it, first," she said.

"Consider it done," I replied. "Leslie will forward it to you after she edits it."

"What's next?" Savannah asked.

"I plan to stop by the art gallery to see Tony Dell this morning."

"Fine with me." Savannah sounded preoccupied. "Anything else?"

"Yes. I wonder if anyone still calls you *Sissy*? One of my friends was your second-grade teacher, and she said you and Maryann were besties in high school."

Savannah sighed before she answered. "I wondered how long it would take you to figure that out," she said. "Yes, Maryann and I were friends. She still called me *Sissy*."

"I saw a photograph on Maryann's nightstand. She and Dr. Lang posed on a hiking trail. Did you know she was dating him?"

"You're on the wrong track, Josie," Savannah said. "Maryann and David never dated."

"Then why the framed photo?"

Again, Savannah sighed. "It was a 'fake boyfriend' picture," she said. "Maryann wanted her mother to stop bugging her about her social life, so she framed the picture and set it where her mom would notice it. People do it all the time."

I was flabbergasted at Savannah's explanation. "They looked like a happy couple," I protested.

"That's the point of a 'fake boyfriend' photo," Savannah said. "I have one of the original prints of that same picture. The three of us went together on that hike. We had our photo taken at the top of the trail. Maryann cut me out of the picture before she framed it."

"So, Dr. Lang isn't Maryann's ex-boyfriend?"

"Definitely not."

I could tell Savannah was growing weary of my questions, but I still had a few more minutes before she arrived at the coffee shop. "Can I see your picture?"

"Sure. If you promise you won't mention it to her mom, I'll text it to you."

"I promise," I said. "Two more questions?"

"What now?" Savannah asked.

"Did you introduce Maryann to Tony Dell? And has Johnny Depp ever scratched you with his claws?"

Savannah giggled into the phone. The sound was like music in my ear, and I realized it was the first time I'd heard her laugh.

"I don't know where you get these questions, Josie," she said. "No. I didn't introduce Maryann to Tony. *She* introduced Tony to *me* after I told her the Cleeve Hill Garden Society wanted to do a Garden Tour highlighting Peru."

"Oh!" I said, surprised. "And the cat?"

"Sorry to disappoint you, but no, JD has never attacked me."

"What about—" I began another question, but Savannah interrupted.

"Time's up," she said.

And just like that, she dashed all my theories into pieces. Now I had more questions to add to my growing list. If Dr. Lang wasn't Maryann's "ex," where did she send the break-up messages?

Determined to make progress on the case, I spread Maryann's phone records across my kitchen island for a closer look at the discrepancies I'd found earlier. This time, I noticed two of the calls went to a familiar number—the Village State Bank.

Since the chief had previously approved my contact with Maryann's employer, I decided not to ask for additional authorization. *No need to bother him about a simple follow-up call.* With my pen in hand, I contacted Maryann's talkative supervisor, Corky Markham.

"I have a few more questions about Maryann Penny, if you don't mind," I said when she answered her phone.

"Again?" The woman's voice held more than a trace of irritation. "That lovely officer, Bonnie Jackson, just left my office. Was there something we didn't cover?"

"I'm sorry to trouble you, Corky. The chief has me reviewing paperwork. This is a minor item related to Maryann's phone records. You understand how important it is to check every detail!"

"Of course," she answered in a friendlier tone. "What do you need to know?"

"The week before she died, Maryann called the bank around eight o'clock in the morning on two different occasions. Can you tell me why she might have done that?"

"Do you have the dates? It was probably related to her work schedule. She would have clocked in for her shift at approximately that time."

I read the dates to her, providing the specific times of each call.

"Yes, here it is," Corky said. "I remember now. I answered the phone both times. Maryann had car trouble. Something about a bad battery. She called to let me know she would arrive late to work."

"Thank you, Corky," I said. "Can you explain why one call lasted only sixty seconds and the other for six minutes?"

"Six minutes?"

"Yes. The second day her call was considerably longer than the first. I want to understand why."

"Clearly, you must be mistaken, Ms. Posey," Corky said. "Neither call was a long one. Maryann told me she would be late, and I made a note of it on her timecard. End of story."

"But the phone records show a six-minute call," I repeated.

"Not my problem," Corky retorted. "I had no reason to keep her on the phone. You'll need to question the phone company about their error."

I rolled my eyes in an exaggerated gesture Ms. Markham would never see. "Yes, ma'am," I said. "I'll do that."

Another question unanswered, I thought, marking it for further research.

I drained the last drop of coffee from my mug and pondered the purpose of the longer call, to no avail. Moe and Johnny Depp snoozed side-by-side in front of the refrigerator, so I stepped over them to refill my cup. *Maybe more caffeine would help clear the cobwebs from my mind.* Silently, I regretted that Chief Marshall refused to discuss the case with me. In situations like this one, I could always rely on him for a logical explanation.

Shoving the bank calls aside, I moved further down my list to a series of calls Maryann had made to the Kitty Cat Hotel. I assumed the boarding facility had Johnny Depp on their waiting list, and Maryann called each day to check for cancellations. I dialed their number to corroborate my theory.

The receptionist answered on the fourth ring, multiple cats meowing in the background.

"Kitty Cat Hotel," she said. "How may I help you?"

"I'm calling about a boarding appointment for Johnny Depp," I said.

"I'm sorry, but we're still fully booked." The woman rushed through her answer, an annoyed whine in her voice. "As I explained to you more than once, we will call if anyone cancels. Johnny is right here, on my waiting list."

"Thank you. I understand." I hung up without pushing her for additional details. Then jotted a notation beside their number: *Calls verified.*

"At least I can check Kitty-Kats off my list," I said aloud, which prompted Moe to raise his head and scramble to his feet. He sauntered to my barstool, rested his head on my lap, and looked up at me with sad eyes.

"Not *real* kitty cats," I reassured him. "Having one of those around the house is enough, right?"

Moe cocked his head, and I had the uncanny sensation that he understood every word I said. Before I could ask him, my cell rang. It was Kate, calling to check on me.

"Are you still off the case?" she asked.

"Yep," I acknowledged. "I've spent most of the morning at home in my pajamas, making phone calls and feeling sorry for myself."

"You're not alone," Kate said. "The chief revoked my Citizen Patrol Badge this morning."

"It's so unfair," Sharon called out from the background.

"That's terrible, Kate," I said, "What happened?" I knew my friend had worked hard to earn her position on the chief's volunteer unit.

"I'll tell you all about it at lunch," Kate said. "Are we still meeting at noon?"

Sharon chimed in, an edge of excitement in her voice: "Trust me. You need to hear what we discovered, even if you aren't *officially* working the investigation. This is too juicy to ignore."

"Wouldn't miss it," I said. "I have one other stop to make, but I'll see you at Cozy Cups."

* * *

I had dressed and gathered my things to leave the house when Chief Marshall phoned. His call was brief: "I got your text. Could you stop by the station later this afternoon?"

"I'm on my way out the door now," I said, glancing at my watch. "The mavens are meeting for lunch at noon. I have an appointment with a photographer at the Garden Tour afterwards. We should finish around four-ish. Will that work?"

"Glad you can squeeze me into your busy schedule," the chief answered with only a trace of sarcasm. "See you in my office at four o'clock, sharp."

I started to answer, but he had already hung up the phone. I wished Chief Marshall would make up his mind. *First, he doesn't want to see my face again, then he calls to set an appointment. What next?*

Instead of brooding about it, I jumped into my car and headed to the English Village Art Gallery. If I hurried, I could spend a few minutes with Professor Tony Dell before I drove to Cozy Cups for lunch.

Chapter Twenty

Any doubts I harbored about Professor Tony Dell's credentials disappeared when I walked into the main hall of the art gallery, where vast murals and lighted exhibits transformed the space into a colorful representation of Peruvian culture. Every inch of the hall invited visitors to explore the rich history, diverse landscapes, and vibrant traditions of the country. I was pleased to see displays of artifacts, textiles, and art from various periods, including pre-Inca civilizations, the Inca Empire, and colonial and contemporary Peru.

One section focused on the Amazon rainforest, and another on the majestic Machu Picchu, an ancient Incan city high in the Andes mountains. As I strolled through the exhibits, I jotted a few notes to include in my feature article about the Garden Tour. Within a few minutes, a tall man with wavy dark hair entered the hall from the side door. I recognized him as the professor from Kate's brochure, except that he looked more strikingly handsome in person. He walked with a confident swagger and carried a clipboard with a thick sheaf of papers attached.

I approached him with a smile. "It appears you and I are both note-takers," I said. "You must be Professor Dell."

"Tony," he said, extending his hand to shake mine. "And you are?"

"Josie Posey. I believe we briefly texted each other Saturday evening," I said. "I'm a local news reporter with questions about Peru and the Garden

Tour."

"Ah, yes. Thank you for stopping by, Josie," he said, with a charming trace of a Peruvian Spanish accent. "You are in the right place; I am always happy to talk about my homeland."

He gestured toward a small cafe table near the gallery's entrance. "Come. Sit with me," he said. I followed him to the table, where he pulled out my chair deferentially. Then, taking a seat across from me, the professor removed a few pages from the back of his clipboard and handed them to me.

"After Flo called, I prepared several information sheets on the Garden Tour art pieces; you can take them with you for reference."

I tucked the pages into my notebook and set my phone on the table. "Okay if I record our interview?"

"Of course," he said. "Shall we begin with coffee?"

"Another time—when I'm not taking notes," I said, smiling. "I am told Peruvian coffee is a drink to be savored."

The professor laughed. "You have spoken to one of my students."

"Yes," I admitted. "Maryann Penny."

The smile left his face. "I was sad to learn of her death," he said. "Maryann was a bright young woman. She will be missed."

"That's another reason I wanted to see you," I admitted. "To learn more about Maryann. What can you tell me?"

Tony crossed his legs and leaned back in the small chair. "We met when she enrolled in the coffee class. After she tasted the coffee, she was eager to learn *everything* about Peruvian culture. I did my best to teach her."

"She became a volunteer, assisting with the exhibit?"

"Technically, yes. But she contributed far more than the average volunteer. She devoted many hours to cataloging the artifacts. She never missed a detail. I would have offered her an apprenticeship, but we didn't have the funds."

"We never have enough money for the arts," I said.

"That's true," the professor said. "While others make a killing in business ventures, artists live on a shoestring."

"Do you consider yourself an artist?" I asked.

Tony gestured to the ID card affixed to the lanyard around his neck. "I am a lowly museum curator with the heart of an artist, but not the talent," he said. "My father hoped I would join him in the family business, but I gravitated toward the nonprofit world. It broke his heart."

"What was the family business?"

The professor waved his hand. "Nothing important," he said. "Imports. Exports."

His vague description made me more curious about his background. "Did your family support your decision?"

"Not in the beginning," he said. "But they have taken a tremendous interest in my work here."

"It's a wonderful display," I said. "Too bad Maryann won't be here for the grand opening."

"Yes. It's terrible that she died in such a mysterious way. Do the police have any leads?" His tone was casual, but his sharp eyes studied my face. Instead of answering his question, I asked another of my own.

"The day before she died, Maryann seemed anxious and confused. She brushed me off when I asked about *you*. Later that evening, she sent me a note about where to find instructions on how to make Peruvian coffee," I said. "What happened? Why did Maryann stop working with you? Were you dating? Was there a quarrel?"

"No. Absolutely not." Professor Dell clasped his hands on top of the clipboard. "She became distracted a few weeks ago," he said. "I assumed she was busy with other things. It happens with volunteers. They begin with energy and enthusiasm, but drift away when the job becomes tedious."

"Something caused her to quit." I stared at him, waiting for a better explanation.

"If you must know, we had a brief commotion over one artifact; it belonged to a local collector but was mistakenly shipped to the gallery. Maryann opened the crate before we noticed the error."

"Why the uproar over an address mix-up?" I asked.

"The item broke in transit." The professor shrugged. "Maryann hand-carried the vase to the correct address. She explained it arrived in damaged condition, but the collector made a fuss about it."

"How did you resolve it?" I asked.

"Maryann insisted the gallery should pay for the damages. I disagreed. No one blamed Maryann for the breakage, but she still felt responsible. She knew the collector personally, which left her between 'a rock and a hard place'—as Americans say."

I recalled the text messages Maryann had sent, trying to extricate herself from what I had assumed was a dating relationship. *Perhaps they referred to her volunteer position, instead,* I thought.

The professor continued. "We sorted it out with the collector and her insurance company, but the conflict caused too much stress for Maryann. She quit a few days later."

"Was she angry with you?"

"No. We ended on friendly terms. In fact, Maryann introduced me to Sissy Sweet, who became the intermediary between the gallery and the garden society—saving me a ton of headaches." He smiled ruefully. "I prefer not to work directly with the Cleeve Hill Garden Society."

I assured him I understood the challenges of pleasing the matriarchs of Cleeve Hill. "They speak highly of you, however," I said.

He dismissed the compliment with a wave of his hand. "I've done my best to help with their event—including persuading some of my Peruvian contacts to donate several priceless art pieces for the upcoming Garden Tour. It hasn't been easy, but I have convinced them there is value in promoting our Peruvian culture."

The professor picked up his clipboard and stood to signal the end of our conversation, so I slipped my notepad and pen into my purse and turned to ask one more question.

"Tell me, Tony," I asked. "With your credentials, you could find work in a much larger city. Why did you choose English Village for your stint as a visiting curator?"

He grinned at me. "Didn't you know? I graduated from Wichita State University with a Master's Degree in International Business and Museum Studies. A local guy, Stan Hermann, was in several of my classes. We have stayed in touch."

"Stan Hermann?" I hoped the professor did not detect my surprise at the mention of the plumber whose name appeared on my suspect list.

"You know him?" Tony asked. "Stan serves on the art gallery board. He's the one who invited me to apply for the curator job here."

He tapped a finger on the face of his watch and smiled at me. "Sorry, but I'm late for a meeting with a donor. I hope to see you again at one of the Garden Tour events."

I nodded my agreement and walked with him to the exit. As I watched him cross the parking lot, one thought circled in my mind: *Everyone knows everyone in a small town.*

* * *

Kate and Sharon waved to me when I walked through the door of the Cozy Cups Cafe. The lunch crowd already filled most of the tables, but my friends had saved our favorite spot near the front window.

"You're late," Sharon said. "We thought you'd never get here."

I took my seat, and Lorene hurried over with our menus. The chief's wife had become a good friend to our Mahjong Mavens over the years. She loved to cook, and we loved to eat, so we spent a fair amount of time in her restaurant. Somehow, she ran the business as tightly as a four-star general, but still kept the place comfortable and inviting. Lorene took her order pad from her apron pocket and leaned down to console us about the chief's latest decisions.

"Sorry Earl is being such a stickler about this murder case," Lorene said. "I heard he banned you from the investigation."

"No need for *you* to apologize," Kate said.

"You know how it is," she said. "My husband takes his job seriously. If he believes you're at risk, he will do all he can to distance you from the action."

"I understand his reasoning," I said. "But we can help in ways his officers can't."

"Give him time, Josie. He will call you when he gets in a pickle; he always does." She took our orders, and we waited for our food to arrive before my friends shared their news.

"Don't panic, but we ran into a snag with the plumber," Sharon began the tale. "His receptionist balked when we requested information."

"Uh, oh." I braced myself for the news.

"No worries," Sharon continued. "Kate pulled out her Citizen Patrol badge from the community awareness program Chief Marshall taught last year. She flashed it in the receptionist's face and, suddenly, Stan-The-Man's office staff was happy to answer her questions."

Kate raised her hands to silence Sharon. "We could tell you more about how it all went down, Josie, but it's best that you don't know *everything*—in case the chief asks."

"Don't tell me." I agreed. "I get into enough trouble on my own. No sense in stirring up more."

"Anyway, you were right about the plumber. Stan Hermann could be an accomplice in Maryann's murder," Sharon said.

Kate handed me a copy of a page from the plumber's appointment book. "We don't have details, but his scheduler confirmed a service call in Maryann's neighborhood the morning of her murder. Although it wasn't supposed to be on her street, his van was in the vicinity about the time you arrived at Maryann's home."

"Did you talk to him?" I asked.

"We can't," Kate said.

"He's *missing*," Sharon added. "His wife says he went fishing."

"The chief already knows," Kate announced. "After we gave him the appointment calendar details, the chief put out a BOLO on the plumber's van. Then he told me he no longer needed our services."

I took another bite of Lorene's homemade chicken pot pie and dabbed my mouth with a napkin. "I can't believe he *fired you* from your *volunteer* position," I said. Kate loved serving as a community liaison to the police department, and now she was off the team. I felt responsible.

Sharon shrugged her shoulders. "It's okay, Josie. We can accomplish more without the restrictions of the police department."

She and Kate shared a "shall-we-tell-her?" look across the table and I pounced on them

"What is it?"

Kate leaned closer, keeping her voice low. "Stan's wife says he often loans his van—the one he drives—to an old friend. It shows up again in a couple of days."

"Yes," Sharon explained. "She thinks his buddy from high school might know something about it."

Kate handed me another slip of paper. "Here's the name and number, so you can call."

"You didn't give this to the chief?" I clutched the folded note in my hand.

Sharon and Kate looked at each other, and then back at me. Sharon sighed. "We tried, but he was so angry about Kate using her badge to get the plumber's schedule that he didn't let us talk."

"Anyway, the whole thing is probably a dead end. The van you saw might have been another vehicle. The plumbing company owns several."

"Can't hurt to check it out," I said. "At least the high school buddy might rule out the plumber, by confirming the van's location at the time of the murder."

"You track down the van," Sharon said. "Meanwhile, Kate and I are headed to the lake this afternoon. Thought we might take our poles and a bucket of worms."

"Stan's wife told us where to catch the big ones," Kate added, winking at me. "If the plumber is off fishing, like she said, we'll see him there."

I shook my finger at the two smiling ladies. "Don't do anything foolish," I said. "Stan-the-Man is a potential murder suspect."

Kate scoffed. "We're driving around to look for his pickup, Josie. Not making a citizen's arrest."

"He won't even notice us," Sharon assured me.

I thanked my friends and paid our lunch tab. "I have to meet a photographer for the Garden Tour," I said, standing to leave. "Call you later if I learn anything new."

Before I turned the key in my ignition, I glanced again at the note Kate had given me. *CJ Drake. I've never heard of him. So, why does his number seem familiar?*

When my brain refused to make a connection, I gave up, tucked the note into my pocket, and drove to Cleeve Hill.

The cantankerous gardeners could not be kept waiting.

Chapter Twenty-One

Monday Early Afternoon

The Cleeve Hill matriarchs were in high form as they escorted the photographer throughout their gardens—each vying for spectacular shots that would outdo their competitors. I accompanied them—ostensibly to gather notes for the photo captions, but more to keep the ladies out of the photographer's way.

Although the gardens had been lovely when I toured them on Saturday, they were spectacular today—groomed to perfection. The Peruvian art pieces rested on their pedestals with small plaques beneath each one. Evelyn Greenwood led us directly to the hand-painted Peruvian vessel in the corner of her Secret Garden. "Imagine the scenes the vase has witnessed—and the secrets it has concealed—dating back to around 1200 AD," she said.

While the photographer snapped pictures, I gazed at the two-handled stoneware, with its intricate floral designs and curved body. "It's large enough for a small child to crawl inside," I said to our hostess. "No doubt it has been a family heirloom for centuries."

Evelyn, eager to share her knowledge, explained that art was an important form of expression in ancient times. "The Incas spoke Quechua, pronounced **keh**-*chuh-wuh*, and had no written language. Some textbooks say they also communicated through a system of different knots tied in ropes attached to a longer cord."

I tried to envision the knotted ropes, but could not picture such a foreign notion.

Evelyn gestured again to the antique sculpture. "The artist who created this piece is unknown," she said, "but a signature of sorts—a small painted flower—still exists on the bottom of the vase," she said."

Fascinated by her story, I stepped closer to admire the colorful paintings that covered the outside of the vase. "What will happen to the artifacts after the Garden Tour?" I asked.

"Technically, they now belong to the Cleeve Hill Garden Society," she said. "We will either loan them back to the art gallery or sell them to fund next year's event—though I hope Savannah Sweet will generate the profits she has promised this year, so we can hold on to the Peruvian artifacts as an investment."

"How are your ticket sales so far?" I asked.

"Frankly, it's difficult to tell. Savannah is *not* a bookkeeper. All I can say is that I'm doing my part to ensure we make a big profit." She made no further comment as we retraced our steps toward the center of the garden. There, Evelyn made an unexpected turn down yet another pathway.

"Follow me," the stately woman said. "I can lead you through an adjoining gate directly into Leticia's garden."

"There's a shortcut?" I recalled my earlier visit, where I pranced the full length of every sidewalk to enter through each gardener's front door.

Evelyn laughed at my expression. "Yes, Josie," she said. "You'll find it's much easier to move from one garden to the next."

She reached into an opening in the trellis wall, turned an invisible latch, and the door swung open. I walked through with the photographer following behind. Leticia Cornwell waited for us on the other side.

The spry little woman was all smiles as she guided us directly to her reflection pond and pointed to a gorgeous leather trunk. Sun sparkled on the dome-shaped top, adding a rich sheen to the 1767 piece. An 18th-century artist had designed the trunk as though he envisioned it would someday grace a garden; engraving the hand-tooled leather with motifs of lush plants—leafy artwork that suited the English garden Letica had designed.

"The trunk *belongs* here," I said.

Leticia clapped her hands. "Yes, yes, yes!"

When the photographer moved away from us to take a wider shot, Leticia stepped closer to my side.

"Can you spot a secret compartment?" she asked, barely containing her excitement.

I studied the trunk but found no hidden drawers. "No." I shook my head. "I would never guess."

"I found it quite by accident shortly after the trunk arrived," Leticia confided. "A false bottom releases with the touch of an invisible button!"

Her enthusiasm was contagious. "Was anything inside?" I asked.

"A few hundred dollars," she said, with a gleam in her eye.

"You're kidding," I said.

"No, it's true!" Leticia winked at me. "But don't tell anyone. It's our secret."

"What did you do with it?"

Leticia clasped her hands on her lap and smiled like the Cheshire cat from *Alice in Wonderland*. "I called Tony Dell, of course. He said to keep it as a donation to the Cleeve Hill Garden Society."

"How generous of him," I said, impressed at the curator's gift.

Leticia lowered her voice to a whisper. "Yes, Josie, especially since I don't have the financial resources of my neighbors. We may appear to be equals, but I often struggle to match their donations. Frankly, I was relieved when Tony Dell said the trunk and its contents belonged to us now."

"Still, he didn't have to donate it," I said.

"Well, he's not taking it back," Leticia declared. "Finders keepers."

We both laughed at her childish response until, on that cheerful note, the photographer returned, and Leticia walked us across her flagstone paths to a gate that opened into the final garden. The sweet fragrance of roses filled the air, and Florence Crocket waited for us there.

Like the other matriarchs before her, she made no comment but led us straight to the art installation. Delfin's sculpture, El Beso II, rested on a white marble ledge in the ultimate tribute to the Garden of Love.

I stood in awe of the piece, finally turning to Florence. "You have outdone yourself," I said. "This is the highlight of all the gardens."

She beamed at me. "Did I tell you I visited Delfin's original, life-sized El Beso sculpture when I traveled to Peru last year? That's when I convinced him to create a smaller one for my garden."

"No," I said. "I thought this was Tony Dell's idea."

"Posh!" Florence scoffed. "That man doesn't have enough imagination for a project of this scope. He's an embarrassment to his family. They even encouraged him to Americanize his name when he accepted the curator position here—that's why he goes by Tony Dell instead of Tony Delfino."

Aha! Tony Dell's contacts in Peru weren't merely acquaintances—they were family. I hoped my surprise didn't show on my face as I processed the new information. "So, *you* suggested the Peruvian theme," I repeated, "not Tony Dell."

"Yes. I fell in love the moment I saw this piece in Lima. The Delfino family hosted a lovely event while I was there. I've been quietly collecting artifacts from Tony's father since then. There's quite a market for Peruvian art here."

"How wonderful for you, Florence," I said warmly. "And Professor Dell? How should I describe his contributions to the Garden Tour, when I write my article?"

Florence Crockett cocked her head to one side as she considered her answer. "Refer to him as our international consultant," she said. "We selected the artifacts. Tony Dell placed the orders. But *I* am the reason his family *donated* the items to the Cleeve Hill Garden Society."

Confused, I repeated the organizational structure back to her. "*You* chose the Peruvian Gardens theme. *Savannah Sweet* coordinated the event details and marketing. And Tony Dell ordered the artifacts through his family's business."

"Yes!" Florence said. "The Delfino family generously donated the items in appreciation of my business dealings with their import/export company."

We stood to admire the piece for a few minutes more while the photographer packed his equipment. I said my goodbyes, retired to my car, and drove away from the mansions on Cleeve Hill.

Halfway down the block, my cell phone buzzed, and I pulled to the curb, thinking it might be Florence, with an additional note for my article. I swiped to answer, "Hello?"

I heard someone breathing ominously into the phone.

"Who is this?" I demanded.

I heard a click, followed by an ominous metallic voice, "Don't trust the gardener," the voice intoned.

"What?" I shrilled into the speaker, attempting to engage the caller. "I didn't catch that–"

But the call had ended.

I sat for a moment in my car, wondering at the contrast between this sunny day and the dark tone of the call. A chill ran up my spine at the sensation that someone was watching me. I turned to stare at the mansions behind me, but could see no one lurking in the windows.

Shaking off the fear, I put away my phone and shifted into drive. If I hurried, I could still make it to my appointment with Chief Marshall on time.

Chapter Twenty-Two

Monday Late Afternoon

The chief had just completed his interview of Lois Penny when I arrived. He called me into his office and closed the door.

"Coffee?"

"No, thanks. I've had plenty today. If I drink another drop, I won't sleep tonight."

Chief Marshall eyed the shoebox I carried. "You came bearing gifts?"

"Nothing fancy," I said. "Just a few thoughts about the case."

The chief motioned for me to place the box on the table. "First, let's talk about why you spoke to Lois Penny before I gave you permission."

"You told me not to call her, and *I didn't*," I said. "*She* called *me*. It would have been rude to refuse to speak to her."

"Uh-huh." The chief's eyes bored into mine. "Are you going to tell me what you learned?"

"I already sent you a full report," I said.

"Tell me again," Chief Marshall said.

"She wants me to keep Johnny Depp." I tried to lighten the moment.

"Ni-i-i-ce." Sarcasm wasn't pretty on the chief. "Anything else?"

"Probably the same stuff she told you," I said.

"Repeat it, in case I missed something." His dark eyes never left my face.

I pulled my notepad from my purse, flipped to the page where I'd jotted information from Lois Penny, and read the list to Chief Marshall. "Maryann had few friends. No brother or sister. She was closest to someone who lives near here. Lois referred to her as Sissy. I didn't ask for details, because I promised I wouldn't pry into the case."

The chief rolled his eyes. "Keep reading."

"Lois said Maryann dated a dentist for a while. I assumed he was the one in the photograph on her nightstand—the same guy I saw later in the park with Savannah Sweet. She also said Maryann mentioned someone new. A professor, maybe. Again, I didn't ask more, because…"

"Right. You didn't want to pry," the chief said. "Anything else?"

"Lois is ill, just as Maryann told me. Breast cancer. She begins radiation treatments soon."

The chief nodded. "Thank you for the report, Josie."

I dared to turn the tables and ask the chief a question. "How did I do?"

"About the same as I did," he said. "Except I didn't offer to keep the cat."

Ignoring the chief's attempt at humor, I pulled the shoebox closer. "Are you ready for the latest information?" I asked. "Inside, I have evidence of a curious phone record, updates on Maryann's relationships, several unsolved riddles, and a foolproof plan to flush out our killer."

"All this, even though you are off my murder case?" The chief raised one eyebrow.

"Yes, sir." I ducked my head to avoid his eyes. "I found it while doing research."

He glared at me until I spoke again.

"You *told me* to share anything interesting," I said.

Chief Marshall muttered something about an "exasperating woman" under his breath, then motioned for me to open the box. "Let's see what you brought."

Sitting straighter in my chair, I reached into the container and pulled out a single index card. "Here is a phone number we should trace," I said. "Maryann sent text messages to *this number*, stating she 'couldn't do this anymore.'"

The chief nodded. "I remember the text from her phone records," he said. "We presumed it was a break-up message to her boyfriend."

"Yeah, well. It must be a burner, because the calls go to a message saying the number is disconnected."

"You called the number?" Chief Marshall stared at me again, his already dark eyes turning to black.

"I figured Dr. Lang would answer and I could hang up," I said. "But then I talked to Savannah Sweet. It turns out I was all wrong about the boyfriend thing."

"Leading to the update on Maryann's relationships, I assume?" The chief appeared to be enjoying my discomfort.

"Yes." I cleared my throat. "So, Kate and I were talking about small towns, and she told me a story about her sister, who she always called 'Sissy,' and then, later, Lois Penny mentioned someone named 'Sissy,' on our phone call–"

The chief interrupted to add, "You mean the call you weren't supposed to make?"

"Right," I agreed, my head bobbing up and down. "Anyway, Maryann's school friend 'Sissy' is now known as Savannah Sweet, who is promoting the Cleeve Hill Garden Society event."

"And you know this from Lois Penny?"

"No, chief. I told you I didn't pry into details on that call."

"My apologies," the chief said. "Please continue. How did you know Savannah Sweet was Maryann's childhood friend 'Sissy'?"

"Because my maven friends came for a pajama party on Saturday night and we were talking about high school days. Nellie brought a yearbook from the year Maryann was a senior. Just—you know—for fun. To get a glimpse of Maryann's past."

"A pajama party. For fun," the chief sounded doubtful.

"Yes," I confirmed. "But when I wondered if the yearbook showed anyone named 'Sissy,' Sharon spoke up and said it was probably Savannah Sweet— she was seven years old when Sharon taught second grade at the elementary school. Can you believe it? Sharon was Sissy's teacher!"

"It's a small world," the chief said.

"Then we also found a picture of Maryann with Sissy Sweet in the yearbook!" I pulled a photocopy of the yearbook page from the box and handed it to Chief Marshall.

He studied the photo I had circled, then placed the page on the battered metal table of the conference room. "Got it. Maryann and Savannah Sweet were friends," he said.

"Yes," I said. "The big news is I talked to Savannah, and *she said* Dr. Lang was never Maryann's boyfriend, so he is no longer a suspect."

"No?" Chief Marshall asked. "What about the nightstand picture?"

"Savannah said Maryann used the picture as a 'pretend-boyfriend' so her mom would stop asking about her social life."

"A fake boyfriend photo?"

"Yep. Happens all the time, according to Savannah. Would you like to see the original picture?" I showed him the copy Savannah had texted to my phone, the three smiling hikers beaming at the camera.

Chief Marshall stood to refill his coffee cup. "I will look into the burner phone angle," he said. "Maryann wanted out of something. The person who owned that phone may be our killer."

"I agree," I said. "And there's something else…"

The chief stirred two cubes of sugar into his coffee. "There's more? What is it now, Josie?"

"When I reviewed Maryann's text messages, I noticed one she wrote to me the night before she died."

"We saw that," the chief said. "Something about coffee. It didn't seem relevant."

"That's what I thought, when I read it the first time. But it seemed peculiar, so I studied it again…"

"And?" Chief Marshall's voice held an edge of impatience.

"And so, when I went to Maryann's yesterday to pick up cat food, I peeked inside her coffee canister."

"Go on." The chief snapped at me in a sharper tone,

I looked him in the eye. "And she left me a page of riddles in the canister."

"Did you intend to share them with me?" Chief Marshall glared across the table.

"That's why I'm here." I glared back at him.

Pulling the zippered plastic bag from my shoebox, I removed the blue paper and smoothed it onto the table. "This is what Maryann hid in her coffee canister," I told the chief.

Chief Marshall wrinkled his forehead. "I don't understand," he said. "They must be important. Why didn't you search for them immediately?"

"She told me to try the Peruvian coffee, Chief. I didn't know she had hidden riddles that could help us identify her murderer!"

The chief grabbed the blue paper and hurried to read the riddles. I watched as he came to the dead end I had. "These make no sense," he said.

I read the first riddle aloud. *"If you wish to dig for gold/Do not waste your time/Rare dollars for the bold/In antique vessels, you will find."*

Chief Marshall shrugged. "She's talking about counterfeit money, but where are the antique vessels?"

"I don't know," I admitted. "I considered her claw-foot bathtub, but why tell us something so obvious?"

The chief read the second riddle. *"If vast profit is your goal/You cannot trust your eyes/For when the truth be told/The money-tender lies."*

"Someone was making a killing off the counterfeit money," I said. "Maryann wanted us to know, in case something happened to her. If we can find the source of the money, we will locate her killer."

"Would Wayne Wentworth be the money tender?" the chief asked. "His name is the first to pop into my mind."

"Listen to riddle number three," I said. *"If you are confused/And don't know what to do/Read between the lines/For the answers to the clues."*

The chief took a flashlight from his belt and studied the paper from top to bottom, front and back. "I don't see any pencil marks," he said. "What are we missing? Was there anything else in the plastic bag?"

"Only a blue marker," I said, handing him the bag.

"I'll have our detective study it," Chief Marshall said. "Maryann may have used a heat-sensitive ink they can decipher."

"I didn't think of that," I admitted.

The chief pushed his chair away from the table and stood to stretch.

"What's next?"

"My foolproof plan for catching the killer," I said.

"Nothing is foolproof, Josie," he said.

"This plan is," I said.

Chief Marshall sighed heavily. "Tell me the plan, and *I* will decide how foolproof it is," he said.

I stood, walked to the whiteboard, and wrote three words: *Operation Rumor Mill.*

The chief rolled his eyes but motioned for me to continue.

"It's simple," I said. "The mavens circulate a rumor that I have discovered evidence pointing to the intruder's identity, and his motive for Maryann's murder—and that I'm meeting you at the scene of the crime, to show you what I have found."

"*That* should get his attention," Chief Marshall said sarcastically.

I ignored his tone and continued. "Yes. The killer will attempt to remove the evidence from Maryann's home before we arrive for a noon rendezvous. You will have the house under surveillance and catch him in the act."

Chief Marshall shook his head. "Sorry, Josie. This is far too dangerous."

"Let me finish, Chief," I said. "If Bonnie Jackson is willing, I will hide out at the station while she takes my place. She can wear a protective vest and drive my car to the meeting. Or skip the meeting altogether—the rumors will lead the killer to Maryann's house, and you can arrest him."

I handed him the list the mavens created—complete with the proposed rumors, names of the identified rumor-spreaders, and our recommended methods for initiating the contacts. "Here are the details," I said.

"I'll think about it," he replied in the polite voice that meant he would rather walk across hot coals barefoot than implement *Operation Rumor Mill.*

"Okay," I said in a tone that meant it was NOT okay at all. I stomped back to the table and closed the lid of my empty shoebox.

Ignoring my mini tantrum, the chief smiled at me. "So," he asked, "where will you go next?"

Although I knew he was inquiring about my plans to continue nosing around his investigation, I chose the simpler path. "I'm headed home to take

Moe for a walk," I said.

"What about *that cat?*" Chief Marshall asked. "Has he found a comfortable spot in your favorite chair?"

"Don't worry about Johnny Depp," I said. "We bonded when Maryann's intruder tossed him onto my face."

"Rough way to begin a relationship." The chief's broad grin reminded me that we were still friends, despite our disagreements.

"Johnny was probably more scared than I was," I said. "You should have heard him yowl. I bet he scratched the killer good, trying to get away from him."

The second the words were out of my mouth, something clicked in my brain. "Wait," I said. "Chief, is it possible we could use Johnny Depp as a witness?"

The chief stared at me like I'd lost my mind. For a moment, he was speechless. The corner of his mouth twitched. I could see he struggled to keep from laughing at my suggestion.

"Hear me out," I said. "Johnny Depp has vicious claws. Maryann told me she planned to have the vet trim his nails soon. Meanwhile, she trained the cat to use his scratching post and stay away from her bedspread and drapes."

"You want us to check all our suspects to see if they have scratch marks on their arms?" the chief asked. "It might be hard to prove the marks came from Johnny Depp, unless the cat wants to ID the intruder in a lineup. How would he point out the bad guy? Meow or twitch his tail?"

"No," I said. "I'm suggesting the vet could check Johnny's claws the same way forensics scientists look for skin cells under a victim's fingernails to determine whether they fought with a specific assailant."

Chief Marshall blinked. He stood up and paced the floor. Finally, he spoke. "I hate to admit it, but this idea may have merit. I have never heard of using a veterinarian's skills to retrieve human skin cells from underneath a cat's claws, but there's a first time for everything."

He continued to pace the floor as he considered my somewhat unorthodox suggestion. I waited, hands folded, while he muttered to himself.

At last, he turned to face me again. "Josie, you are brilliant. I don't know if this notion is feasible, but I'm willing to check it out. We'll call Doc Swinson. He can answer our questions. The cat may not qualify as a witness, but Doc Swinson would."

I waited, fingers crossed, while he made the call. Minutes later, the chief walked back into the room.

"Go," he said. "Get the cat and take him to Doc Swinson's clinic. He's waiting for you."

He shooed me out the door, where I did a happy dance in the hallway. *The chief said I'm brilliant,* I thought. *I will be back on the case in no time.*

Chapter Twenty-Three

Early Monday Evening

I had barely returned from dropping JD at Doc Swinson's clinic when my caller ID announced a call from Chief Marshall. A surge of hope made my heart beat faster. I figured he was ready to offer me my job back, but I tried not to show my excitement.

"Hello, chief," I said. "I'm glad you called."

"We've made progress on the case," he said.

"Yes, we have," I agreed.

"No, Josie," Chief Marshall said. "I meant our investigative team has made progress in the time since you left my office."

"I just walked into my house," I protested. "What could you have learned in the half-hour it took me to drive home, load Johnny Depp into his crate, drive to the clinic, and return home again? Is it about the plumber? Kate told me he is still missing."

The chief growled, and I pictured him twirling his pen through his fingers. "Kate is not authorized to search for missing persons," he said. "She and your mavens need to back off."

It's a good thing he doesn't know about the fishing trip, I thought.

"If it's not about the plumber, why are you calling?" I asked.

"If you listen for a minute, I will tell you."

"Okay, Chief." I zipped my lips and waited for Chief Marshall to come to the point of his call.

"Earlier, you theorized that the counterfeit money was the key to Maryann's death."

I nodded my head even though the chief couldn't see me. "Yes, my best guess is that whoever killed Maryann did it because she was about to expose them for crimes related to the money. If we can find the source of the money, we can locate our killer."

"We're on the same track," the chief said.

"Have you found a connection?"

"Only one, so far."

I hated when the chief gave me cryptic answers. He forced me to keep pushing for details.

"Who is it?"

"We have identified one person, besides Maryann, with access to the money. It isn't good news."

His comment baffled me. "How bad could it be? Was it Maryann's mother?"

"I'm afraid it's worse."

"How?"

Chief Marshall hesitated for a fraction of a second before he asked, "When you paid for your friends' lunch today, did you give Lorene a one-hundred-dollar bill?"

"Yesss." The word emerged in slow motion as my brain finally understood where the chief was leading.

"The money was counterfeit," he said, and the weight of his words fell heavily onto my chest.

The insistent thrumming of a headache began in the back of my neck, but I refused to acknowledge it. "What do I do now?" I asked.

"Get back to the station ASAP for an interview with Agent Evans," the chief said before he ended the call. "And bring a friend."

Do I need an attorney?

I dialed Kate's number. If I had to be interrogated by a Secret Service Agent, I wanted my Harvard-educated U.S. Marine friend by my side.

She answered on the first ring and listened to my panicked voice.

"Remember the money I mentioned in Maryann's bathtub?" I asked, without waiting for her to answer. "It was counterfeit."

"Wow," Kate said. "We guessed the cash would lead to her killer. But I never suspected a counterfeit scheme."

"I've been summoned to an interview with a U.S. Secret Service agent about my involvement. Want to ride along?"

"What involvement?" Kate asked. "You've done nothing wrong."

"I may have passed fake money to the police chief's wife," I said.

"Say no more, Josie." Kate sighed. "We will go together. I'll drive."

* * *

Kate took a chair beside me in the cramped conference room at the police station. I shoved my hands into my pockets to keep them from shaking. A crumpled piece of paper in one of them reminded me I still hadn't contacted CJ Drake to verify his use of the plumber's van. *Probably not a good time to ask permission to make a phone call,* I decided.

Secret Service Agent John Evans sat unblinking at the head of the table, with the chief next to him. A tape recorder rested on the table between them. Agent Evans pressed "record" before he recited the date and time, and a brief statement.

"Today, we are questioning Josephine Posey regarding the distribution of fraudulent currency at the Cozy Cups Café, in English Village, Sunflower County, Kansas. Ms. Posey, please state your name and address, for the record."

"Josephine Eleanor Posey, 15 Primrose Lane, in English Village, Kansas," I said.

"Did you pay your lunch bill today with a hundred-dollar bill?" he asked.

"Yes, sir."

"Were you aware the bill was counterfeit currency?"

"No, sir."

"Where did you get the bill you gave the cafe's proprietor?"

"From Maryann Penny," I answered.

"You took cash from the bathtub, at the scene of the crime?" The agent's question was a slap in the face. The chief's eyes widened, his pen poised over the pad in front of him as he waited for my reply.

Tears stung my eyes and threatened to spill over. "No, I did not."

Chief Marshall paused the recording and turned to the agent. "We agreed that Ms. Posey is a witness, not a suspect," he said. "Please phrase your questions appropriately."

I blew my nose and took a deep breath.

Pressing "play" again, Agent Evans spoke to me in a gentler tone.

"Tell me, Ms. Posey, where were you when Maryann gave you the bill?" he asked.

"In the drive-through teller window at the Village State Bank," I answered.

"Maryann Penny gave you counterfeit cash in her capacity as a teller?"

"She must have," I explained. "I still had my deposit slip in the envelope she gave me that day. I pulled a hundred-dollar-bill from the envelope to pay for lunch. Most places in the village don't give change for a hundred, but I knew Lorene would."

"Did Maryann know the bill was fake?"

"I don't know," I said. "She was preoccupied that day."

"But *you* believed it was real?"

"I had no reason to think otherwise."

Agent Evans asked one last question. "Do you think you may have any additional counterfeit bills in your possession?"

I stared at him, wishing I'd thought to consider that possibility. "I don't know."

While he watched, I opened my purse and retrieved the deposit envelope I had tucked into my billfold. One additional hundred-dollar bill was still inside. I handed the bill to him.

Agent Evans removed a small scanner from his briefcase and tested the bill. He turned to the chief and shook his head. "It's good."

Maryann gave me two bills—one real and the other fake? I shrugged my shoulders. "I can't explain this."

Agent Evans concluded with a brief lecture on protecting the United States currency, and a reminder that if found guilty of the federal crime of counterfeiting, I could serve jail time. My car—if used while I was committing the crime—could be confiscated.

Kate and I were free to go, but we requested a word with the chief before we left the building. We followed him into his cluttered office.

"We still don't have a suspect," I reminded him. "Shall we implement *Operation Rumor Mill?*"

Deep circles ringed the chief's eyes, and he sank into his chair with a groan. "This investigation is giving me nightmares. Every bone in my body says the cash we found at Maryann's house originated from the same place as the counterfeit bill you gave Lorene. But we don't want the whole town to make the connection."

"No one knows yet," I said, "except Kate."

"I won't tell anyone," Kate said.

"It won't be long before the word spreads." Chief Marshall massaged his temples as he spoke. "Now that the counterfeit bills are in circulation, we must alert the community. I've scheduled a news conference in thirty minutes."

The words were barely out of his mouth when my phone beeped with a text from my editor. "Be at the police station in thirty minutes," she wrote.

"Already there," I texted back, with an apologetic shrug to the chief.

"Leslie wants me at your news conference," I explained, holding my phone up, "for a story in tomorrow's edition."

"Don't mention your involvement," the chief advised. "And avoid any reference to Maryann as the employee who handed out the illegal currency."

Kate wrinkled her forehead. "Since you never released the information about the tub filled with cash, the news media will see this as a separate story, right?" she asked.

The chief shook his head. "Maryann was a teller at the bank's drive-through, and the counterfeit bill surfaced shortly after her death. Someone will put the two together."

"You're right," I said. "Everyone will speculate about it."

"We need to move fast to convince the killer that we're close to an arrest," the chief said. "If we can entice him with this rumor scheme of yours, he will implicate himself."

"Does that mean we're doing it?" I held my breath, waiting for the chief to continue.

Chief Marshall stroked his chin and leaned back in his chair. "I'm inclined to approve the rumors, but nix the high-noon rendezvous," he said. "There's no need to put you, or Officer Jackson, at risk as decoys."

Kate shook her head. "Won't the rumors that Josie has found additional evidence of the killer's name and motive send him directly toward her?" she asked.

"Make sure your rumors stress that the evidence is hidden inside Maryann's home," the chief said. "The killer will most likely go there to retrieve it." He jotted notes on his spiral pad. "I'll assign one officer to watch the empty house, and another to tail Josie wherever she goes."

I sighed. "I don't need a police escort, Chief. I've got your number on speed dial, remember? Meanwhile, I promise to lock my doors and windows; Moe can take care of any intruders."

The chief fixed his dark eyes on mine. "Let's compromise," he said. "Same instructions as I gave you earlier: We will patrol your block. You keep the porch light turned on to indicate all is well. At the first sign of any trouble, flip off the light. But be prepared—that porch light goes out and my officer will show up at your door with a gun in his hand."

"Agreed," I said, extending my hand.

Chief Marshall gave me a firm handshake. "Don't start *Operation Rumor Mill* until I give you the final word," he said. "During the news conference, the bank will offer a reward for information about the bogus bills—so the town will already be buzzing."

Kate left the station through the front door, promising to retrieve JD from Doc Swinson's, then return to give me a ride home after the news conference.

I ducked out the back door of the station as the local news crews arrived at the front entrance. Keeping my head down, I crossed the parking lot, then proceeded to the alley between the bank and the cafe.

Within three minutes, I had scooted through the alley to Main Street, reversed directions, and arrived at the front door of the police station, where

I signed in with the other media.

Three television stations sent cameramen and reporters that afternoon. I showed up representing *The Village Gazette*, and a DJ for the local radio station did double-duty as a news guy—asking a few questions so he could grab sound bites for the next day.

Chief Marshall stepped up to the podium, flanked by Secret Service Agent John Evans and Village State Bank Manager Wayne Wentworth. Although the agent and the banker were dressed in nearly identical dark blue suits, the two men were a study in contrasts. The agent, clear-eyed and youthful, bounced on his toes, like an eager recruit on his first assignment. The banker, hollow-eyed and experienced, faced the room squarely, with the bearing of a weary man tossed into an unwelcome battle.

The chief cleared his throat and tapped the microphone. "Thank you for your attention," he said to the media gathered before him. "We are here today to announce that a one-hundred-dollar counterfeit bill turned up at Cozy Cups Café this afternoon. We are asking our merchants and the public to be on the lookout for illegal currency."

Reporters shouted questions; the chief raised his hands until the noise faded into silence.

"One counterfeit bill may not sound like a crisis, but we believe others may follow. The individual involved shall remain unnamed."

Next, he read a formal statement from the U.S. Department of the Treasury. "If you suspect a counterfeit note or have information about counterfeiting activity, please report it immediately."

Chief Marshall motioned to the agent on his left. "This is John Evans, a Secret Service Agent assigned to the case. He will assist us in the protocols involved in gathering evidence and will be available to answer questions at the end of our announcements."

Agent Evans stepped to the microphone. "If you suspect you have counterfeit money in your possession, please follow the protocols listed on our website," he said. Pointing to the slide deck on the screen beside him, the agent read eight guidelines for handling counterfeit bills.

CHAPTER TWENTY-THREE

1. Do not put yourself in danger.
2. Do not return the bill to the passer.
3. Delay the passer with some excuse, if possible.
4. Observe the passer's description—and their companions' descriptions—and write down their vehicle license plate numbers if you can.
5. Report the information to your local police department OR the U.S. Secret Service Office.
6. Write your initials and date in the white border area of the suspected counterfeit note.
7. DO NOT handle the counterfeit note. Place it inside a protective cover, a plastic bag, or envelope to protect it until you place it in the hands of an IDENTIFIED Secret Service Agent.
8. Surrender the note or coin ONLY to a properly identified police officer or Secret Service Special Agent, or mail it to your nearest U.S. Secret Service field office.

The agent concluded his formal announcements with a request for help in locating the perpetrator of the crime. "In case you are wondering, there is no financial remuneration for the return of the counterfeit bills, but you are doing the *right thing* to help combat counterfeiting."

Reporters scribbled on their pads, and one petite blonde wearing a royal blue blazer raised her hand. The chief waved her off. "Not yet," he said, reclaiming the podium.

Motioning for the banker to step forward, he said, "Please give your full attention to Mr. Wayne Wentworth, manager of Village State Bank, for an important announcement."

The chief stepped back from the podium and exchanged places with Wayne, who lowered the microphone to adjust for the height difference between the chief and himself. He cleared his throat and sipped from a bottle of water someone had placed on the shelf below the podium.

"We believe the counterfeit money, passed by one of our citizens, was given to them at Village State Bank's drive-through window," he said.

The reporters exploded into a frenzy of questions:

"How much phony money did the bank distribute?"

"When did this happen?"

"Who is responsible?"

"What about other customers who may have received counterfeit bills?"

Chief Marshall stepped in front of the banker and raised his hands. "Quiet, please. Allow Mr. Wentworth to complete his formal remarks. We will take questions in an orderly fashion."

When the crowd settled into silence, the chief turned again to the banker. "Mr. Wentworth?"

Visibly shaken, Wayne returned to the podium. "We are as baffled by this occurrence as you are," he said. "Village State Bank is cooperating fully with the police—and the Secret Service—to investigate details."

Mr. Wentworth removed a handkerchief from his pocket and dabbed the beads of sweat from his forehead. "We have had no other report of counterfeit money in circulation. The bank's cash-on-hand is lawful currency. Our goal is—and has always been—to earn the trust of our customers. I take full responsibility for this lapse. We will determine how it happened and pursue legal actions to prosecute the person, or persons, who involved the bank in this scheme."

Eager reporters waved their hands in the air, but the banker took another sip from his bottled water.

"To aid in the investigation, Village State Bank is offering a $25,000 cash award to anyone who provides information leading to the arrest and conviction of the criminal or criminals who printed or distributed counterfeit bills in our community."

I watched from my place in the press corps behind the TV cameras while the reporters scrambled to ask questions and rush back to their newsrooms.

This should get the party started, I thought.

Chapter Twenty-Four

Monday Night

Kate and I ate carryout from Pedro Chang's new Chinese/Mexican restaurant. Lost in our own thoughts, neither of us said much during dinner. Moe stretched out on the kitchen floor, hoping for a scrap of egg roll. JD dozed in his crate, still woozy from the light sedative Doc Swinson had used, when he extracted the human skin cells from beneath the cat's claws and trimmed his nails.

As we tossed the empty food cartons into the wastebasket, Kate broke the silence. "I know you have your hands full with this counterfeit money story, but I have to tell you something," she said.

"What is it?"

"We saw him."

"Who?"

"The plumber," Kate said. "Today. We took our fishing gear and tried to look inconspicuous, just like you told us. Stan-the-man was there. He had a pop-up tent on the bed of his truck, and a couple of rod holders so he could fish two lines at a time off the shore."

"That's wonderful, Kate. It verifies his wife's statement. We can take him off the suspect list."

"Yes. Maybe. I don't know." Kate threw up her hands and stared at me. "The thing is, he wasn't alone."

"For goodness' sake, don't keep me guessing," I said. "What did you see?"

"It was the professor," Kate said. "Tony Dell arrived in a Jeep, leaned out the window to speak to the plumber, then drove away."

"Huh," I said. "When I met with the professor this morning, he mentioned his friendship with Stan. He said the plumber is a board member for the art gallery—but it's odd that he would drive all the way to the lake to speak with him."

Kate clasped her hands on the countertop. "There's more," she said. "Sharon and I fished near some trees about a hundred feet from Stan's spot. About the time the professor pulled up, Sharon's line gave a sharp tug and the tip of her rod bent toward the water. She shrieked, then fought the whopper till she dragged it to the shore."

"Tell me the plumber didn't notice the commotion," I said.

I could read the answer on Kate's face. "Sorry, Josie. When we turned around, the plumber and the professor stared directly at us."

Kate looked so miserable, I couldn't bear to scold her. "Never mind, Kate. You were in a public place, with valid fishing permits, right?"

"Yes."

"And you accomplished your mission."

"Yes. We confirmed the plumber was fishing, as his wife claimed."

"With everything that's happened, I still haven't called the number his wife gave you for CJ Drake," I said.

"Do it now," Kate said.

I spread the wrinkled note on the counter and put my phone on speaker mode to dial the number. We both listened as the phone rang several times, then went to a robotic recorded message. "This mailbox is full. Please try again later."

Kate shrugged. "Another failed effort to track down details," she said. "At least we didn't share this number with Chief Marshall. It leads nowhere."

"Let's hope nobody mentions your fishing trip to the chief," I said. "He won't believe you *coincidentally* ran into the plumber."

Kate signaled to me with crossed fingers. "It will be our secret," she said.

We tuned in to the local TV station at six o'clock to see the coverage from Chief Marshal's news conference. My eyes focused on the blonde anchorwoman who still wore the royal blue blazer she'd had on earlier in the day. She spoke from the parking lot of Village State Bank, with a view of the drive-through window as a backdrop.

"Chief Marshall says this is the first time in recent history that counterfeit money has surfaced in English Village," she announced in a somber tone. "So far, only a single hundred-dollar bill has been reported. He urges shop owners to be on the lookout for more."

After the newscast switched to a screen with the list detailing how to handle questionable bills, the reporter concluded with a sound bite from Wayne Wentworth, offering the cash reward for information leading to the arrest of criminals involved in the counterfeit scheme.

Kate set her empty coffee mug on the table. "It wasn't a long story," she said.

"No."

"Is that good or bad?"

"Good," I said. "When I saw the reporter standing in front of the bank drive-through, I thought she had made the connection between Maryann's death and the counterfeit currency."

"Only a matter of time," Kate said. "Have you finished your article for the *Village Gazette?*"

"I wrote a draft earlier, but now I will add the information Agent Evans shared with me after the news conference. It will give more depth to the story—which is what people expect when they read a report in the newspaper."

"What did he tell you?"

"Nothing new about this case, but some fascinating details on counterfeiting operations."

I picked up my notes and read a few passages aloud. "United States currency is the easiest in the world to counterfeit because it is made from fabric. Even third-world countries in Africa have switched to polymer bills already; US paper currency is 75% cotton and 25% linen."

Kate raised an eyebrow. "You've captured my interest."

"Then you might also be interested to know that more fake American money comes from Peru than any other country," I said.

"Peru?" Kate stared at me. "Professor Dell's homeland?"

"Yep," I said. "Counterfeiters in Peru produce and distribute about 60 percent of the counterfeit U.S. notes distributed worldwide. Interesting."

"Agent Evans knows his stuff," Kate said.

I flipped the page on my notepad and skimmed down a few paragraphs. "Here's the interesting part," I read. "Since the 1980s, the feds have been tracking high-quality counterfeit hundred-dollar bills. They call them *super-dollars* or *super-bills*."

"Now I'm super-confused," Kate said. "These fake bills have been in circulation for over fifty years, and we haven't located their source?"

"Some of them," I said. "Various organizations and governments have been suspected of being the mastermind behind the super-bills—including North Korea, Iran, and even the CIA."

"Sounds like the makings of a spy thriller," Kate said.

"Listen to this," I continued. "Law enforcement agencies across the globe have made several high-profile raids with the U.S. Secret Service. They have seized huge stockpiles of funny money. In 2002, the British police apprehended an organized group that had printed $35 million in fake U.S. hundred-dollar bills. Experts from the Bank of England confirmed that the quality of their product was even better than the real deal, printed by the U.S. Treasury."

"Whoa. What is our government doing about it?"

"Back in 2010, they introduced a redesigned hundred-dollar note, including two new features: a blue 3-D security ribbon with images of bells and *100s* that change as you tilt the note, and a bell in the inkwell that alternates colors from copper to green. But the older bills are still in circulation. It will take a long time to remove them."

Kate stood and stretched.

"Too much information?"

"It makes me wonder who's responsible for the counterfeit bills at Maryann's."

"Me too." I rubbed my eyes and flipped another page of my notepad. "They were all hundred-dollar bills. With *super-dollars* flooding the world, that's the most popular denomination, followed by the twenty."

"What about the lowly one-dollar bill?" Kate asked. "Too common?"

I smiled at her. "Good question. Technically, a one-dollar bill is the easiest to counterfeit. It has fewer security features, but it isn't cost-effective for counterfeiters to spend their time and resources on it."

"Makes sense," she said as she gathered her things. "I think I'll head home now and let you get some rest."

"Thanks for coming to the rescue when I needed you," I said.

"Hanging out with you is always an adventure." Kate smiled at me. "Besides, I've never met a secret agent before."

"We can both cross that off our bucket lists," I said, walking her to the door and bolting the lock behind her.

After Kate had gone, I completed the counterfeiting article for Leslie Anderson. As I pressed "send" on the email, Nellie phoned.

"The mavens are champing at the bit," she said. "Has the chief agreed to *Operation Rumor Mill?*"

I laughed at her enthusiasm. "Unfortunately, no. Tell everyone to stand down. I'll be in touch."

Seconds later, Chief Marshall phoned to postpone the plan. "Let's wait until we see if the reward announcement produces any leads, Josie. I appreciate your suggestion—and the mavens are perfect for the job—but we need to consider all the risks. I'll talk to you tomorrow."

As I ended the call with the chief, I realized I owed his wife, Lorene, an apology. I called her cell. When she answered, I heard a cacophony of pots and pans banging in the background and realized Lorene was in the thick of dinner hour at Cozy Cups.

"Sorry to call while you're busy," I said. "But I wanted to apologize for paying my lunch tab with fake money. I will come by tomorrow with legitimate cash."

Lorene laughed. "It's okay, Josie. I felt terrible showing your hundred-dollar bill to Earl, but I knew it had to be related to the case."

"Can I look at it?" I asked. "I want to avoid counterfeit bills in the future."

"Sorry. I turned it into the Secret Service for the investigation."

"Yes. Of course," I said. "Maybe they will give me a lesson when I go to the station in the morning."

* * *

I cleared all my messy paperwork from the table, my mind still grappling with the fact that Maryann had passed me a counterfeit bill, and I had given it to Lorene. The whole thing puzzled me. Any criminal with half a brain would avoid circulating fake money through a bank teller window or handing it to a friend.

Maryann was honest and smart. She could not have known the hundred-dollar bill was phony, any more than I did. I decided. *Something else upset her that day at the bank.*

I sat in my favorite reading chair with Moe at my feet and JD on my lap, mulling over our lack of leads. Searching for Maryann's killer was like catching fireflies in the dark. Every time I glimpsed a sliver of light and reached for it, the light disappeared.

It had been four days since I had discovered my friend's body, and I was still at square one. I hoped the bank's offer of a reward would yield results.

My cell phone rang so loud in the silence that I jumped in my chair, startling both Moe and Johnny Depp. I grabbed the phone and peered at the screen. "Caller Unknown."

Preparing for the potential of another threat from a robotic voice, I switched on my recorder before I answered. "This is Josie Posey," I said.

"Ms. Posey, this is Leticia Cornwall. Do you have time to talk?"

I pictured the little gardener with her wisps of white hair and friendly smile. "Yes, Leticia. What is it?"

"I saw the news report about counterfeit money."

"Yes?"

"The police chief said they found just one counterfeit bill. Is it possible there are more?"

I felt the hair rise on the back of my neck, but I kept my voice calm.

"Anything is possible, Leticia. Why do you ask?"

"Because I'm holding seven one-hundred-dollar bills in my hand, and they don't all look the same."

"They may still be genuine currency," I said. "They changed the design of the hundred-dollar bill a few years ago, so it's common to see both the older bills and the newer ones in circulation."

Leticia hesitated before she replied. "Aha. That could be the explanation. How do I tell if these are real?"

"You'll need to run them through a scanner to be sure."

"Isn't there another way?"

"Agent Evans said the counterfeits are difficult for a novice to detect," I said. "You can have it scanned at the police station or the bank."

"Oh dear, I don't want to be associated with fake money. I will look like a foolish old woman."

"Leticia, you are neither foolish nor old."

I heard her chuckle before she answered. "Could you go with me?"

"Why don't I mention it to the chief when I see him in the morning, instead?" I suggested. "He might prefer to come to your home."

"Thank you, Josie."

"Leticia?"

"Yes."

"Who gave you the suspicious bills?"

"I don't know," she said. "They were in the locked cash box where Savannah keeps our Garden Tour fees."

"Who pays those fees?"

"Sponsors and host gardeners." Leticia lowered her voice. "Including *me*. I would feel terrible if the cash I paid was phony money."

"Everyone pays in *cash*?" My voice came out as a squeak, as I absorbed the astonishing news.

"Savannah says it's easier to manage that way. She writes receipts for every donation. I re-count the money to confirm her totals, and she takes it to the bank once a week to deposit into our account. Tomorrow is deposit day."

"Why worry now, if you haven't had a problem with previous deposits?"

"The agent said the fake bill came from Peru," Leticia's frail voice wobbled. "This deposit includes my donation of the money I found hidden inside the Peruvian trunk."

I stifled a gasp with my hand and spoke as calmly as I could. "Don't panic, Leticia," I said. "Hold on to the cash box until we confirm all the money is genuine. I'll get back to you in the morning."

* * *

I paced the floor of my living room, trying to decide whether to text Chief Marshall right away, or wait until morning. After the bank's reward offer, the hotline was likely inundated with calls from everyone in the village in possession of a hundred-dollar bill. Leticia's cash may be legitimate—or a link to the counterfeiters, through the charming professor, Tony Dell. Either way, I was reluctant to sound a midnight alarm without more evidence.

The chief will not race to Leticia's home before dawn to scan the questionable currency, I decided. *This will wait until daylight.*

Chapter Twenty-Five

Tuesday Morning

I tossed and turned beneath the fluffy feather comforter that normally lulled me to sleep. Moe snored on his bed in the corner. Johnny Depp purred at my feet. The grandfather's clock in my living room chimed two resounding notes. Wind blew the loose shutter on my bedroom window, startling me with a repetitive tapping noise that sounded like a stranger rapping on the back door.

Finally, I gave up. I climbed out of bed and slipped into my robe. Johnny stretched, but stayed where he was, nestled in the blankets on my bed. Moe raised his head, then lifted his fluffy body to follow me. I paced the room as I had the night before, barefoot, searching for whatever nibbled at the corners of my mind.

At six o'clock, I turned on the morning news channel. Chief Meteorologist Lisa Teachman flashed a broad smile as she announced another beautiful day. "Temperatures will be in the mid 70s, with plenty of sunshine until later this evening. If you plan to be outdoors after dinner, better take an umbrella. A spring downpour will saturate your new flowerbeds, but it will be gone by morning."

While I always appreciated Lisa's perky forecasts, today I wanted an update on the news. True to form, the station's promotional team had already named our latest newsworthy event.

The morning anchorwoman read from her teleprompter: "We have breaking news on *The Counterfeit Currency Caper*," she announced, and the words blazed across the screen to emphasize her point.

After replaying the previous night's video clip, the announcer returned to the air. "Police Chief Earl Marshall refused to identify the individual who attempted to pay a local merchant with the phony money," she said. "Confidential sources have confirmed the counterfeit bill links to the death of bank teller Maryann Penny, discovered dead in her home five days ago. Officials have declined to comment."

I stared at the screen, wishing the news teams had not connected Maryann to the counterfeit money, and hoping her mother had not watched the report. When I reached for my phone to call the chief, it rang in my hand; he was one step ahead of me.

"Did you see the morning news?" The chief asked.

"Yes. We need to talk to Lois Penny."

"I've already reached out to her," he said. "The coroner has verified Maryann's cause of death. Lois will be here in two hours. She has asked that you join us."

"I'll be there," I said.

"Good. Lois is counting on it," Chief Marshall said. "Meanwhile, the guys at the crime lab deciphered your riddles."

"Did Maryann use heat-sensitive ink?"

"Nope. Turns out, she wrote the clues in common, over-the-counter invisible ink, available at many toy stores. This one was slightly more sophisticated."

"The ultraviolet kind?" I felt foolish for not considering the simplest of methods.

"Yes," the chief said. "She even provided us with a flashlight to shine onto the words."

"Where?" I asked.

"It was in the zippered plastic bag," the chief said. "The blue pen had a dual purpose: writing the clue with one end, and reading it with the ultraviolet pen light on the opposite end."

I slapped my hand on my forehead. "How did I miss that?"

"Nobody's perfect," Chief Marshall said. "The light was hidden by an ordinary push-on cap. I missed it, too."

"We couldn't see the answers in front of our eyes," I said.

"I'll summarize the clues the lab provided," the chief said. "Riddle One mentioned rare dollars and antique vessels—which we guessed referred to counterfeit money and Maryann's bathtub. But Maryann wrote: 'Find phony money inside artifacts.'"

My mind leapt to the currency Leticia Cornwall had discovered in her garden, but I hesitated to interrupt the chief's report. "Hmm," I said. "Someone connected to the Peruvian artifacts may be involved in the counterfeiting scheme."

"Yes," he said. "Tony Dell can provide a list of people in our area who collect them."

"What about the second riddle?" I asked. "It mentioned a vast profit and a lying money tender."

"The hidden clue suggests Wayne Whitworth may be involved," the chief said. "Maryann wrote: 'My boss is making big money. You should investigate.'"

I was confused. "Why would the bank president offer a reward for information leading to his own arrest?"

"I agree that sounds odd," the chief said. "Makes me wonder whether Maryann had some of her facts wrong."

"Either way, we have to investigate him," I said. "We should also start *Operation Rumor Mill*. When the killer returns to search Maryann's house for the evidence, you can arrest him."

Chief Marshall grew quiet on the other end of the call.

"Chief? Do you agree?" I asked.

"Yes, Josie. Every time I eliminate a suspect, new information pops up. Then I return them to the list again. Tell the mavens to implement *Operation Rumor Mill* later this morning, stressing the fact that the new evidence remains, untampered, where you found it. Maybe add something about a forensics expert who can't get here until tomorrow."

"Good idea," I said. "That will explain why we haven't already moved it."

"Glad you approve, Josie." If the chief was mocking me, I didn't detect it in his voice. Instead, I felt he genuinely believed in our rumor plan.

"Our officers will wrap the whole house in new crime scene tape; a couple of guys will take turns watching the place from a patrol car parked out front."

"Perfect," I said. "The suspect will believe the rumors and attempt to sneak into the house from the back."

"We hope so," he said, "Meanwhile, you stay inside your locked house tonight, with an officer checking it periodically. We need to make progress on this case. The list of suspects keeps growing instead of shrinking."

"Okay, Chief," I said. "Er, speaking of growing…" I allowed my sentence to trail away.

"What *now*, Josie?" The chief grumbled.

"Leticia Cornwall called me last night. She thinks someone may have given the Cleeve Hill Garden Society some counterfeit bills, but she wants to stay out of the spotlight."

"She's an old woman, Josie."

"So?" I hated when the chief implied older citizens were less knowledgeable than others. His attitude was precisely why Leticia hesitated to reach out to the police department directly.

"She's probably overreacting to the news report," he explained, talking in the singsong tone he likely used when he spoke to his six-year-old daughter.

"I'd suggest you talk to her," I said in my grown-up Mom-voice.

"I'll send someone with a scanner to check the bills," he attempted to appease me.

"Fine." I said, leaving no doubt that I thought he should go himself.

"We'll talk later," Chief Marshall tried to end the call.

"Fine," I repeated. "But Chief?"

"What?"

"Make sure the officer asks Leticia about the Peruvian trunk featured in her garden this season."

Chief Marshall groaned. "I'm not assigning an officer to tour her garden, Josie. What's so important about the trunk?"

"It has hidden compartments," I said as sweetly as I could muster. "That is where she discovered the suspicious currency."

My phone went silent. I waited until the chief spoke again.

"Point taken," he said. "I'm on my way to see Leticia Cornwall."

* * *

Thanks to the TV news reporter's "confidential sources" linking the counterfeit bill to Maryann—and the bank's reward offer—everyone in English Village was already speculating about the young teller's death.

My watch read 7:00 a.m., but we had no time to waste. I sent a group text to the mavens. "Launch *Operation Rumor Mill.*"

I added the chief's instructions to stress the *location* of the evidence, as well as to mention an out-of-town expert on his way to retrieve it. Within sixty seconds, the ladies responded with two thumbs-up emojis and a bright green checkmark. I smiled. Rumors would speed through the town before breakfast, spurring the murderer to return to the scene of the crime and destroy the unknown evidence I had supposedly discovered.

We're about to catch a killer, I thought.

* * *

I arrived at the police station early, but Lois Penny was already there. She and Wayne Whitworth sat together on one side of the battered metal table; both had deep shadows below their eyes. I wondered whether Wayne was here as Maryann's employer, or her biological father, but did not feel it appropriate to ask.

Lois must have read my mind, because she provided an introduction. "Wayne is here at my invitation," she said. "I felt he should hear the details of his daughter's death, firsthand."

The banker bowed his head. "I wish I had found the courage to tell her of our relationship before she died," he said. "Perhaps she would have turned to me for help."

I had dozens of questions to ask, but they would have to wait until the chief arrived. "She was a lovely young woman," I said. "I'm truly sorry for your loss."

Chief Marshall walked briskly through the door, sparing us any additional awkwardness.

"Coffee?" he offered.

I eyeballed the new coffee machine and decided one more cup couldn't hurt. "I'll serve," I said.

The fragrant aroma of the fresh brew almost covered up the "burnt coffee" smell that still lingered in the room. Chief Marshall had abused the old coffee pot for many years before Lorene insisted he replace it. In minutes, we each had a full mug in front of us. Two sugars, no cream, for the chief. Two creams, no sugar, for me. Straight black for Lois and Wayne.

The coroner arrived precisely on time. Dr. Flavin was a bald man. Tall, with a slight stoop from bending over his work for the last twenty years. He wore a gray jacket and carried a clipboard in his hand. Turning down coffee, he shook hands with each of us and took his place at the head of the table.

"Thank you all for your patience," he began. "As the forensic pathologist on this case, I appreciate this is a difficult time for you. I hope knowing the cause of Maryann's death will bring you some peace of mind."

He removed a pair of wire-rimmed reading glasses from his front pocket and opened the file folder. "Maryann Penny died of complications resulting from a severe anxiety attack," he said. "Most likely, she panicked; her system was overwhelmed with adrenaline, causing ventricular fibrillation."

Lois spoke in a wobbly voice that betrayed her emotions. "You're saying my daughter was not murdered? She died of a heart attack?"

Dr. Flavin nodded. "Yes. We found no signs of a struggle; Maryann had no mortal wounds. Our toxicology tests were negative; she was not poisoned. Without another underlying ailment to blame, we must assume your daughter suffered a major shock—something, or someone, frightened her. Maryann's fight-or-flight response mechanism kicked into high gear, triggering the adrenaline rush that ultimately led to her death. It's an educated guess, although I must tell you Maryann's heart did not exhibit the damage we normally find after a myocardial infarction. Under the circumstances, we may never know what actually happened."

"What circumstances?" Wayne asked, and I realized neither of them had been told the details of the crime scene.

Dr. Flavin looked at Chief Marshall, and the chief clasped his hands in front of him. Taking a deep breath, he spoke in the gentle voice he reserved for the families of victims. "Someone confronted Maryann, rendered her unconscious, and laid her on a bed of cash in her bathtub."

Before I knew what was happening, Lois screamed. Her face turned white, and she slid to the floor in a dead faint. Wayne jumped from his chair, lifted Lois from the floor, and laid her on the table. I pushed my chair out of the way and stood like a useless statue, staring at Lois. Dr. Flavin removed his jacket and rolled it into a cushion to prop the woman's feet above her head.

"This is all my fault," Wayne murmured as he hovered over Lois. "I killed Maryann."

Chief Marshall glanced sharply at the banker, and I knew the "money-tender" riddle had raced to his mind, like it had to mine.

Dr. Flavin pulled a small atomizer from his pocket and spritzed the air near the woman's face. "It's peppermint," he said, "almost as effective as smelling salts, for situations like this one."

A few seconds later, Lois opened her eyes. "What happened?"

"You fainted," Dr. Flavin explained, helping her off the table and into her chair. "Sit here for a few minutes. If you feel faint again, drop your head between your knees."

The chief removed a bottle of water from the mini fridge near the coffeemaker and handed it to Lois, who drank several swallows before she set it on the table.

Wayne had returned to his chair, where he hung his head and repeated, "This is my fault. I killed my daughter."

Lois spoke softly to the banker. "No, Wayne, don't say that."

Then Chief Marshall separated the two. "Be silent. Both of you."

He walked to the phone, punched the intercom button, and called Officer Devon to report to the conference room. The young officer appeared at the door before the chief had returned the phone handset to its cradle.

Chief Marshall introduced the officer, then addressed Mr. Whitworth. "Wayne, we need a formal statement from you. Officer Devon will explain your rights and begin the process. I encourage you to have an attorney present, if you would like."

Wayne nodded without speaking. He walked to the door, looked back at Lois to mouth the words, "I'm sorry," and followed Officer Devon down the hall.

Stunned by the scene we had just witnessed, the rest of us waited for orders from the chief. Lois blew her nose. The coroner sat upright in his chair. I kept my head down and scribbled notes on the pad I had taken from my handbag.

Chief Marshall paced the floor before he returned to his seat. "Lois, I want to ask you a few questions about your reaction to Dr. Flavin's report, if you feel up to it."

Lois set her jaw and nodded. "I'm ready," she said.

The chief, the doctor, and I relaxed into our seats, thinking we were ready, too. *But none of us realized the bombshell Maryann's mother was about to reveal.*

Chapter Twenty-Six

Tuesday Late Morning

Lois Penny sipped her water and repeated her statement. "I'm ready," she said.

Chief Marshall ran his hands through his cropped hair. "Before we begin, I'd like your permission for Josie and Dr. Flavin to remain in the room. Josie discovered Maryann's body, and Dr. Flavin has found no logical cause of death. Both are searching for answers."

"They can stay," Lois said. She raised her head. "I have nothing to hide. But first, tell me why no one informed me of the bathtub filled with cash."

"We wanted to protect Maryann's reputation," I said. "With so much cash in her home, the media might have assumed she had stolen it."

Chief Marshall pointed his thumb at his chest. "It was my decision, Lois. We told no one about the money because we wanted to screen leads we received on the hotline. Only those with insider information would know to mention the bathtub filled with cash."

Lois sighed. "I could have saved you a great deal of time and trouble, as you attempted to determine my daughter's cause of death," she said.

"Please," the chief implored. "Tell us."

"It was the cash," Lois said, her voice hoarse as she spoke. "The cash killed her."

"The cash?" I stared at her, waiting for a better explanation.

"Yes." Lois sat wringing her hands as her eyes filled with tears. "Maryann had allergic contact dermatitis."

"What?" Dr. Flavin asked. "Maryann was allergic to the ink used in paper currency?"

The irony of Maryann's condition hit me in the face. "A bank teller, allergic to money!"

Chief Marshall buried his head in his hands. "No wonder we couldn't identify a murder weapon," he said. "I never considered an allergic reaction."

"Most people understand that money is dirty," Dr. Flavin said. "Paper currency changes hands often; it's not surprising that it would carry dust—and sometimes mold or other allergens—depending on where it has been. However, an allergy to the inks and dyes applied *in the production of currency* is rare."

Lois dabbed at her eyes with a tissue. "We tried to protect her," she said. "Maryann was aware she might get a rash or become ill from handling currency. She didn't realize how severe the reaction could be."

Dr. Flavin adjusted the wire spectacles on the bridge of his nose. "Currency manufacturers use dyes made from the most protein-rich parts of plants, which—like peanuts and soy—are the most likely to cause allergies. Inhaling the fumes from these dyes can lead to anaphylactic shock, just the same as a peanut allergy."

"Wayne has the same allergy," Lois said. "He knew the severity of the reaction Maryann would likely have if exposed to large quantities of currency."

I placed a fresh cup of coffee in front of Lois. "Is that why Maryann wore gloves when she handled money at the teller window?"

"Yes," Lois said. "All the tellers wore white gloves. Not long after Maryann began working at the bank, Wayne introduced *white-glove service*. Publicly, he announced it as a new image campaign to illustrate how carefully the bank handled each customer's money. Privately, he began the program to protect Maryann from the effects of her allergy."

Dr. Flavin studied the report he had prepared for Chief Marshall. "I will revise this and return it to you," he said. "It is now obvious that Maryann's heart failure resulted from the effects of her allergic reaction to the dye in the counterfeit currency."

"She is still the victim of a crime," Chief Marshall said. "When a death occurs during the commission of a felony, the law holds the perpetrator accountable."

∗ ∗ ∗

After our meeting with Lois, the chief pulled me aside to tell me about his visit with Leticia Cornwall. I sat across from him in the cluttered office where we had sparred over many topics since I had moved to English Village.

"Mrs. Cornwall was correct," he said. "The bills she found in the Peruvian trunk were counterfeit."

I raised my eyebrows. "She wasn't just an old woman overreacting to the newscast?"

Chief Marshall squirmed in his chair. "I stand corrected, Josie. I apologize."

"Have you told her yet?"

"No," the chief said. "I promised to get back to her tomorrow. The Secret Service Agency wanted time to consider how the money found its way into her trunk."

"What will you do with the bills?"

"I've already given them to Agent Evans. His team oversees all leads related to counterfeiting."

"I hope they talk to Tony Dell," I said. "He provided the trunk. When Leticia poked around and found the money in a hidden compartment, Tony told her to keep it, as a donation to the Cleeve Hill Garden Society."

The chief shrugged. "We don't need to tell the U.S. Secret Service Agency how to conduct their investigation," he said.

"Whatever you say, Chief," I said.

He glared at me. "Promise you won't tell anyone about these additional counterfeit bills."

"Mum's the word," I said, pinching my thumb and forefinger together to slide them across my closed lips.

"Get out of my office," Chief Marshall said, rolling his eyes. "Find something useful to do."

I walked from the police station to the Cozy Cups Cafe for lunch. Lorene seated me near the front window, where I could entertain myself by observing people outside the cafe, or inside.

A bright yellow Fiat pulled into a parking spot, and I watched as the lovely red-haired real estate agent climbed out of the driver's seat, tossed her Gucci bag over her shoulder, and walked toward the cafe. I ducked behind my menu as Savannah Sweet entered the front door and swept her eyes across the room. Spotting her lunch partner, she made a beeline to the corner table, where Professor Tony Dell stood to greet her.

As soon as she was seated, Savannah took a manila folder from her bag, handing it to the professor. He removed a single sheet of paper and studied its contents, nodding his approval as he read. While I ate my lunch, the two of them carried on an animated conversation, bending their heads over the paper as though it held the key to all the world's treasures. The professor made several notes as they talked.

After Lorene cleared the dishes from my table, I paid the tab and handed her an additional one-hundred-dollar bill. "Consider it a tip," I said, smiling at her.

"Thank you, Josie," she said, giving me a wink.

I stood to leave, but I couldn't resist the opportunity to speak to Savannah and Tony. Neither of them appeared surprised when I showed up at their table.

"Hi, there," I said. "Could I join you for a few minutes? I'd love an update on the English Village Garden Tour."

"Well, bless your heart, Josie," Savannah's voice dripped with sweetness. "We just completed a few more details, but I doubt they would interest you."

I flashed a bright smile. "You're mistaken, Savannah," I said, pulling out a chair, "*everything you do* interests me."

"Please sit down," the professor said as my rear end hit the seat. "We are always happy to answer questions from the media."

"I'm not," Savannah said. "I never speak to reporters without an appointment."

"Pretend I'm a garden society VIP," I retorted, pulling a notepad from my purse.

Tony Dell smothered a smile with his hand as Savannah pouted at me across the table.

"That's a lovely Gucci bag, Savannah," I said, pointing to the designer tote hanging from the back of her chair. "Is it a replica?"

She rolled her eyes. "Surely you don't want to talk about purses again," she said.

"No," I agreed. "I want to know about the Garden Tour sponsors. Do you have a list of donors to mention in my next article?"

Tony leaned forward in his seat. "Good idea," he said. "I'm sure the underwriters would appreciate the exposure."

Savannah shot him a withering look before turning to me with a forced smile. "I'll send it to you," she said. "Anything else?"

"Thank you for offering," I said. "How about a copy of your budgets? It occurred to me that the Garden Tour is a major event. People might be interested to know how much money it brings into our community."

"Absolutely not," she said, taking a sip of coffee from her mug. "Our financial reports are confidential."

I shrugged. "Okay. Whatever you say."

"Besides," Savannah said, "Haven't you stirred up enough talk about money this week? The town is in an uproar about counterfeit bills."

"*Bill*," I corrected. "They've only verified *one* counterfeit bill, so far." I crossed my fingers behind my back, since the chief had made me promise not to mention the phony money he found at Leticia Cornwell's.

"Where do you think it came from?" Savannah asked. "Do you know who gave the counterfeit hundred-dollar bill to one of our merchants?"

She stared at me until I wondered whether she knew I was the guilty one. "I really can't say," I said. "Can *you*?"

The professor interrupted our squabbling. "I'm sure Chief Marshall will track it down," he said. "Meanwhile, I'm late for another meeting."

When they stood to leave, I followed behind. Savannah had parked closest to the entrance, so I walked a short distance beside the professor toward his car. "Did you know the best U.S. counterfeit currency comes from Peru?" I asked.

He smiled. "I read about it in your article."

"And *you* are from Peru," I added.

"Yes," he said. "I have dual citizenship. I am one of 750,000 Peruvians living in the U.S.A."

"How many of them live in English Village?" I asked.

The professor brushed aside my question. "You're an excellent reporter, Josie," he said. "But you're looking at the wrong person. Back off before you get hurt."

I watched as he drove away.

Was that a threat? The professor knows more than he pretends, I thought.

Chapter Twenty-Seven

Tuesday Afternoon

I parked in my garage and sat at Piper's steering wheel, stewing about the unsuccessful encounter with Tony Dell and Savannah Sweet. *Both knew Maryann,* I thought. *And both are hiding facts that could identify her killer.*

With no additional leads, I climbed out of the car and went in search of Moe. We could use a walk to clear our minds. Grabbing his leash, I slipped my keys and phone into my pocket, and we headed out the front door toward the park.

I carried on a rambling conversation as we walked. Moe pranced beside me, pretending to be interested. Mostly, I talked about the weather, flowers, and the upcoming Garden Tours. We both knew I was making noise to keep from thinking about Maryann, dying from allergic contact dermatitis.

We entered the shady gazebo, where I settled onto a bench, and Moe rested at my feet, moments before Harvey Jacobs walked out of the blacksmith shop. He spotted us and strolled in our direction.

I watched as he approached. Although we had spoken on the phone, we had not seen each other for nearly three months. *Maybe it's time to extend an olive branch,* I thought.

"Hey," Harvey said, "long time, no see."

"It was a long winter," I answered, smiling at him. "Moe and I waited for warmer weather to venture outside."

"Okay if I give him a biscuit?" Harvey reached into his pocket for the treat.

"He's expecting one." I released my hold on Moe's collar, and he took the biscuit from Harvey's outstretched hand. "Some things never change," I said.

"Like friendships." Harvey shoved his hands back into his pockets and smiled down at me. "We *are* still friends, right?"

"Yes," I agreed. "Good friends are hard to find." I patted the bench, and Harvey sat down beside me.

"I heard you're also making friends with the Cleeve Hill Garden Society ladies," he said. "That must be interesting."

I rolled my eyes. "Don't get me started," I said. "Those frail little gardeners are tougher than they look."

"No doubt you can handle it," Harvey said. He threw his head back and laughed. "I'm *rooting* for you."

"Ha, ha. Thanks a lot, Harvey," I said. "I can use all the moral support I can get."

"Seriously, Josie," he said, "I'm here if you ever want to talk. No strings attached."

"No strings?"

"Nope," he said. "I'm a superb listener. Let me prove it to you over dinner at the Philbrook tonight. We'll go Dutch, so it's not a date."

He looked so hopeful that I couldn't disappoint him. "I would like that," I agreed.

The relaxed conversation lightened my mood and reminded me of why I had welcomed Harvey as a friend when we first met. I felt a sense of relief that we were on speaking terms again. Refreshed by the walk—and our brief visit with Harvey—Moe and I returned to the cottage in high spirits.

My phone pinged with a text from Chief Marshall as we stepped onto our front porch. "Doc has isolated human skin cells from JD's claws," he wrote. "The crime lab has them on file. All we need is a sample from a suspect to compare. Good work, Josie."

I appreciated his praise but regretted that we still had no suspect in Maryann's murder. Moe followed in my footsteps as I moved through the cottage, tidying the kitchen and starting a load of laundry. I cleared away the remnants of papers piled on one end of the dining room table, then crawled underneath it to retrieve a note card that had fallen to the floor.

Flipping it over, I read: "Injured Hand. Park Bench. Yellow Fiat."

I smacked my forehead with the palm of my hand. "How could I forget these?" I said aloud, and Moe poked his head under the table to see what was wrong.

I had been so focused on Savannah Sweet's lack of bookkeeping skills that I neglected to follow up on the three items that originally landed her on my suspect list.

There is nothing so messy as a crime with gaping holes where information should be, I thought, picking up the phone.

Savannah answered on the first ring. "What now, Josie?" she asked.

"I wanted to apologize for barging in on your lunch," I said. "I was rude, and I'm sorry."

Savannah remained silent, so I kept talking. "I saw an opportunity to talk to Tony Dell and took advantage of it. I shouldn't have interrupted you."

When she still didn't answer, I said, "Sometimes I push too hard for answers."

"Stop talking," Savannah interrupted my rambling. "I accept your apology. I've been guilty of interrupting people at lunch, too. I know what it's like to need answers and hit a brick wall."

"Really?"

"Maryann had been my best friend since the first grade." Savannah's voice cracked with emotion. "You aren't the only one with questions, Josie."

"Then you won't mind answering some of mine?"

"Nothing I say will bring Maryann back, but I will answer anything that will help catch her killer. What do you need to know?" Savannah asked.

"Why were you at Maryann's house the night before she died? I drove by and saw a yellow Fiat in her drive. I would have asked earlier, but I wasn't sure the car belonged to you…and we weren't exactly on good terms."

"There's nothing to tell," Savannah said. "Maryann and I were friends. When I dropped off a deposit at the bank Wednesday morning, she said she was leaving town for a few days. She wasn't herself. I was worried about her."

"You went to see her that evening?" I prompted.

"Yes. I tried to talk to her about whatever was bothering her. She refused. Told me I should mind my own business, not to worry. She could handle her own problems. Maryann shut me out, Josie. She said I shouldn't tell anyone that we had talked. In hindsight, I believe she wanted to protect me."

"Did she say anything else?" I asked.

"One thing," Savannah said. "As I left her house, she hugged me and said, *'Don't trust anyone.'* It was the last thing she said to me."

Maryann's warning sent chills up my spine. I wanted to believe Savannah, but she had lied to me before, so I didn't fully trust her.

"Remember the first time we met?" I asked. "You told me you had injured your hand on a broken screen door. Was that true?"

"No," Savannah said. "If I had been truthful, you would have known I'd talked to Maryann—and she had insisted that I not mention seeing her."

"Please tell me now," I said. "How did you hurt yourself?"

"Maryann was in a rush to get packed. JD was meowing for dinner, so I offered to feed him." Savannah explained. "I cut my hand opening the can of cat food. It was clumsy of me. Maryann saw the blood and went into full first-responder mode. She doused it with peroxide and wrapped it in a huge wad of gauze."

"She took care of you," I said.

"Yes," Savannah's voice was low. "I wanted to help Maryann, but I only caused her extra trouble. I still felt bad about it the next day. I wasn't in the mood to answer a nosy reporter's questions."

"Did you talk to her Wednesday morning before she left town?"

"No. Maryann promised to let me know after she solved her problems. She said it wouldn't take long. All day, I waited. She never called. Later that night, I heard the police had responded to a disturbance in her neighborhood. I *knew* something bad had happened to her."

Listening to Savannah talk about her friend, I believed her story. "There's just one more thing bothering me," I said.

"It's always *one more thing* with you," Savannah said.

"I know," I admitted. "It's a character flaw. My friends tell me it drives them crazy."

Savannah sighed into the phone. "What do you want to know?"

"I was positive I saw you last week, but you denied it. Late Wednesday afternoon, in the park?"

"I remember," Savannah said. "I finished my appointment with a home buyer early and stopped at the park to gather my thoughts before I drove to Maryann's house. It's a good place to relax."

"Then why lie about being there?"

"Because it wasn't your concern, and I preferred not to discuss it."

"Because it was a secret rendezvous with Dr. Lang?" I asked.

"Holy guacamole, Josie," Savannah practically shouted into the phone. "Don't you ever quit?"

"No," I said. "I saw him drop something shiny. You picked it up, slipped it into the book you were reading, and walked out of the park."

"That was a private matter," Savannah said. "It wasn't important."

"If it wasn't important, why pretend you didn't see each other?" I asked.

"Believe me, Josie," Savannah said. "This is not relevant."

"Can you give me a hint?" I pressed.

"If you must know, every time David and I cross paths, the whole town thinks we're engaged. That causes problems for his fiancée. So, we try not to be seen together."

"But I thought–" I stopped mid-sentence.

"You thought we were a couple," Savannah said.

"Everyone does," I said.

"That's the problem," Savannah said.

"Then, why were you dating him, and where is his mysterious fiancée?"

"I wasn't dating him—although sometimes I let busybodies come to their own conclusions. I was selling him a house." Savannah said. His fiancée is attending graduate school abroad. This summer, she will complete her degree, join David for a surprise engagement party in Kansas City with their unsuspecting friends and family, and return here to meet his business associates. They plan to marry and move into a home in English Village."

"I see," I said, although I still didn't have a clear picture of why they staged the convoluted key exchange.

"David borrowed the house key so he could take another look at the home he had selected. He forgot to put it back into the lockbox, so he asked if he could return it to me in the park."

"Seems a little over-the-top, to me," I said.

"Not the way rumors fly around here," Savannah said. "David wanted to purchase the house as a surprise for his fiancée. I met him for lunch one day to talk about the type of home he wanted. Before I returned home that night, my social media accounts had exploded with questions about the 'handsome hunk' escorting me to lunch."

"People *do* like to talk," I admitted.

"Some posts included photos," Savannah said. "At first, we both thought it was funny. David even allowed his office staff to think we were dating; he had not announced his engagement to anyone. Then his fiancée saw the pictures and threw a fit. David had to tell her about the house hunt."

"I guess you're right," I said. "It had nothing to do with Maryann."

"Right. Except that when I told her that evening how upset David's fiancée was about the rumors that he had cheated on her, Maryann became worried about using his photo on her nightstand. She already felt guilty about being dishonest with her mom. She tore up the photo and tossed it in the dumpster."

"No wonder I didn't see it the next day," I said. "It makes sense that she wouldn't want to cause David any additional problems."

Moe laid his head on my knee, and I knew he thought my phone conversation had lasted way too long. I hoped Savannah had more patience than he did.

"Tell me," I asked, "where did Maryann turn when she needed information or advice?"

"That's easy. She usually asked one of four people for their opinions: Her mom. Me. Her boss. Or Professor Dell."

"Anyone else?"

"No. Why are you asking?"

"Because someone she trusted betrayed her," I explained. "Otherwise, she wouldn't have told you to 'trust no one.'"

"Well, it wasn't me!"

Savannah had thoroughly answered all my questions, but I still had one small request. "Would you do me a favor?" I asked.

"You can't be serious," she said.

After I explained that Maryann's cat had most likely scratched her intruder, and the crime lab needed skin samples to compare to the scrapings found beneath JD's claws, Savannah surprised me with a laugh.

"Only *you* would suggest that the police investigate Johnny Depp's claws," she said. "If it will rule me out as a suspect, I'll go there now."

* * *

JD napped on the couch, while Moe and I, inspired by the beauty on Cleeve Hill, spent the rest of the afternoon planting flowers in the beds that bordered the front of our cottage. A few puffy clouds gathered overhead. Moe supervised from the porch; I raked the soil, breaking up the clods into small pieces. Next, I prepped the dirt with fertilizer, dug holes for each plant, and tucked them all into the rich earth. After I tamped the soil into place, I watered the beds and put away my gardening tools.

The Cleeve Hill Garden Society would approve, I thought, arching my back to relieve my fatigued muscles. It had taken only a couple of hours to plant the flowers, but I already felt the effects of the physical labor.

I drained the last of my water bottle, noting the grime beneath my fingernails—although I had worn gardening gloves—and the splotches of dirt that dotted my shirt and jeans.

Mrs. Abernathy waved from across the street and walked over to admire my handiwork.

"Audrey Hepburn used to say, 'to plant a garden is to believe in tomorrow,'" she said.

"I agree with her," I said, brushing a dried clod from my pants.

"Would you like to come over for a chat?" Mrs. Abernathy asked. "I have fresh lemonade."

I wiped my brow with the back of one dirt-streaked hand. "I would love to," I said. "But I'm far too grimy to enter your home. Could I have a raincheck?"

"Anytime," she said. "But let's make it soon. I want to hear all about your investigation."

"It would be a brief conversation," I said. "The chief has forbidden us to talk about it."

"I heard you're close to identifying a suspect," Mrs. Abernathy said, pushing for details.

"Still can't talk about it," I smiled back at her. "But I appreciate your interest."

"Maybe tomorrow?"

Her hopeful expression made me laugh out loud. "We'll see," I said. "Right now, I need to shower and run some errands."

"No worries," she said. "I always monitor the house when you're out."

"Thank you, Mrs. Abernathy. It's good to know you're looking after me."

Moe and I watched from our porch as she made her way back across the street. A half-hour later, I was on my way to the Philbrook Inn for dinner. Pulling into a spot next to Harvey's old blue pickup truck, I parked Piper, swung my purse over my shoulder, and walked inside.

Harvey waved at me from across the room—his lopsided smile a welcome sight, after so long an absence. We had both dressed for comfort: Harvey was in blue jeans and a plaid shirt, and I wore my black pants and a gray sweater.

True to his word, Harvey kept the conversation appropriately "non-dating" casual. It wasn't long before we slipped into the natural rhythm of our earlier days, as friends. Harvey shared funny stories about well-meaning customers who frequented his hardware store, and I bemoaned the antics of the gardeners on Cleeve Hill. He mentioned the investigation of Maryann's death only once, to say he had confidence that I would solve the case.

By the time we'd finished our meals and paid the tabs, our friendship was on firm ground again. Harvey and I had put our differences behind us. *If only solving Maryann's murder could be as easy,* I thought.

Chapter Twenty-Eight

Tuesday Night

Dusk had already fallen when I pulled into my garage. The rain Lisa Teachman had predicted arrived precisely on time; sprinkles turned into a steady shower moments after I parked Piper for the night. It had been a long day. I was tired and discouraged, despite the dinner I had shared with Harvey. Every clue I followed led to a dead end. *At least we know what caused Maryann's death,* I thought, reflecting on the weird allergy Lois Penney had revealed.

I climbed out of my car, walked the few paces in the darkened garage, and trudged up the short flight of steps, still mulling over the lack of a suspect in Maryann's case. Like always, I turned the knob of my kitchen door, expecting to find my fluffy sheepdog waiting for me on the other side. When Moe failed to greet me, a chill ran up my spine, and I hesitated in the doorway. Rain noisily pelted the roof in the darkened sky outside, but *inside,* all was quiet.

The house is too silent...too still, I thought.

I waited. Listened to the silence. Nothing stirred.

Don't be a fraidy-cat, Josie. The childhood taunt echoed in my head. *Turn on the light.*

Swallowing my fear, I tiptoed into the shadowy kitchen. "Moe?" I called out, but he did not appear, and my eyes had not adjusted to the darkness.

When I flipped on the light switch, I was so startled that I dropped my handbag to the floor and squealed like a little girl. Then I froze in place, taking in the scene before me.

Corky Markham sat alone at my kitchen island, dressed head-to-toe in black, a duffle bag at her feet. She held a silver Glock in one hand; the barrel pointed my direction.

"I hope you don't mind that I let myself in," she said. "I wanted to speak to you privately. Just a quiet conversation between friends."

Her tone was so cordial I might have believed her, except for the gun she grasped in her palm.

"Where is Moe?" I demanded. "If you have hurt him—"

"No need for threats," Corky said. "Your watchdog growled incessantly on my arrival. He forced me to sedate him with a dose of melatonin. He is resting in your laundry room with Maryann's cat." She waved the gun in the air. "Go. See for yourself."

I glared at her and raced to the utility room, where Corky had confined both animals—JD in his kennel, and Moe stretched, as if lifeless, across the floor. The cat batted a paw at me, wanting attention, but sweet Moe was out cold. I placed my hand in front of his nose, to be certain he was still breathing. Then, I whispered in his ear, and he attempted to open his eyes.

"It's okay, boy," I told him. "I'm here."

I filled his water bowl, leaving it near his head so he could drink as soon as he woke up. I backed into the hallway and left the laundry room door wide open. Moe needs a chance to escape, I thought.

Corky hadn't budged from her seat in the kitchen.

"How did you get into my house?" I confronted her, hoping she could not sense the fear growing inside me.

She shrugged. "With a key, Josie. I borrowed it from your neighbor, Mrs. Abernathy. She's a bank customer, like you. The nosy old woman once mentioned that she 'keeps an eye on' your place when you're away. I knocked on her door and explained you had asked me to check on Moe. She happily handed me the key."

I pictured Mrs. Abernathy giving this banker the key to my front door while protecting my home from strangers. Corky had duped my well-intentioned neighbor.

"What do you want?" I asked.

"I hoped you would offer me coffee," she said. "I have a proposal to discuss."

"Fine," I said. "Peruvian blend okay?"

She smiled. "Perfect."

I started the coffeemaker and set a platter of cookies on the counter. "Mind if I turn on some lights?" I asked. "The neighbors will notice if my house stays dark."

Corky nodded. "Whatever you would normally do," she said, "as long as you're ready to consider my proposal when the coffee is ready."

Walking through my cottage, I turned on two lamps in the living room, the chandelier over my dining room table, and the lamp on my nightstand. I hoped Corky wouldn't notice that I turned *off* the switch for the porch lights. *If the chief has anyone patrolling my neighborhood, they will recognize our prearranged sign that something is amiss,* I thought. *I must stall this deranged woman until help arrives—or until I can devise a way to escape.*

Returning to the kitchen, I motioned to my handbag—still on the floor near the garage door, where I had dropped it. "I'll retrieve my notepad and pen now," I said.

Corky eyed me suspiciously. "Hand me the purse," she said. "I'll get them for you."

I made a big show of rolling my eyes, then marched to the bag— intentionally blocking Corky's view with my body. Without hesitation, I bent over the purse, grabbed the strap with one hand, and reached inside a side pouch with the other. *Yes! For once, I remembered to store my miniature tape recorder where it belonged.*

Grasping the tiny recorder in my palm, I pressed what I hoped was the 'on' button and hid the machine in the pocket of my sweater—while simultaneously spinning back around to face Corky. I strode back to the kitchen island as casually as I could, considering that my heart pounded furiously in my chest.

"Here," I said, dangling the bag by its handle. "You'll find a life-threatening spiral notepad inside, along with a pink ballpoint pen."

Corky waved the Glock at me. "No need to be snippy," she said, removing the pen and pad and setting them on the counter. "I doubt you'll need to take notes, anyway."

I poured the coffee and pulled a barstool to the opposite side of the kitchen island, so I could face my foe. "Please put the gun away, Corky," I said. "I can't think clearly with a weapon pointed at my face."

"If you hadn't poked your nose into Maryann's death, all of this would have blown over by now," she said. "The police would have assumed Maryann became embroiled in a counterfeit money distribution scheme, and—wracked with guilt—took her own life to escape from the shame. I even took her sweater to plant in the delivery van."

"You're the *CJ Drake* who borrowed Stan's van!" I pointed my finger at her. "Was that your plan?" I asked, "to let an innocent girl take the blame while you and your plumber friend walked away with the cash?"

Corky leaned toward me and spat the words out of her mouth. "You think you're smart," she said. "But you have it all wrong."

"Enlighten me," I said, crossing my arms across my chest.

"I was nothing but an intermediary," Corky said. "I received shipments of what I thought were genuine Peruvian artifacts. I delivered them to a private investor who paid me for each delivery. I didn't know the vases and trunks in those crates contained counterfeit currency."

"That's poppycock," I said. "Why would a private investor hire a small-town bank employee to deliver precious artworks in a borrowed plumbing van?"

Corky sat up straight on her barstool and lifted her chin. "Because no one would expect it," she said. "He wanted to keep his purchases confidential. No one is suspicious of a trusted bank officer from a tiny town."

"And the plumber?"

"Stan was an innocent bystander," she said. "He let me borrow his van about once a month to drive to a spot near the Mexican border, where I met the investor. I never told Stan where I went—only that I had another shipment for the art collector."

Corky's story was so ludicrous I might have believed it, if she hadn't been sitting across from me with a gun in her hand.

"Who was this mysterious art collector?" I asked.

For the first time, Corky's defiant attitude dialed down a notch. She ducked her head and mumbled, "Er, I can't tell you."

"You can't, or you won't?" I asked.

"I can't, because I don't know who he is," she said. "I never saw him without a mask. We both wore them to protect his privacy, and mine."

"Where did you meet him to unload the van?"

"The back parking lot of a Big Mart store—in a different location each time. We used a burner phone to communicate. He texted me the location before each drop off."

"Let me get this straight," I said. "You delivered truckloads of art you never saw, to an investor you never met, at a secret meeting point each month, in return for enormous sums of money. Yet you never questioned the legality of those deliveries?"

Corky squirmed in her seat. "I needed the money," she whined.

"How did this benevolent art collector approach you?" I asked.

"He called me at the bank," Corky said. "He said a mutual friend, who wished to remain anonymous, had referred him to me. The friend assured him I was trustworthy. The guy asked me to make one delivery a month, for six months. I was to be compensated for each delivery."

I listened to the bank officer's story, astounded at her naïve acceptance of the stranger's offer. "How much did he pay you?" I asked.

"One hundred thousand."

I fought to keep my jaw from dropping wide open. "For six trips?"

"No," Corky lowered her eyes. "Per trip. I only made five trips."

"Half a million American dollars for five deliveries?" The words caught in my throat.

"Yes," she said. "But I had expenses."

"Expenses?"

"I missed work for a few days," Corky explained. "Plus, I paid Stan for the use of his van, and I filled it with gasoline each time."

"Right." My well of sympathy for the woman was running dry. "How much did you pay Stan?"

"Five thousand."

"Per trip?"

"No." Corky looked away from my gaze. "Total."

"You made five hundred thousand dollars for five days of work, and paid out five thousand to Stan, plus some gas money?" I shot her another withering look. "I'd say it was worth your time, wouldn't you?"

She shoved the gun aside and clasped her hands together. "I didn't think anyone would get hurt."

As I stood to refill our coffee cups, I heard a low moan from the laundry room and rushed to check on Moe. He had rolled onto his side and lay, snoring, in his sleep. *The sedatives are wearing off,* I thought.

My anger toward Corky had faded as Moe improved, but the woman still held me captive at gunpoint. If I could keep her talking until help arrived, I might get answers about how Maryann ended up in a bathtub full of cash. I marched back into the kitchen, took a sip of the fresh coffee I'd left on the counter, then added more cream to offset a slight bitter aftertaste.

"You said you had a proposal for me. What is it?" I studied the woman across from me.

"You agree to concoct a story the chief will believe, placing Maryann to blame for the counterfeit money, and I'll share the wealth."

"Forget it," I said. "I won't cover up your crimes."

Corky waved her gun in the air. "Then get me a deal," she said. "I'll tell the chief everything I know, in return for immunity in the murder charge. I didn't kill Maryann."

"From what I've heard, you don't have any bargaining chips," I emphasized her position by counting her weaknesses with three fingers. "One: you don't know who was behind the smuggling scheme—or whatever you call this distribution of counterfeit money hidden within the artifacts. Two: you can't identify the collector who took possession of your deliveries. And three: you don't even have addresses for the drop-off points. I doubt your *art collector* lives anywhere near the Big Mart stores."

"I have more than you think," Corky said.

I was growing weary of her cat-and-mouse game. "How did Maryann get involved?" I asked.

Corky rolled her eyes. "The girl couldn't mind her own business," she said. "First, she opened one of my shipments—mistakenly delivered to the art gallery. Then, she jostled it into the trunk of her car like a sack of potatoes, cracking the base."

"Did she see the counterfeit bills hidden inside?"

"No, she did something worse. She overheard my conversation explaining the mishap to my contact. Afterwards, she wouldn't stop asking questions. I tried to bargain with her. Offered her some money. Gave her a burner phone so we could communicate outside of the bank."

I took another sip of my coffee. "She figured out that you were smuggling phony money into the country and planned to blow the whistle," I said.

Corky shrugged her shoulders. "She gave me no choice. When she refused to take a payoff for her silence, I slipped a counterfeit hundred-dollar bill into her cash tray at the drive-through window, making her an accomplice."

"No wonder she was nervous the day I made my deposit," I said. "She didn't know which bill was counterfeit."

"The little ninny still refused to cooperate," Corky said. "Maryann planned to see an attorney, so I went to her house that morning to reason with her. I had a friend drop me there so no one would see my car in her driveway. He also dragged in several large plastic bags I'd stored in his van—but I didn't tell him what was in them."

"Let me guess," I said. "Maryann turned you down again, so you staged a scene that would pin the entire counterfeiting scheme on her."

Corky nodded. "Clever idea, huh?"

"I doubt the chief will think it was clever," I said.

"Chief Marshall has no imagination," Corky said.

I massaged my temples where a throbbing headache had begun. "I still don't understand one thing," I said. "I know Maryann's cause of death, but not the details of how she fell into a bathtub filled with cash. Did you hit her with the wrench?"

Corky gave me a cagey grin. "Surely you can figure it out," she said.

Her face softened around the edges, and I felt like I was seeing her through an aquarium. I rubbed my eyes, and she became clear again. "Wait," I said, and my tongue felt thick in my mouth. "Did you sedate Maryann the way you did Moe?"

"You're getting warmer, Josie," Corky said in a distorted, slow-motion voice. "I mixed a sedative in her coffee and helped her to the bathroom when she was too weak to walk on her own."

As the meaning of her words sank into my mind, three things happened: I felt myself slip off the stool and onto the floor. The squeal of a police siren careened onto my street. And Moe launched himself over my body toward the woman who pointed a gun at my head.

Chapter Twenty-Nine

Early Wednesday Morning

The last thing I remembered was the "pop" of a gunshot and the whistle of a bullet past my ear. I awoke to shrill beeping sounds— the steady rhythm of my heart verifying that I was alive and well, in a room so bright it hurt my eyes to open them.

Chief Marshall spoke to the nurse in a whisper. "Is she awake?"

"Almost," the woman replied. "Her vitals are good. She was given an overdose of the melatonin your suspect used to spike her coffee."

I squinted my eyes and joined their conversation in a croaky voice I didn't recognize. "Moe–?"

The chief rushed to the side of my bed. "Moe is fine, Josie," he said. "When we arrived at your house, Moe had knocked Corky to the floor and was sitting on her chest. As soon as you're able to walk out of here on your own, we will take you home to see him. The two of you can rest and recover together."

I was too weary to form long sentences. "Time?"

"Two o'clock. You've been in the hospital for five hours."

Blinking against the bright lights, I struggled to raise my head. "Corky?"

"She is in our jail cell at the police station," Chief Marshall said. "Tomorrow, we will charge her with the distribution of counterfeit currency and involuntary manslaughter. Doc Swinson has already positively matched Corky's skin scrapings with those he found under JD's claws. This, combined with the confession she made to you, will be enough evidence to convict her."

I swallowed hard, thinking of how the greedy bank officer inadvertently took Maryann's life. She had intended for me to discover Maryann asleep in the tub filled with money. The girl might have struggled to convince a jury that she was innocent.

"Why did Corky come after me, instead of falling for our fake evidence rumor?" I asked the chief.

"She believed you were the one key witness who could place her at the scene—or help set her free. When you refused to accept Corky's proposal to incriminate Maryann, she was prepared to stage another murder—this time with you as the victim. She intended to plant the gun in Stan Hermann's van and let the plumber take the blame."

I shook my head to clear the remaining cobwebs from my brain. "And Tony Dell?"

"Agent Evans will contact him. I'm sure the professor will cooperate with the investigation."

* * *

Chief Marshall returned me safely to my cottage at 3:00 a.m., where I spent the first ten minutes praising Moe for his bravery. After all the hugs and kisses, Moe cocked his head and gave me a puzzled look, as if to say, "You're *my human,* Josie. It's my job to protect you."

Then, with the house secure and my cell phone on the nightstand beside my bed, I pulled the covers over my head and tried to sleep. In the darkness of my dreams, Corky Markham chased Moe around my kitchen island with a gun in her hand. I raced behind them in slow motion, stretching my arms as far as they would reach, to capture Corky before she caught up to my sweet dog. In the nightmare, my arms turned to rubber bands, cartoon-style, but they were still not long enough for me to grab her.

The dream rambled on throughout the wee hours of the morning until— after tossing and turning for hours—I woke up. I heaved a sigh of relief when

I realized Moe lay snoring at the foot of my bed, oblivious to the dangers of my dreams. The clock on my nightstand read 5:45 a.m. I had slept fitfully, but was now wide awake, my brain spinning from all that had occurred in the past twenty-four hours.

Johnny Depp meowed from his kennel, hungry for breakfast.

I tiptoed around Moe, released JD, and walked into the kitchen for coffee. The cat followed behind me, swishing his tail until I filled his bowl and set it on the floor.

Turning on the TV, I settled into my favorite chair, where Johnny soon sauntered over to drape himself across my lap. The local station began with "Breaking news on the *Counterfeit Currency Caper*," the blonde reporter looking crisp and professional in her bright red blazer.

I pumped up the volume.

"Police have apprehended a person of interest in the circulation of phony money earlier this week," she announced. "Although they have not released the individual's name, our confidential sources suggest the person is an employee of the English Village State Bank—the same place where Maryann Penny worked before she was found dead in her home one week ago." The news reporter motioned to a video screen behind her, where Maryann's photo appeared side-by-side with a picture of the bank's exterior.

"Bank President Wayne Whitworth had offered a reward for information leading to the arrest of those responsible for the counterfeiting scheme," the newscaster continued. "Mr. Whitworth has not returned our calls for an update on the reward."

The anchorwoman turned to the camera again. "Police Chief Earl Marshall has scheduled a news conference at noon today, where he will update us on the case," she said.

As I turned off the program, my phone pinged with a text from the chief: "You awake?"

"Yes."

Seconds later, he called. "We have a news conference scheduled at noon today. Do you feel well enough to attend?"

"I wouldn't miss it," I said.

"We've arrested Corky Markham and will charge her with Involuntary Manslaughter—causing a death while committing an unlawful act."

"What about the counterfeit charges?"

"Agent Evans will handle that," the chief said. "He has already confiscated Corky's burner phone, downloaded footage from the Big Mart security cameras, and enlisted Tony Dell to help track the origins of the suspicious Peruvian artifacts."

Images of Professor Dell flashed into my mind as the chief spoke. *Tony Dell, charming as he explained the Peruvian exhibits at the art gallery. Tony Dell, admitting that Maryann had caused problems by opening a crate from a misdirected shipment. Tony Dell, conspiring with Savannah Sweet at the cafe, and warning me to 'back off' when I asked questions about Peru.*

"Chief," I asked. "What do you know about Tony Dell?"

"You can stop searching for suspects, Josie," the chief said. "We found the person responsible for Maryann's death. She admitted it to you, and we have the recording from your phone to prove it."

"I know, but–"

"But, what?"

"Corky couldn't pull off the counterfeiting scheme by herself," I said. "Tony Dell had access to the Peruvian artifacts. His last name isn't even Dell; it's *Delfino.* He's *from Peru.* In my first conversation with Corky at the bank, she mentioned Maryann was involved with the professor—something about a foreigner who couldn't be trusted."

"You want to point a finger at the professor based on something our suspect said several days ago?" Chief Marshall's tone left no doubt that he disagreed with me. "Corky was likely trying to send you on a wild-goose chase."

"Tony Dell dodged my questions," I said. "He's hiding something, and I don't trust him."

Chief Marshall must have been drinking a fresh cup of coffee because I heard a gurgling cough, as though he had swallowed too fast and spewed some of the hot brew out of his mouth.

"You okay, Chief?" I asked.

"Fine, Josie," he said in a gruff voice. "Just do me a favor and leave the counterfeit money case to the Feds. Be happy that we solved Maryann's murder. Your persistence and bravery paid off."

My face flushed at the compliment, and I felt a surge of pride that the chief appreciated my work. Thanks to our small team of investigators, Maryann's intruder—her murderer—would pay for her crimes. When the U.S. Secret Service completed its investigation, Corky Markham would face federal counterfeiting charges as well.

"Thank you, Chief," I said. "Sometimes I get focused on details and forget to celebrate the big victories."

"Details are important," the chief said. "I'm working on a few of them now. Show up early for the news conference. There's someone I want you to meet."

* * *

Fueled by adrenaline from the late-night face-off with Corky, I skipped my morning yogurt and splurged on a hot breakfast of scrambled eggs and an English muffin. Harvey called as I poured my second cup of coffee.

"Congratulations, Josie. I heard you cracked two cases in one," he said. "Is it true that Maryann's killer was also our local counterfeiting kingpin?"

"Where did you hear that?" I asked.

"The morning newscast." Harvey said. "You solved the *Counterfeit Currency Caper.*"

"Hmm. I believe the story credited Chief Marshall with apprehending the counterfeiter," I said. "No one mentioned Maryann's murderer. And they certainly didn't call out *my name* in connection with the arrest."

Harvey chuckled at the other end of the call. "This is English Village, Josie. The whole town knows you're responsible for capturing the suspect who committed both crimes. They say you chased him down and badgered him until he confessed. You're a hometown hero."

I laughed at his description. "Don't believe everything you hear at the coffee shop, my friend. After our dinner last night, the suspect was waiting for me in my kitchen. I just kept asking questions until the cavalry arrived."

"Ri-i-i-ght," Harvey said. "Are you going to tell me who was behind all of this?"

"You'll have to watch the news conference," I said. "The chief would never forgive me if I stole his thunder before he made an official announcement."

"Anyway, I'm proud of you, Josie. Good job."

When we ended the call, I realized Harvey had never scolded me for putting myself in danger, as he had in our "almost dating" days. He had spoken to me like a friend, not an overprotective father figure. *Well done, Harvey,* I thought.

The Mahjong Mavens took the opposite approach. Nellie showed up at my door before I'd cleared away my breakfast dishes. She marched into the cottage with fire in her eyes. "What were you thinking?" she said.

"Good morning, Nellie," I answered, giving her a hug. "It's good to see you, too."

"Don't be smart with me, Missy," she said. "I've heard all about your latest encounter with a killer, and I won't be mollycoddled."

I poured her a cup of coffee and motioned for her to sit. "Calm down, Nellie. I would never attempt to appease you with less than the truth."

"I should hope not." Nellie huffed, peering at me over the rim of her cup.

Pulling up a barstool to sit beside her, I studied Nellie's worried face. "What do you want to know?"

"They say you attacked Maryann's killer in your own home and ended up in the hospital with a brain concussion," Nellie said.

"I didn't attack anyone," I said. "It was more like a business meeting. The suspect wanted to make a deal. I tried to negotiate while I waited for Chief Marshall to arrive. But before we could come to any agreement, I fell asleep and slid out of my chair onto the floor. Moe leapt onto the suspect. He was the brave one."

Nellie's eyes narrowed as she considered my story. "I heard there was a gun involved."

"There might have been," I conceded. "I try not to look into the barrel of a weapon. Especially when some crazy person is waving it in the air."

"No concussion?" Nellie asked.

CHAPTER TWENTY-NINE

"No. Nothing wounded, except my pride."

"Why would you fall asleep in the middle of a confrontation with a killer?" Nellie probed.

"The chief says the intruder drugged my coffee," I explained.

"Probably tired of your incessant questions and ready to end the conversation," Nellie said, the shadow of a smile on her lips. "At least you got the bad guy."

I grinned at her. "All's well that ends well, right?"

"When will you tell us the full story?"

"As soon as Chief Marshall approves."

"Harrumph," Nellie grumbled, but she wrapped me in a warm hug before she left me alone to prepare for the news conference.

Kate and Sharon rang me with a video call just as I was ready to step into the shower. I grabbed a towel and answered anyway.

"Oops, did we catch you at a bad time?" Kate asked.

"I can give you thirty seconds," I said. "Then I have to focus on getting ready to head to the police station."

"Everyone says you fought off a murderer and landed in the hospital," Sharon said.

"Half of that is true," I said. "There was no hand-to-hand battle, but I still ended up in the hospital."

"You okay?" Kate asked.

"After several hours in the ER, they sent me home."

"We want to know every detail," Sharon said. "See you at mahjong this afternoon?"

"I'll be there," I said.

After another round of congratulations, my friends promised to watch the noon broadcast for official details. Then I showered, dressed for the news conference, and drove to the police station where Chief Marshall was waiting for me.

Chapter Thirty

Wednesday Noon

I parked in the back parking lot, where the chief had instructed me to enter the staff door. He met me there and escorted me to one of the small interrogation rooms. I stepped inside to find Professor Tony Dell deep in conversation with a stocky man who looked vaguely familiar.

The two were total opposites. Tony Dell wore pressed khaki pants, a designer polo shirt, and polished leather Carducci shoes. The stranger was in navy blue coveralls and work boots. They stood as we entered.

"Josie, I believe you already know Professor Dell," he said, tilting his head toward the art curator. "But I wanted you to meet Stan Hermann."

The man extended his hand and clasped mine in a firm handshake. "I'm pleased to meet you, Ms. Posey. The Chief has told me about the valuable consulting you and Professor Dell do for the police department."

The plumber's brilliant blue eyes shone with sincerity, and I glanced at the chief for a clue on how to respond.

Chief Marshall took charge. "I know you had a few questions for the elusive Mr. Hermann," he said with a smile. "So, we arranged for a brief interview before the news conference."

"Thank you, Chief," I said, taking a notepad from my shoulder bag. "And you, Mr. Hermann."

"The professor and I will leave you now, but we would like you to join us after the news conference, if you have the time," the chief added.

Without a word from Professor Dell, the two men exited the room and closed the door.

Stan Hermann smiled broadly at my obvious confusion. "Chief Marshall said you'd be surprised to meet me," he said. "He's a real character."

"I suppose you told him my friends went to great lengths to find you on your fishing trip?" I asked.

"Oh, yeah," Stan said. "Even casting a line to catch a big one. It took both of those ladies to reel-in a *snapping turtle.* They hightailed it out of there, squealing like banshees." He chuckled. "Tony and I had to laugh at that one."

"Yes, well, you're here now," I said. "Ready for my questions?"

His face grew serious. "Shoot."

"Tell me about your friend Corky," I said. "How long have you known her?"

"We called her CJ in high school," he said. "Her last name was Drake, back then. Feels like I've known her forever. She was always a tomboy, hanging out with me and the guys after school. Playing baseball in the sandlot behind the house where she grew up. The only girl in the neighborhood back then."

"You're still friends?" I asked.

"Always will be," he said. "She's not a bad person. She just wanted to make some extra money. I wish she'd confided in me."

"You didn't suspect that Corky was into something illegal?"

"No," Stan answered. "She's borrowed my vehicles for years—always trying to make a buck. When we were kids, she'd take my truck for a few days and deliver produce for a local farmer. She would always say, *'You're the Man, Stan,'* and I would laugh and give her my keys."

"She's the one who created your slogan?" I asked.

"Yep. That's how it all started. Later, she talked me into trading my van for her little sedan for weekend shopping trips to Kansas City."

"You never asked questions?"

"Didn't have to," Stan said. "She was a friend. She always returned the van in good shape, washed inside-and-out, full of fuel."

"What about the money she paid you?" I asked.

"It wasn't unusual," he said. "Over the years, I loaned her a few hundred dollars whenever she got into a bind. I figured she wanted to repay me."

"Did Chief Marshall tell you he arrested Corky last night?"

The plumber shifted in his seat. "Yeah. I was sorry to hear it. The worst part is, a woman died because of Corky's mistakes. I'm sure she never meant to hurt anyone."

"How about you, Mr. Hermann?" I asked. "Has Chief Marshall charged you as an accomplice?"

"No," he said, his blue eyes fixed on mine. "They could have confiscated my vehicle for transporting the counterfeit money, even though I wasn't driving it. I told the chief the same thing I told you, and he believed me. Plus, Corky stepped up and took full responsibility."

"She's been a good friend to you," I said. "But *you've* been a *better one.*"

"You have some good friends, too," Stan said, handing me a shopping bag from beneath the table. "I brought hats for you to give them. Maybe they'll wear them the next time they go fishing."

I pulled the bright red ball caps from the bag and read the bold message: "When you need a hand, call Stan, The Man."

We shared a laugh, and I promised to deliver the caps to the mavens.

"There's one for you, too," he said.

I considered wearing my hat to the chief's news conference, but carried the bag to my car instead. When I returned from stowing the caps in my trunk, Officer Devon was rounding up reporters for the news conference.

The TV stations had arrived, spreading their camera equipment and cords across the front of the room, and leaving the rest of us to jostle for a space. I knew most of them from my days with the *Kansas City Star*, but noticed a few rookies among the crowd. The mayor and a smattering of other elected officials gathered near the back of the room to hear the announcements first-hand.

Authorities from four organizations filed into the room: Secret Service Agent John Evans, Forensics Pathologist Arnold Flavin, Bank President Wayne Whitworth, and Police Chief Earl Marshall. The chief stepped up to the podium and tapped his microphone to silence the room.

His dark eyes grew serious as he spoke. "We are here today to update you on our progress. I will make a brief statement, followed by comments from each of the experts gathered here beside me. At the conclusion of these remarks, we will take your questions."

The chief cleared his throat and leaned forward, resting his hands on the podium.

"Our small village has been in the spotlight for the past week as we have investigated two crimes: a home invasion, where we found a woman dead in her bathroom, and a counterfeit money case, where a local merchant discovered a phony hundred-dollar bill," he said. "Either of these events would have caused a commotion in any town our size."

A ripple of heads nodded as the chief's audience acknowledged the truth of his statement.

"I'm proud to say that our residents responded to these crimes like true neighbors and friends," Chief Marshall said. "They showed concern for those who lost a loved one, and a willingness to assist law enforcement officers in the search for a counterfeiter in our midst."

If the chief had not chosen police work, he might have had a successful career in public relations, I thought, watching the elected officials who attended the event in a show of support. Mayor Minter beamed in the back row, her eyes glued to Chief Marshall.

"Although we investigated these incidents as separate crimes, the evidence points to a single perpetrator," the chief announced.

He paused for the whispers of surprise to ebb, then plowed forward with a 30-second sound bite perfect for the nightly news: "In cooperation with the U.S. Secret Service Agency, the English Village Police Department has arrested a 54-year-old female on charges of distribution of counterfeit currency and involuntary manslaughter." He paused only slightly before adding, "Ms. Corky Markham is currently in custody, awaiting arraignment."

The room erupted as reporters recognized the name of a respected bank employee many of them knew. Anticipating their reaction, the chief took a sip of bottled water while the crowd settled. He motioned again for silence.

"We are grateful to the officers who assisted us in this effort," the chief continued, "as well as to the citizens who called our hotline with leads, and to those who responded to our requests for information or support."

He turned to catch the banker's eye. "And now, Wayne Whitworth, the President of English Village State Bank, has an announcement." The chief stepped away from the podium to make room for the banker.

Mr. Whitworth stood for a moment without speaking; his drawn face still had dark circles beneath his eyes, and I wondered whether he had slept since we had talked the previous morning. "Barely one week ago, a talented young bank teller lost her life, after an unknown intruder left her to die, alone in her own home," he said, his voice fraught with emotion. "Maryann Penny deserved better."

I choked back tears as he continued.

"When our bank offered a reward for information leading to the apprehension and arrest of the individual responsible for Maryann's death," he said, "we never imagined the perpetrator would be another of our trusted employees."

Whitworth removed a white handkerchief from his coat pocket and dabbed beads of sweat from his forehead. "Nor did we suspect that a counterfeit money scheme would tarnish the reputation we have worked diligently to build."

The banker squared his shoulders and leaned into the microphone. "Please know that the English Village State Bank is prepared to restore your trust in us," he said. "Meanwhile, we are pleased to announce the recipients of our reward offer. Four citizens earned the money through creative police work, which resulted in dozens of calls to our hotline. These ladies will share the reward: Josie Posey, Nellie Nester, Kate Jones, and Sharon Fitzpatrick."

Chief Marshall caught my eye and gave me a slight nod of approval. I couldn't wait to tell the mavens *Operation Rumor Mill* had resulted in a cash prize. No doubt they would be ecstatic.

Dr. Flavin was next to the podium. His statement was brief. "Several of you requested details of the victim's cause of death. We have confirmed that Maryann Penny died of heart failure, caused by side effects of her severe allergy to inks and dyes used in paper currency. I would like to stress that Maryann was not a willing participant involved in counterfeiting money, but an innocent victim of that crime. At the request of her family, we will provide no additional information on this matter."

Finally, Secret Service Agent John Evans took his turn in front of the cameras. I'd never imagined him as the *James Bond*-type, but today he dressed for the occasion. His tailored black suit, starched white shirt, and red tie made me wonder whether he carried a pair of reflective Aviator sunglasses in his pocket. He addressed the reporters in just a few short words.

"The United States Secret Service Agency extends gratitude to Police Chief Earl Marshall, his investigative team, and the city of English Village, for their quick actions in the apprehension of Corky Markham. The Secret Service and the Federal Bureau of Investigation will share the responsibility for prosecuting this crime."

After all the announcements, reporters waved their hands in the air, pleading for more details. I listened from the sidelines as the chief and others dodged most of them. Only one comment caught my attention. The blonde news anchor asked Agent Evans whether additional arrests would be forthcoming in the counterfeiting case.

The agent nodded. "Yes. We fully expect to identify, apprehend, and prosecute any others identified as accomplices to Ms. Markham in this crime."

Tony Dell's face flashed in my mind. *Will the professor be the FBI's next target?* I wondered.

Chapter Thirty-One

Wednesday Afternoon

I couldn't shake the idea that Professor Dell had played a role in the counterfeit money that led to Maryann's death. It had most likely originated in his home country of Peru and arrived in Sunflower County inside artifacts like those displayed at the art gallery. In my experience, this was too coincidental to ignore. Apparently, Chief Marshall saw something in Tony Dell that I didn't. Every time I raised my suspicions, he pooh-poohed them.

After the news conference, I returned to the chief's office, as he had requested. The professor arrived there ahead of me.

"Come in, Josie," he said. "The chief will be here soon."

I took the empty chair and set my purse at my feet. "I didn't see you at the news conference," I said, making conversation.

"No, I had some business to complete," he said. "I wanted to do it before we accompanied Chief Marshall to Leticia Cornwall's home."

I hoped my surprise didn't show on my face. *No one had mentioned a visit to Letica's place.* "Are you sure he expected me to join you?" I asked.

"Actually, Letica requested your presence," Tony said.

"Hmmm," I replied as briefly as I could.

The professor grinned at me. "Guess she trusts you more than she does the Police Chief," he said.

"I *heard* that," Chief Marshall said, walking through the door.

Tony shrugged. "It's true," he said.

Watching their friendly exchange, it occurred to me that Tony and the Chief had developed a camaraderie based on some level of mutual respect. Again, I wondered what the chief saw in this newcomer to our team.

"I'll drive," Chief Marshall said. "Did you bring the cash?"

"Yes," Tony answered, and I was too stubborn to ask what cash they were talking about.

Ten minutes later, we pulled into Leticia Cornwall's drive and walked to her front door. I rang the bell.

The slight woman opened the door and ushered us inside. "Come, let's sit on the dining terrace," she said. "I've arranged tea cakes. You must join me."

We trailed behind her through the French doors and onto the flagstone path, her silver hair blowing softly in the wind. She motioned for us to sit at a white patio table covered with a linen tablecloth. A pitcher of iced tea and two trays of fancy cakes rested in the center.

"I do hope iced tea suits you," Leticia said, pouring each of us a glass. "Hot tea seemed too formal for our little meeting."

"It looks wonderful," I assured her, as we helped ourselves to the cakes.

"Tell me, Chief Marshall," Leticia said, fidgeting with her napkin. "Was I correct? Were the bills I found in my trunk *counterfeit* money?"

"I'm afraid so, Ms. Cornwall. You were wise to be suspicious."

"Good heavens," the distraught gardener exclaimed. "What will I tell Florence? I've already pledged an additional $500, to support the Garden Tour."

"I'm sure she will understand," I said, placing my hand on her arm.

"You don't know *Florence*," she said, clearly upset. "She can become quite disagreeable when things don't go her way."

"Perhaps I can help," Tony Dell offered. "Would you allow me to examine the trunk where you found the money?"

"I don't see how that will change anything, but you're welcome to see it," she said, rising from her chair. "Follow me."

The three of us tagged behind as Leticia guided us beyond a row of hedges to the lily pond. She gestured to the rocky ledge where the artifact rested in a beam of sunlight. The hand-tooled leather trunk was as beautiful as I remembered it on my last visit.

Professor Dell stepped closer to the trunk. "May I?" he asked.

Leticia nodded.

With a quick flick of his wrist, the professor reached beneath the trunk and pressed. A narrow drawer released from what appeared to be the bottom of the trunk. He turned to Leticia, "Is this where you found the money?"

"Yes!" she said.

"You have a keen eye, Ms. Cornwall," he said. "Did you explore the exterior of the trunk for any additional hiding places?"

"No," she said, "I never thought of that."

Professor Dell rocked back on his heels and studied the trunk from all angles. "The design was popular in the 18th Century, when hidden compartments concealed personal documents, or valuables like jewelry or cash."

"Compartments?" I asked.

He nodded. "Travelers preferred to separate their possessions, believing a thief would steal only what he discovered in one compartment, never suspecting additional trays or pockets hidden inside."

Leticia listened, wide-eyed, to the professor's history lesson.

"What do you think, Ms. Cornwall?" Chief Marshall asked. "Shall we have Professor Dell search for more spring-loaded buttons?"

"Please!" she said.

In quick order, Professor Dell felt the seams of the trunk from top to bottom. He popped open the false bottom of a compartmentalized tray, but it held no surprises. A deep side panel lined with velvet brought better results. He reached into the pocket and withdrew a delicate ring. The band was gold, with a polished emerald stone in the setting.

"This is a Cabochon gemstone," the professor said, placing it in Leticia's hand. "See the smooth, rounded shape with a dome top and flat bottom?"

"It's beautiful," Leticia said, placing it on her finger.

"It's a treasure," I said.

"Can you estimate the value?" Chief Marshall asked the professor.

Professor Dell shook his head. "I'm not a jeweler, but I would guess the value to be many thousands of dollars." He turned to Leticia. "If you would allow me to display the ring at the art gallery this summer, I would gladly pay a leasing fee of $500 in advance."

Tears filled Leticia's eyes. "Yes!" she said, dabbing at her face with a pink handkerchief she pulled from her pocket. "I accept your generous offer."

The professor counted five bills into her hand, and Leticia took his arm to lead him to Florence Crockett's rose garden next door. Chief Marshall and I followed them.

"I love a happy ending," I said.

"We all do," the chief said.

After Tony Dell's unexpected kindness toward Leticia, my conscience nagged at my brain. "I guess I was wrong about Professor Dell," I said. "He's exactly what he appears to be—a respected curator of Peruvian art."

"Maybe," the chief said. "Maybe not. Everyone has secrets."

"What do you mean?"

"Always trust your instincts, Josie," the chief said, shooting me a look I didn't understand.

Before I could get an explanation, we entered the aromatic garden. Roses filled the air with the scent of love. Florence Crockett strutted about like a peacock, adding flower buds to table vases and tying satin ribbons that flowed from the arbor, while she chatted nonstop with Professor Dell and Leticia Cornwall.

When she noticed we had entered the gate, Florence rushed toward us. She shook Chief Marshall's hand and gushed about his quick resolution of the counterfeit money case. "I never trusted that *Corky* woman," she said. "I can't believe she orchestrated the whole thing."

"Neither could we," Chief Marshall said, his eyes focused on the woman's startled face. "That's why we believed her when she named *you* as the mastermind in charge."

I stood with my mouth open and watched Florence burst into tears. In a fit of rage, she spun around and pointed her finger at Tony Dell. "This is all *your fault*," she said. "Your family business shipped the artifacts to us. You should have known the cost was too good to be true."

"You are a smart businesswoman, Ms. Crockett. You understood what you were doing," Tony answered in a firm tone.

The next thing I knew, Florence made a dash for the garden wall, scrambling over the trellises like an Olympic track star.

Chief Marshall dived for the woman, grabbed her by the ankles and dragged her to the ground. Tony Dell stood over both, laughing like he'd never seen an old woman and a police officer tangled up in a bed of roses—Florence scratching and kicking to get free.

Meanwhile, Leticia Cornwall fainted, and I raced to kneel by her side, splashing water from a garden fountain into her face. That did the trick. She sat straight up and screamed at Florence. "You're ruining your roses, Florence Crockett!"

Suddenly, Florence stopped fighting. Tony Dell extended his hand to pull her to her feet. The chief stood up and whipped his handcuffs from his belt, fastening them around the old woman's wrists as he recited her Miranda rights.

Tony Dell pulled a badge from his pocket, identifying himself as an undercover agent for the U.S. Secret Service. "Florence Crockett, you are under arrest for counterfeiting."

"I only wanted to help the Cleeve Hill Garden Society," she whined.

"Tell that to the FBI when you plead your case," Agent Dell said.

"You!" I shook my finger at him. "When I asked if you knew anything about counterfeiting, you denied it."

Tony shrugged. "At least I gave you a call alerting you not to trust the gardener," he said.

"You, you, you—," I sputtered at him.

Chief Marshall smiled at my outburst. "We captured the perps, Josie," he said. "It's a happy ending—just like you wanted."

"Except for Maryann's death," I said.

"Yes," the chief nodded, his dark eyes filled with sadness. "Justice can't bring her back to life; but it's all we can do, to avenge her."

* * *

The Mahjong Mavens waited for me on Nellie's front porch when I arrived, carrying the bag Stan Hermann had given me.

"You're late," Kate said.

"Yes, but I brought gifts," I replied, handing each of them a "Stan, The Man" ball cap, which they promptly put on their heads. "Stan wanted to express his admiration of your fishing skills."

"I'll bet he did," Sharon laughed.

"We heard the news of his friend Corky's arrest," Kate added solemnly.

Nellie wrapped an arm around my waist. "Get inside. Tell us everything!"

I gave them the short version: "Maryann's cause of death was a heart attack caused by a reaction to the inks used in paper currency."

"We never would have guessed that!" Sharon said.

"The coroner was stumped, too," I said. "Until Lois Penny and Wayne Whitworth explained their daughter's allergy."

"What will happen to Corky?" Kate asked.

"She will face charges of counterfeiting and involuntary manslaughter," I said. "The *big* surprise came after the news conference—when Secret Service Agent Tony Dell arrested Florence Crockett as the ringleader of the *Counterfeit Currency Caper*."

"Good gracious, Josie," Nellie exclaimed, "Why didn't you tell us Professor Dell was a secret agent?"

"He apprehended Florence, the grand dame of the gardening circle?" Kate asked. "Nobody will believe this story."

I spread my arms in a gesture of surrender. "Sorry, ladies, it all came together so fast it made my head spin. I suspected Tony had something up his sleeve, but he and the chief kept his true occupation a secret till the end. His undercover position as a curator at the art gallery gave him inside information on artifact shipments, as well as the garden society's suspicious activities."

Sharon wrinkled her forehead. "Why would Florence Crockett risk her reputation by getting involved in a federal crime?" she asked.

"People do strange things for money," I said. "The Cleeve Hill Garden Society spent thousands of dollars every year to stage the Garden Tour. Their treasury was running low, and Florence saw an easy way to replenish it."

"By circulating phony money?" Nellie's voice rose an octave.

"She described it as a bona fide investment," I said. "She visited Peru on vacation last year and fell in love with their beautiful gardens. While she was there, a handsome stranger offered her a deal she couldn't refuse. It turns out, he was a black-sheep cousin who was secretly running a counterfeit hustle from within the Delfino family business—a legitimate company owned by Agent Tony Dell's *father*."

"Oh, no," Nellie said.

"Tony's crooked cousin signed Florence up as a wholesale customer. She paid a low monthly price for shipments of Peruvian artifacts. The only catch was that she had to deliver every crate—unopened—to a specified location. Before the first crates arrived, Florence enlisted Corky to transport the goods to the designated distributor."

"She paid for items to give the appearance of a legitimate purchase!" Kate exclaimed.

"Florence never touched the merchandise, but she received a huge payment for each completed delivery." I shrugged my shoulders. "She claimed it was a business deal. Said she knew nothing about counterfeit currency hidden in the crates. The payments to her bank account were reimbursements for her initial investment, and for being the intermediary in the deal."

"What about Corky?" Kate asked. "She was a banker. She had to know this deal was too good to be true."

"Yes," I said. "Corky thought she could make quick money and then get out. She panicked when a shipment mistakenly went to the gallery, instead of to her private address. After Maryann overheard Corky's incriminating conversation with the distributor, there was no turning back."

"She staged Maryann's death to connect the girl to the phony money?" Sharon asked.

"That's the sad part," I said. "Corky didn't plan to kill Maryann. She hoped to frighten her into keeping the counterfeit scheme a secret. Corky was stunned when Maryann died of a rare allergic reaction to the currency."

"Speaking of cash," Nellie said, "we didn't expect to be paid for circulating rumors."

Sharon added. "We nearly fell over when Wayne Whitworth called to tell us *Operation Rumor Mill* fit the criteria of 'creative community police work.'"

"We want to donate the bank's reward money toward an art curator scholarship in Maryann Penny's name," Kate said. "Do you agree?"

Hot tears sprang to my eyes, and I swallowed a lump in my throat so I could speak. "Yes. She would be pleased," I said.

"What shall we do now, Josie?" Nellie asked.

"Is everyone up for a game of mahjong?" Sharon suggested.

"Count me in," Kate said.

As the three ladies stood waiting for my response, I saw the concern in their eyes. *They know the game will distract me from the turmoil surrounding Maryann's death,* I thought.

I smiled at them. "Of course," I agreed.

"We always play mahjong on Wednesdays."

SHARON'S LEMON STRAWBERRY TRIFLE

Prep Time: 10 minutes
Servings: 12

INGREDIENTS

- 6.8 ounces instant lemon pudding mix
- 2½ cups milk
- 16 ounces whipped topping thawed, divided
- 2 pounds strawberries sliced
- ⅔ cup lemon curd
- 14 ounces Angel food cake (Or, substitute **Easy Lemon Cake***, see recipe below)

DIRECTIONS

1. Whisk lemon pudding mixes and milk together for two minutes. Fold in 8 ounces of whipped topping. Refrigerate for at least 5 minutes.
2. Cut angel food cake into small, bite sized pieces. Set aside.
3. In a separate bowl, combine remaining 8 ounces of whipped topping with lemon curd, folding together again thoroughly combined. Set aside.
4. Layer half of the angel food cake in the bottom or a large bowl (Or spoon a layer into bottom of a trifle dish.)
5. Top with half of the pudding mixture, half of the sliced strawberries,

and half of the lemon curd mixture. (Or, layer appropriate amounts of pudding, strawberries, and lemon curd into trifle glass, and repeat layers until filled.)

6. Decorate top with sliced strawberries and a sliver of lemon, or a dollop of whipped cream.

*EASY LEMON CAKE

Prep Time: 10 minutes
Bake Time: 25 minutes + Cool for 1 hour
Servings: 12

INGREDIENTS

- 16 ounces Angel food cake mix
- 21 ounces lemon pie filling
- ½ cup powdered sugar

DIRECTIONS

1. Preheat oven to 350 degrees.
2. Coat inside of a 9"x13" pan with cooking spray or butter.
3. In a mixing bowl, stir dry cake mix and pie filling until thoroughly combined.
4. Pour batter into the cake pan and bake for 20-25 minutes, until edges are lightly browned.
5. Let the cake cool, then sprinkle top with powdered sugar.

LORENE'S HOMEMADE CHICKEN POT PIE

Serves 4

INGREDIENTS

- 2 cups, cooked chicken (Use rotisserie chicken from the grocery store)
- 4 Tbsp. unsalted butter
- 2 cloves minced garlic
- 1 small onion, diced
- ½ cup frozen corn, thawed
- ½ cup frozen diced carrots, thawed
- ½ cup frozen peas, thawed
- 1/3 cup all-purpose flour
- 1 cup low-sodium chicken stock
- ¾ cup whole milk
- ½ to 1 tsp. dried thyme (to your taste)
- 1 tsp. poultry seasoning
- 1 tsp. salt
- 1 tsp. pepper
- 1 Tbsp. cooked bacon diced (optional)
- 1 pastry crust from refrigerated section of grocery store

DIRECTIONS

1. Preheat oven to 350 degrees.

2. Lightly oil or coat with cooking spray, the inside of 4 10-ounce ramekins or one large round casserole dish.

3. Melt 2 Tbsp. of butter in a large skillet over medium heat.

4. Add garlic, onion, corn, carrots, and peas, and cook, stirring occasionally, until onions become translucent (about 2 minutes). Do not overcook, as you want the vegetables to be a little crunchy.

5. Pour ingredients into a heatproof bowl and set aside.

6. In the same skillet, melt the remaining 2 Tbsp. of butter and whisk in the flour until lightly browned. Gradually whisk in the chicken stock, milk, thyme, parsley, salt and pepper.

7. Whisk constantly until thickened. This may take several minutes.

8. Then, add chicken and vegetables, and cook for another 3-4 minutes.

9. Pour into ramekins or casserole dish and cove with the piecrust.

10. Put several slits in the top of each crust, and bake for 30-45 minutes until the crust is golden brown and filling is bubbling. (You can cover the crust loosely with foil if it appears to be getting done sooner than the pie filling).

11. Let sit to cool for 5 minutes, and serve.

—Simple Cooking with Chef H, by Harry Pape

PERFECT PERUVIAN COFFEE

INGREDIENTS

- Freshly ground coffee beans (Medium grind similar to regular sand or kosher salt)
- Water

DIRECTIONS (Drip Coffee Pot)

1. Grind beans to a medium just before brewing.
2. Fill the drip coffee machine's water tank with clean, filtered water.
3. Place a paper filter in the basket.
4. Add medium-ground coffee to the filter. (2 T of coffee per cup desired)
5. Turn on the machine and let it brew.

Tip: If flavor is too strong for your taste, fill your cup halfway with hot water and pour the brewed coffee into the water. You can also store the undiluted brewed coffee in a carafe to keep it fresh. Have another cup anytime during the day by pouring boiling water into a cup and adding the brewed coffee to the heated water.

PASADO PERUVIAN COFFEE

Peruvian filtered coffee (Cold Brew)
12 hours/also known as long brewed

Pasado is basically a very strong extraction of coffee. So instead of getting instant coffee with your boiled water, you get a carafe of cold coffee extraction that you add to the water to your taste. Be careful though, start with a small amount and build up with more if needed as the strength will vary.

INGREDIENTS

- 1 cup ground coffee
- 2 cups cold water
- 1 glass jar with lid

DIRECTIONS

1. Pour water into a jar.
2. Add cup of ground.
3. Seal jar and shake it a few times to mix the grounds thoroughly.
4. Let the mixture 'brew' for 12 hours, shaking/stirring it a few times.
5. Pour through a sift and place in an easy pouring container, preferably one that can seal to preserve it.
6. Prepare one cup of coffee: fill cup halfway with boiling water. Then add your coffee extraction to the cup.

This process ensures a 'fresh' cup of coffee every time by just boiling water. You also do not get the 'burned' coffee taste of the second or third helping out of a filter coffee machine.

—"Coffee: Peruvian Style", by Elesbie Olivier, *Piki Piki Magazine*, 2018, https://www.pikipikioverland.com/coffee-peruvian-style/

Acknowledgments

As always, I am most grateful to the readers who have discovered the *Josie Posey Mystery Series.* Your time and feedback are generous gifts. I hope you enjoyed solving the mystery alongside Josie and her meddling Mahjong Mavens. I would love to hear from you, so please feel free to reach out through my website or social media.

It is impossible to mention everyone who has supported this book, but I would like to try.

First, to the writing community who gave professional guidance, suggestions, editing, and encouragement: thank you. This includes my wonderful agent, Cindy Bullard, of Birch Literary Agency, and the entire team at Level Best Books—especially my talented editor, publisher, book cover designer, and friend, Shawn Reilly Simmons who makes every story better. A special thanks to Deb Well for her editing guidance and insights into cats. Thanks, also, to all the LBB "Besties" and Birch Literary authors who willingly shared their time and their wisdom when asked.

Sincere thanks to my photographer friend Steve Rasmussen, for the "mysterious author" photo. To artist Lyndsey Mbawuike, for her wonderful book cover illustration. And to Wendy Pope for her editing skills.

I am also indebted to other authors across the country, most of whom I have met through Pitch to Published, Pitch Perfect, Sisters in Crime, or Mystery Writers of America. The list has grown too large to include without me forgetting someone's name. You know who you are, and I appreciate each of you.

To the real Mahjong Mavens—Diane, Susan, Karen, June, Carolyn, Jane, and Cheri—thank you for inspiring me every week, and for cheering me on at book talks and other events. As always, you may recognize yourselves in some of this story.

My gratitude also goes out to those who contributed to the content of this story by sharing their expertise, allowing me to use their names, or providing a recipe. This includes Chief Meteorologist Lisa Teachman of KSN-TV in Wichita, KS, for allowing me to reference her in the book. The family of Les Anderson, who approved my tribute to his memory through a female character bearing his name. To Barbara Chamberlin, for the use of her name, again. In memory of my good friend, Harry Pape (Chef H), who we lost way too soon, I am happy to share the Chicken Pot Pie recipe from his wonderful cookbook.

A big shout-out to a friend from our high school days, Linda Witkoski, for readily agreeing I could drop her name into this story, even though she had no idea how it might be used. And to Dan Edwards, another school friend, for serving as an advanced reader/reviewer. I appreciate both of you.

Several close friends have followed this writing journey from the beginning. I'm lucky to have them by my side for the adventure. Hugs to Sharon, Janet, Jane and Karen.

Special thanks to my sister Teresa, who always provides encouragement when I need it most. And to the rest of the family: my sisters, aunts and cousins—including Winona, Jeneva, and Martha—as well as other nieces and nephews who have cheered me forward (you know who you are).

I can't forget Oliver, our sweet and silly Old English Sheepdog who patrols our property to protect us from birds and squirrels, and who prompts me to head for the gym every morning and the park each afternoon. He is the inspiration for the most popular character in the books—Josie's dog, Moe.

Most of all, I want to mention those closest to my heart: Son Matthew and Tatiya, and granddaughters Madeline and Matilda. Son Zachary and Sarha, and grandchildren Zander, Magnolia, and Zoey. We treasure our time with you.

And, always, I am thankful to be spending my life with my husband Bruce, who makes me believe all things are possible.

About the Author

Anna St. John writes the Josie Posey Mystery Series, featuring a mature yet feisty former crime reporter as the amateur sleuth. *Cashed Out Cold* is book four of the series. A former journalist, award-winning advertising copywriter, and ad agency owner, Anna loves small towns and is married to her high school sweetheart. Their Old English Sheepdog, Oliver, inspired the character of "Moe" in the Josie Posey series. Anna is a member of Mystery Writers of America, Sisters in Crime, and the Kansas Authors Club. She is represented by Cindy Bullard of Birch Literary Agency.

AUTHOR WEBSITE:

https://www.anna-stjohn.com/

SOCIAL MEDIA HANDLES:

https://www.facebook.com/cozyauthor

Also by Anna St. John

Doomed by Blooms, A Josie Posey Mystery, 2023

Clocked Out, A Josie Posey Mystery, 2024

Dolled Up for Murder, A Josie Posey Mystery, 2024